In memory of Rev. Joseph Kuehnle

Books by Ashton Lee

THE CHERRY COLA BOOK CLUB

THE READING CIRCLE

THE WEDDING CIRCLE

A CHERRY COLA CHRISTMAS

Published by Kensington Publishing Corporation

A Cherry Cola Christmas

ASHTON LEE

KENSINGTON BOOKS
www.kensingtonbooks.com

KENSINGTON BOOKS are published by

Kensington Publishing Corp.
119 West 40th Street
New York, NY 10018

All Kensington titles, imprints, and distributed lines are available at special quantity discounts for bulk purchases for sales promotion, premiums, fund-raising, educational, or institutional use.

Special book excerpts or customized printings can also be created to fit specific needs. For details, write or phone the office of the Kensington Sales Manager: Kensington Publishing Corp., 119 West 40th Street, New York, NY 10018. Attn. Sales Department. Phone: 1-800-221-2647.

Kensington and the K logo Reg. U.S. Pat. & TM Off.

eISBN-13: 978-1-61773-344-4
eISBN-10: 1-61773-344-X
First Kensington Electronic Edition: October 2015

ISBN-13: 978-1-61773-343-7
ISBN-10: 1-61773-343-1
First Kensington Trade Paperback Printing: October 2015

10 9 8 7 6 5 4 3 2 1

Printed in the United States of America

Acknowledgments

In addition to the help I continue to receive from my agents at Jane Rotrosen Agency, Christina Hogrebe and Meg Ruley, and from my editor at Kensington Books, John Scognamiglio, I have some special thanks to give for this, the fourth installment of the Cherry Cola Book Club series.

First, to Jerry Flowers, of Nashville, Tennessee, for his invaluable information on the country music industry and some of its inner workings as I developed the character of Waddell Mack.

Next, to Judy Douglas and Lisa Moonfire Kirchner, of Ashville, Alabama, for their delightful library anecdote, which helped make my chapter of inspirational stories that much more interesting. And to Weaver Cain for his law-enforcement input.

Lastly, to David Gammill, of Fat Mama's Tamales, in my hometown of Natchez, Mississippi, for his willingness to share his hot tamale recipe with the world; as well as to host the debut signing of *A Cherry Cola Christmas* in his nationally famous restaurant. I am very proud of the Gammill family for making such a success of this Natchez enterprise and was happy to work Fat Mama's Tamales into the plot of this novel.

1

Bad News Travels Fast

Who would have guessed that everything would go south so fast in Cherico, Mississippi, during the two weeks Maura Beth and Jeremy enjoyed their honeymoon in Key West? Their sunny, carefree days were filled with hand-holding strolls along Duval Street, a mandatory visit to the Ernest Hemingway House and Museum with its lovely lacework balconies and extra-toed cats lounging around like royalty, and frequent appearances at Sloppy Joe's for margaritas and the Schooner Wharf Bar for shrimp and lots of live music before retiring to the joys of their creative and athletic lovemaking. The bride and groom had a few surprises for each other, but none that was not wickedly delightful and worthy of return engagements. Amazing what a little salt air and lots of salted rims could do for the imagination and libido!

Of course, it was not like they had left things in bad shape prior to their departure. Nor had Maura Beth received any cautionary cell phone calls or e-mails from her trusty assistant, Renette Posey, that The Cherico Library or any other institution was in trouble. Instead, their stay in Florida had tumbled by all too predictably like the tide ebbing and flowing and without a thought of the extreme northeast Mississippi corner of the world that they shared.

To be sure, it had taken a great deal of patience and all the compassion she could muster for Maura Beth to resolve her lifelong issues with her mother, Cara Lynn, which the wedding had brought to a head like an annoying prom night pimple that refused to pop in time for the festivities. But the two women had embraced in tears and exiled their conflict once and for all, and Maura Beth had fully expected to return to Cherico rejuvenated and ready to tackle such ongoing issues as the new library under construction and the always-devious behavior of Councilman Durden Sparks.

In fact, it seemed to be a very good sign that Cara Lynn Mayhew was reasonably restrained in demanding the details of her daughter's honeymoon over the phone that first evening back. "Of course, you know your father and I will want copies of all the pictures you and Jeremy took. But take your time. I remember that it took me forever to wind down after our honeymoon ended."

"We'll get you a copy of the CD soon," Maura Beth told her, pleased with her mother's understanding tone.

"Make that two copies while you're at it," Cara Lynn added. "Your Cudd'n M'Dear wants a copy, too. It's the least you can do after she gave your library that enormous endowment. I assume you've written your thank-you note to her."

"Of course I have. It was the first one I wrote. Not to mention all the postcards I sent her from Key West. So, two copies of the CD it is. And what is our dear cousin up to now?"

"Something outrageous as usual," Cara Lynn continued, practically hissing through the phone. "She's apparently called up all the New Orleans television stations and demanded that they give her time for a telethon to—get this—eliminate static cling and static electricity!"

"What?!"

"I know. And of course, they're having absolutely nothing

to do with her, so she's bending my ear all the time about what a serious issue this is and how she's sick and tired of getting shocked after walking across the shag carpet and having her delicates clinging to her thighs and backside when she pulls them out of the dryer. Face it, Maura Beth, she needs something to do with her life, and this is her latest attempt."

"Well, I'm just happy she gave me the wedding present to end all wedding presents. The library will never want for anything now."

"Isn't that the truth!"

Thus, a new day had truly dawned between mother and daughter. Maura Beth had never gotten off this easy in any long-distance conversation since her college days, and it made her feel like there was nothing out there she couldn't overcome.

Imagine her dismay, then, when the first thing that greeted her upon her return to work was a breathless and anxious-looking Renette, who did not even offer so much as her usual girlish smile or ask for any of the delicious honeymoon details.

"Councilman Sparks wants to see you in his office as soon as you get settled!" Renette told her, the urgency clearly registering in her voice.

"And it's good to see you again, too, Renette!" Maura Beth replied, still managing a smile. Then she welcomed her sweet-natured, teenaged assistant into her open arms for a heartfelt hug.

"Oh, I'm sorry, Miz Mayhew—I mean, Miz McShay. I'm gonna have to get used to your married name now," she continued as the two women walked into Maura Beth's crowded little office and sat across from each other. "It's just that so much has happened since you left—and none of it good."

"Really? I can't imagine what could have you this upset. Although I understand the part about Councilman Sparks. I should have had you wear a garlic necklace until I got back. Did he tell you what he wanted with me?"

"No, he was just very rude with me over the phone. He told me to tell you the moment you got back from Key West, and I quote, 'To get your little gallivanting, honeymooning, librarian self over to his office.' It's not a stretch to say he's probably up to no good as usual."

Maura Beth shrugged, tossing her auburn curls with definite nonchalance. She had been there and done that more than once with Councilman Sparks. She had won a year-long operational reprieve for the old, worn-out library she still occupied, and then with a little help from her friends had boldly finagled the construction of a brand-new, state-of-the-art facility from Cherico's virtual dictator.

So, what could she possibly fear now? Surely Councilman Sparks could not even be thinking about scuttling further construction of the new building! Why, the foundation had already been poured out at the edge of Lake Cherico, and even before she left for Key West, the first of many concrete pillars had risen to outline her pride and joy and the legacy she would leave to the quirky little town of Cherico.

"Of course, whatever Councilman Sparks has in mind is not the only bad news you'll have to deal with," Renette continued after an awkward pause. "Some more stores are closing, and there's also been some unexpected criminal activity since you left. It's almost as if someone was waiting for you to leave to go into action. It happened down at The Twinkle when no one was looking—some big tips right out on the tables were stolen. It makes me so nervous since I was broken into once and had all my electronic stuff carried off. I don't think I could stand going through that again—I couldn't get a good night's sleep for weeks!"

"Yes, I remember you telling me about what happened to

you," Maura Beth said. A thoughtful frown broke across her forehead. "But why didn't you let me know about any of this while I was in Key West?"

Renette drew back, giving her a thoroughly skeptical glance. "And ruin your honeymoon? Now, Miz ... McShay—ha, got it right this time! I was not about to call your cell and tell you stuff you couldn't do a thing about way down there at the tip of Florida—at least not until you got back!"

Maura Beth's laugh was brief and gracious. "Good point. I'm sure I would have been annoyed if you'd actually done that." Her frown lines grew even deeper as she reflected. "Wow! Was anyone hurt at The Twinkle? Is Periwinkle okay?"

"Yes, she's fine. Everyone down there is fine, except for the missing money."

"Have they started investigating it?"

"Yes, they have. It's the talk of the town. Miz Periwinkle can give you all the details when you catch up with her, but I can tell you she's really upset that someone would do some-thin' that mean and low-down!"

Maura Beth was squinting now, trying to visualize crimi-nal activity at The Twinkle, of all places, but there was a com-plete disconnect in her mind's eye. "These days, I'm surprised nothing's been caught on someone's security camera."

"Miz Periwinkle doesn't have one. But she was in here the other day asking if I'd heard anything from you, and she said she was seriously considering adding a camera to protect her restaurant. But she was shaking her head all the time about it and saying things like, what was the world comin' to with people nasty enough to snatch up Miz Lalie Bevins's tips!"

"I don't blame her. Here I was thinking that Cherico, Mississippi, would be the last place on earth to worry about crime of any kind," Maura Beth observed, her face a study in disbelief. "Looks like even we aren't immune to it way up here in the middle of nowhere."

Renette took a deep breath, exhaling the weight of the world she'd been carrying around on her shoulders all the time she'd been in charge of the library. More than once, she'd told Maura Beth that she really didn't like the responsibility, but she'd never had any choice in the matter. The library had no assistant director—not even a children's librarian who could take over in Maura Beth's absence. "So when are you gonna up and go see you-know-who at City Hall?"

"I think I'll keep our favorite councilman waiting a tad bit," Maura Beth said. "I see I have tons of mail to sort through, and I'm sure I have lots of e-mails to answer and so forth. Besides, I don't want him to think he can just snap his fingers and I'll appear like something out of *I Dream of Jeannie* to grant his wishes. I know how he views all women, including that submissive wife of his, but I decided long ago that that just wasn't part of my job description."

They both leaned in and laughed like girlfriends. "Yep, you've really stood your ground with him and the other councilmen, Miz McShay—and it's paid off. You've always been my role model, you know."

Maura Beth's wink reflected the genuine camaraderie the two women had generated in a very short time; then she sighed. "Well, the honeymoon's over, literally. Back to work—and then over to City Hall to deal with the devil."

Renette wagged her brows, but a frown soon followed. "Oh, I forgot some more bad news. Emma's husband is still taking tests to find out what's wrong with him. She's so afraid it might be Alzheimer's. It's got her so upset, she just isn't herself. She said she might have to consider quitting to keep an eye on Mr. Leonard. She said she needed to talk to you as soon as you got back."

Maura Beth suddenly felt even more deflated. Mrs. Emma Frost, her other front desk clerk, was not particularly knowledgeable or educated, but she was always on time and never complained about the long hours or being on her feet during her shift. Plus, the plain-faced, sixty-something grandmother was a holdover from Miz Annie Scott's library regime, and Emma had made a point of emphasizing that she definitely needed her paltry salary to help make ends meet. And she had been very thankful to get the recent raise that had been provided by Cudd'n M'Dear's extremely generous library endowment—Maura Beth's ultra-spectacular wedding present from the most eccentric of her New Orleans relatives.

"I'm so sorry to hear it," Maura Beth said. "I was afraid of something like that when Emma kept saying that Leonard couldn't seem to remember the simplest things these days and would even wander around the backyard looking for something. But he could never tell her what it was. She said he'd even wandered out of the house now and then, and she had to track him down out on the sidewalk, thankful that he hadn't been hit by a car. So, she's taking it all really hard?"

Renette looked completely distraught. "Honestly, Miz McShay, there are times when I've heard her mumbling things to herself during the shifts we shared while you were gone. I know something like Alzheimer's isn't contagious, but she's doin' an awful good imitation of someone who might have it, too. And then, when I've asked if there's anything I can do for her, she just shrugs and kinda pushes me away."

"That isn't like her. She's always worn her emotions on her sleeve here at work, the way she'll get upset if she tells the wrong thing to a patron and comes to me all flustered until I tell her to calm down and that everything'll be just fine."

"I think she's just worried to death about her husband. I'm sure I prob'ly would be, too."

"Same here." Maura Beth paused to gather her thoughts,

genuinely worried. "I'll see what I can do to comfort her when she comes in tomorrow. Meanwhile, Councilman Sparks is over there at City Hall, busy spinning his web. But this is one little fly that won't get trapped!"

The magic spell that Key West had cast over Maura Beth was beginning to fade with each City Hall front step she climbed. The three-story white columns towering above almost seemed to be frowning down upon her. For a brief moment, she actually contemplated how convenient it would be to return to that laid-back, semitropical environment—perhaps permanently. There would be nothing more difficult to deal with down there than the swaying of royal palms in the constant breeze off the Gulf—unless one of those frequent hurricanes came roaring in during the season. Unfortunately, she was about to face Cherico's very own hurricane in the form of Councilman Durden Sparks—always plotting, fomenting discord, and pitting folks against one another in the manner he had perfected over the past several decades. The man had "storm warning" written all over his face.

Before Maura Beth knew it, she was sitting across from the charming rascal himself in his spotless, designer showroom-like office with the smell of the rum-flavored cigar he was smoking lingering in the air. That was a new touch, she observed. Perhaps he thought smoking cigars made him even more of a good ole boy than he already was. Of course, getting all the meaningless pleasantries out of the way as fast as she could was the first order of business.

"Yes, Councilman, you're absolutely right," she was saying, sounding a bit bored. "Jeremy and I thoroughly enjoyed our honeymoon. It was everything we hoped it would be and more. But I'm sure you'll understand what I mean when I say that it was over all too soon."

He nodded perfunctorily, flashing one of his best reelection smiles. "That's the nature of honeymoons, of course. They really don't prepare any of us for the real world we live in, do they? Speaking of which, I have some very bad news to share with you today."

Maura Beth sat up straighter in her chair, looking alert and confident. She was ready for anything he had to throw at her these days. "I already know what you're going to say. It's about the stolen tips down at The Twinkle, isn't it?"

Councilman Sparks looked momentarily surprised, pulling back slightly. "Well, yes, that was a part of what I wanted to discuss with you. And I see you've been properly briefed."

"My assistant, Renette Posey."

Councilman Sparks cast his eyes at the ceiling for a moment or two. "Yes, that sweet little teenaged thing you've got working for you down there behind the front desk. Is she old enough to drive yet?"

Maura Beth refused to bristle. "She's a high-school graduate going on nineteen. But enough about Renette. Why don't you continue with your bad news? I know you're just bursting to tell me."

He cleared his throat loudly and then put the cigar down in the nearby ashtray where the smoke continued to curl upward lazily. "Yes, well, I'll get to the stolen tips bid'ness later. But first I wanted to tell you that Spurs 'R' Us, the cowboy boot manufacturer that was going to locate in our new industrial park, has backed out of the deal at the last minute. Said they're looking into another location up near Nashville. Dillard Mills, their two-faced CEO, had the gall to tell me over the phone he thought their boots would sell better if people knew they were made in the country music capital of the world and not here in Cherico. What an asinine reason! Who'd care about something like that? Anyway, I don't have to tell you that that's a real blow to our economy. It would've meant hundreds of new jobs for us, and we really need them.

Our sales tax is lagging way behind last year, too. The town's in a real slump that shows no signs of ending soon. If it keeps up, Cherico's not gonna have much of a Christmas this year. I guess you could say that Spurs 'R' Us has Scrooged us!"

Maura Beth nodded sympathetically but remained wary. She could not see where he was going with this where she was concerned. "I'm sorry to hear that. I know you were excited about them being the first industry to locate in your park—the park to end all industrial parks."

"It's not *my* park. It belongs to everyone here in Cherico, including you. Hey, we were just about ready to do a presser to announce the construction date of the plant. Instead, it's gotten out around the state that we've been one-upped by Nashville. That's the big story now, and it can't help us with our future industrial prospects!" He paused, looking off to the side at the smoke-filled plane of light streaming through his window, as if he were searching for inspiration to continue. "And since you're so tight with Miz Periwinkle Lattimore, I suppose you already know her ex has closed down the Marina Bar and Grill out at the lake and left town. Another source of consistent tax revenue just sailing off into the sunset on us!"

"Yes, unfortunately I was aware of that," she told him, nodding smartly. "Harlan Lattimore's moved back to his hometown of Jefferson, Texas, to start over fresh. It seems there's nothing much left for him here after Periwinkle turned down his second marriage proposal. These things happen."

Councilman Sparks muttered something under his breath, lightly brushing his silver tie with the tips of his fingers, and continued. "Well, Harlan Lattimore leaving's not all that's happened. Miz Audra Neely is closing down that fancy antique shop of hers on Commerce Street after Christmas, too. And Cherico Ace Hardware is going out of bid'ness. We can't afford too many more empty storefronts downtown. Looks awful when we show these company execs around. Gives the unmistakable impression we're dying on the vine—and if we don't turn this around soon, that's exactly what's gonna happen to us!"

"Oh, I didn't know that about Audra and the hardware store. But Audra did have a lot of high-end items for a small town like Cherico. I know they were all out of my price range. Frankly, I'm surprised she was able to stay in business this long."

"That was why we needed those Spurs 'R' Us jobs. Woudda brought in folks to live here who could've afforded nicer things. Things are looking pretty bleak around here, Miz Mayhew."

"McShay."

"Of course. You're a respectable married woman now. To that young shop teacher, right?"

Maura Beth looked thoroughly exasperated, making no effort to contain her anger. "Please stop doing that, Councilman. You know very well that my husband, Jeremy, teaches English here at the high school. You always do that to needle me, and I'm sick and tired of it."

Councilman Sparks took another puff of his cigar, indulged one of his wicked grins, and chuckled. "You're one feisty librarian. I've always given you that much."

Maura Beth decided it was time to cut to the chase. "Well, I appreciate you keeping me in the loop about all this, but what do you think I can possibly do about it? I'm no elected official or detective. Why am I really here?"

He shrugged his shoulders as his mouth went all crooked—not a good look for such an extraordinarily handsome man. "Actually, Lon Dreyfus asked me to speak to you. He wants to address your book club about the stolen tips thing. He's thinking that you and your cronies could keep an eye out around town so this thing won't get outta hand. Of course, the truth is, he loves to hear himself talk. So, he's addressing all the civic groups, and you've got quite a collection of members there. All ages and interests . . . Connie and Douglas McShay, Miss Voncille Nettles—er, Linwood she is now—and her genealogy following; Justin and Becca Brachle; that black pastry chef and his mother—well, I don't have to tell you who all comes to your meetings, do I? Maybe someone'll see something to help the sheriff and the police department out. More pairs of eyes on the street, you know."

Maura Beth sank back in her sumptuous leather visitor's chair and peered smugly at her longtime adversary. Having the upper hand was sweet, indeed! "So, let me get this straight, Councilman. After all the grief you've given me, the library, and The Cherry Cola Book Club, you actually want our help now?"

He didn't even blink. "That's the gist of it. I mean, you could call one of your club meetings and potlucks and enlist their help. The way I see it, it'd clearly be a civic duty thing. Besides, as I said, it's not my idea, it's the sheriff's. He and I—well, we don't always see eye to eye, but I pretty much agree with him on this one. I mean, what harm could it do?"

Maura Beth's laugh was genuine and prolonged. "And not so long ago, the book club was the proverbial thorn in your side."

"True enough." He leaned in farther, looking almost predatory and ready to pounce on her with his hands palms down and fingers spread wide on the desk. "But you've proven you can hold your own with us good ole boys running things. You got exactly what you wanted out of your newfound political savvy—that big new library going up out at the lake. You and I, we share a few secrets now, don't we? So, I view you as a pretty valuable asset to Cherico."

"To your political reign here in Cherico, you mean."

"Why should I deny it? That's what I'm all about, and you

know it as well as I do. So, are you and the club gonna help out or not?"

Maura Beth took her time. An uneasy feeling gripped her briefly. She had been prepared for another of the councilman's attacks, but cooperating with him on just about any level was awkward and rare territory. Still, she didn't see how she could turn Sheriff Dreyfus down. Unlike with Councilman Sparks, she'd never had an unpleasant experience with him over the years. "Yes, of course, the club will help. I imagine everyone's concerned about it. They all have a stake in our little community."

"Ah! Just what I thought you'd say!"

"You almost always get your way, don't you?"

He pulled back somewhat, drumming his fingers rapidly on the highly polished wood to some hidden rhythm. "Almost always. You're one of my few exceptions. And now—well, you're married and all that goes with that."

Maura Beth's expression was steely. He was no longer able to get to her where she lived. "It was never going to happen, Councilman. Even if you'd burned down the library, I was never going to come work for you as your secretary. And I use the term loosely."

His face went all dreamy and slightly creepy at the same time. "Ah, yes, what could have been!"

"I'll get back to you as soon as I can about when we can work the sheriff in," she told him, ignoring his theatrics. "And I'm sure you're right—everyone who belongs to The Cherry Cola Book Club is very involved in the welfare of our little town. Someone may very well spot something—or overhear something that will help catch the culprit. Then maybe you can find another cowboy boot company to kick up its heels in your industrial park."

"Yee-ha, little lady!" Councilman Sparks shouted, making a lassoing gesture while flashing his legendary white teeth.

Maura Beth gave him one of her weakest smiles as she said good-bye and walked away. Some things and some people never changed.

It was only when Maura Beth and Jeremy were sitting across from each other at their kitchen table that evening having dinner that she felt the full impact of her latest session with Councilman Sparks. "What this boils down to is, the head honcho of Cherico has now put me in the same category as his City Hall lackeys—'Chunky' Badham and 'Gopher' Joe Martin. I'm supposed to do his bidding without giving him an argument like I used to do."

Jeremy swallowed a forkful of the chicken spaghetti she had made for them and took a moment. "Well, at least this time Councilman Sparks is trying to do some good, and the sheriff is only doing his job. I mean, the sooner whoever did this is caught, the better."

Maura Beth moved her food around her plate, looking thoroughly disinterested. "I know. It's just the way he manages to turn every conversation with me into a dirty joke. I always come away feeling like he's made another pass at me and that I need to take a shower."

Jeremy narrowed his eyes and sat bolt upright, looking very territorial. "Maybe I need to go over there and set him straight, then."

"That would not be a good idea, sweetie," she said. "But I appreciate you wanting to be my knight in shining armor. Just trust me on this one—I can handle the councilman by myself."

"Just promise me you won't let things get out of hand with him."

She reached across and gave him her most reassuring smile, gently patting his hand. "I promise."

Then, for not the first time, she sat back with the pride of first-home ownership on her face and surveyed the bright yellow kitchen inside the Painter Street cottage they had bought from Miss Voncille Nettles—now Mrs. Locke Linwood. What a generous wedding present from her parents—William and Cara Lynn Mayhew—the down payment had been! And then Miss Voncille had used their honeymoon period to move what possessions she was keeping into the Perry Street house she now shared with her new husband—Locke Linwood. But some of Miss Voncille's personality still lingered by mutual agreement—a couple of her iconic potted palms she had lovingly maintained over the decades in honor of her MIA fiancé, Frank Gibbons; the big, round breakfast nook table where they were having dinner at the moment; and a comfortable, upholstered chair or two in the living room and master bedroom. At any rate, everything was where it was supposed to be for the newlyweds upon their return from Key West, making for a seamless transition into their new home.

"Everything that's been happening to Cherico reminds me of that old gospel song," Maura Beth said, emerging from her reverie about their little cottage. "You know, the one about Joshua fittin' the Battle of Jericho? Maybe that sounds a little outside the box right now, but it seems to fit."

Jeremy nodded while hitching up one side of his mouth in recognition. "Never sang it myself, but I know the tune."

"Yeah, well, I was wondering if this is the beginning of the end for our little town with all these stores closing. Am I building a brand-new library just as our walls come tumblin' down, so to speak? Councilman Sparks paints such a dismal picture, and he's usually pretty cocky about things."

Jeremy shook off the suggestion vigorously, wagging a finger. "Nah, let it all play out, sweetheart. You and I—we'll stay the course here as we planned. And Cherico'll be the better for it—you'll see."

2

Dreaded Birthdays and Hot Tips

Maybe it was just her overactive imagination, but Maura Beth thought Emma Frost had aged by leaps and bounds over the past few weeks. Her pale, plump face—never what anyone would call pretty—seemed to have acquired folds and creases that were not there before. Yet there remained a certain honesty and determination in the woman's plainness that endeared her to everyone who walked into the outdated, claustrophobic Cherico Library and asked for her help at the front desk. Indeed, no one had ever even thought about registering a complaint.

Maura Beth's goal on her second day back at work was to try as best she could to lighten Emma's load, and she believed she was well on her way to doing that as the two women sat across from each other in her office just before the library was set to open up at nine o'clock. "So, who's looking after your Leonard when you come to work?" Maura Beth was asking.

"Cissy—that's my daughter that's not married yet, ya know—well, she comes over to help me out. She's at my house right now prob'ly watchin' TV with him. We just gotta keep an eye on Leonard, since he just cain't be trusted to know what's best for him. We learned that lesson the hard way first time we found him wanderin' around out on the sidewalk. He just slipped out on us when we weren't lookin', and when we asked him what he thought he was doin', all he'd tell us was, 'I'm just out for a little walk like I used to do before y'all started frettin' over me so. A man needs some fresh air, ya know!' Then he stormed off to his room, mad as an old banty rooster, and slammed the door so hard, there come a zigzag crack in the wall and one a' the pictures of my mother in the hallway fell down with a racket like you've never heard. It scared me near half to death!"

Maura Beth was a bit overwhelmed by Emma's ramblings but managed to maintain her smile. "When will you know something for sure from the doctors?"

Emma turned away, looking pitifully distraught. "Any day now, they told us. I just have this feelin' he's got the Alltimer's. They kinda hinted at it here and there, but they couldn't say for sure 'til they'd checked on a few more things."

Maura Beth let the malapropism pass without so much as a blink. This was no time to tidy up the English language and cause embarrassment. Instead, she concentrated on sounding as soothing as she could. "Maybe it won't turn out that way, though. At any rate, I want you to know that I'll do everything I can to help you out if it comes to that. We'll work out special hours for you so you can keep your job. With the money my Cudd'n M'Dear gave us, I can afford to hire extra clerks to spread the hours around a bit more. I'm going to be interviewing for that very soon."

Emma appeared greatly relieved. "Thank you, Miz Maura Beth. The raise you gave me has already helped us a lot. I cain't keep askin' my Cissy to give up her spare time and such—she's found her a nice young man she's interested in and all and they've been goin' out, so we may have to hire us a sitter for Leonard when neither of us can work it out."

"I understand. But the days of the library and its employees getting the short end of the stick are over," Maura Beth told her, drawing herself up proudly. "You've done your part to help out for decades now, so I'll see you're taken care of as long as you want to work here. Meanwhile, I just wanted to say again what a great job you and Renette did looking after things while I was on my honeymoon. I knew I didn't have to worry about a thing."

Emma waved her off quickly. "Oh, it was mostly Renette, ya know. She's the one that really knows what all you want done. I've always just taken orders—first from Miz Annie Scott, and now from you and Renette." There was an awkward silence during which Emma's face dropped noticeably. "But . . . would you mind if I leaned on your shoulder just a tad bit more?"

"Of course not. What else did you want to tell me?"

Emma took her time, her eyes shifting from side to side, but eventually got the words out. "It's just that it's been real hard on us—seein' Leonard kinda disappear on us bit by bit. I don't mean the time or two he got out of our sight and we had to track him down out in the backyard or sittin' on the front stoop. I mean what's goin' on in his head. Sometimes, he's just not there anymore. He's someplace else, and I cain't seem to pull him back."

"I'm sure that's difficult for you, Emma," Maura Beth said, leaning in to pat her on the hand several times. "But once the doctors tell you what's going on for certain, you'll be able to deal with it all better. These days, they have medications that help with all kinds of conditions."

"I hope so. But . . . there was somethin' else."

"Go on, dear. I'm here for you."

Emma's sigh was pronounced as she folded her hands in her lap, looking lost and forlorn. "The strangest thing is the way Leonard carries on about my birthday. Cain't even remember when he started up, but he sings 'Happy Birthday' to me at the drop of a hat. I mean, I can be comin' outta the shower drippin' wet in my birthday suit, and there he is ready with another chorus."

Maura Beth cocked her head, struggling mightily to suppress a smile. "Things could be a whole lot worse, I guess. He could be snapping your picture. Is your birthday coming up soon? I always get yours confused with Renette's."

"Still six weeks or more away. I'm not too thrilled about it since it happens I'll be turnin' sixty-five. Makes me feel real old, and I know I look every year of it. Now don't lie to me and say I don't. I know better. But Leonard, he forgets practically everything else these days, but he remembers my sixty-fifth birthday of all things. And every time he finishes singin' to me, he winks and says, 'Gonna have us a great little party, aren't we? Just you wait'n see!' "

Emma paused, looking more confused than anything else. "Miz Maura Beth, I'm here to tell you there was years he'd forget all about my birthday until the last minute and then he'd have to run out and buy somethin' real quick off the rack that never fit me or was some god-awful color or print no respectable woman'd ever wear. Of course, I'd smile like it was just what I wanted and all and then give it to the Salvation Army when he wudd'n lookin'. Now I know this sounds kinda ungrateful of me, but I hope when the doctors tell us what's wrong with him, they'll have some a' those pills you were talkin' about that'll make him stop singin' to me. I've been Happy Birthday'ed near 'bout to death!"

In spite of everything, the two women couldn't help laughing, exchanging reassuring glances. "Well, how is he when it comes to your anniversary?" Maura Beth said.

"Now that, he always forgets, and it's been that way from when we was first married. Some men just cain't seem to get that date through their heads!"

Maura Beth looked particularly thoughtful and sank back in

her chair. The remnant emotions of her honeymoon briefly flooded her brain. She hoped they would never stop visiting her. "It's too soon for me to know how my Jeremy will be about handling such things as birthdays and anniversaries. But I have to tell you—so far, he's been pretty romantic about everything."

Emma made a dismissive noise under her breath and threw up her hands. "Leonard, he never was. That's why you'd think I'd really take to the way he's runnin' this birthday thing into the ground. But the truth is, I'd rather have him like he used to be—warts 'n' all—than have whatever craziness is goin' on in his brain."

"I know this is a trial for you, Emma, but try not to get too down in the dumps about it."

Emma glanced at her watch, sucked in air, and quickly rose from her chair. "I'll do my best, Miz Maura Beth. Meantime, that front desk is callin' my name. I do take my job seriously, ya know."

Maura Beth quickly rose and gestured toward the door. "I do—and that's why I'll see to it that you and your family are taken care of no matter what."

Maura Beth and Jeremy had just finished their dinner of trout amandine, garlic new potatoes, and fresh roasted asparagus at The Twinkle and had lingered after closing to catch up with Periwinkle Lattimore and her pastry chef and good friend—perhaps even significant other now—Mr. Parker Place. The four of them were sitting beneath one of the signature metallic star mobiles, lamenting the general state of affairs in Cherico, but particularly the mystery of Lalie Bevins's missing tips.

"Can you tell us everything Lalie remembers about that particular day?" Maura Beth was asking after a sip of the Chardonnay she'd held on to after the table had been cleared and Lalie herself had headed home. "Who else was working that afternoon?"

"Ruby Varnell, my other waitress, wasn't in for lunch service because she was under the weather, and Charlie Marks, my sous chef, doesn't come in 'til the dinner service. I always handle things myself before then unless we've been rented out for a party. Anyway, I'd trust both Ruby and Charlie with my life savings. They're hardworking, salt-of-the-earth people just like Lalie and her son, Barry."

"Who was Lalie serving?"

"The two customers were my lawyer, Curtis Trickett, and Audra Neely. But they weren't sitting together. Curtis came in around one o'clock, and he was entertaining about five of his big-time clients all at once. We had to put a coupla tables together for him, and he ran up quite a bill with the bottles of wine and the drinks and everything else they ordered. Guess it was one a' those 'thank you for the business' things. And then Audra Neely and her assistant came in late, too, from her antique shop. Those two ladies are both hooked on my tomato aspic, just like Connie McShay," Periwinkle explained. "But Lalie said this time they ordered big lunches and cocktails, and even a couple of aspics to go. Both Curtis and Audra have charge accounts with us, which we bill monthly, but they also prefer to pay as they go with their tips. Lalie said Curtis flashed a Benjamin Franklin at her as she was walking away with some of the dishes, and she also saw Audra put down a twenty. They're both really big tippers—I can vouch for that myself."

"Wow! That sure is a lot of money for any waitress to lose!" Maura Beth declared.

"Tell me about it," Periwinkle continued. "Anyway, at that point there wudd'n anybody else in the dining room since it was nearly two o'clock by then. Lalie went into the kitchen with some of the dessert dishes, and when she returned a little bit later to collect the tips, the money was gone. Best we can figure out, somebody must've just walked in and taken it. Pretty all-fired brazen—even risky, if you ask me.

Lalie could've returned at any time and caught 'em red-handed. Believe you me, if I'd seen who did it, I would've pressed charges right then and there. That's a rotten thing to do—stealing money from a hardworking waitress on her feet all day. The very idea just makes my blood boil!"

Mr. Place nudged her gently. "Tell 'em about the theory you had and the detective work you did."

Periwinkle frowned and shook her head. "Ya think?"

"Go ahead."

"Well, it's those two high-school hooligans Lalie's son, Barry, hangs out with all the time. Scott and—I think they call the other one Crispy 'cause he likes bacon so much. I mean, they phoned in that fake delivery order a while back and then tailgated Barry in our delivery van with their high beams on when he got out there in the boonies with all that food nobody ordered. Had us all scared half to death. So I told Lalie she needed to question Barry about those two and see if he could get 'em to fess up. But she said they swore they didn't do it and hadn't been anywhere near The Twinkle in a long time. She even called up their mothers about it, and they said those boys were still grounded from the dirty trick they played on Barry. So it seemed like a dead end. But Barry says he'll bet anything those boys found a way to sneak in here and take that money, no matter what their mothers say."

"So he thinks their mothers are covering for them, then," Maura Beth said, sounding decidedly judgmental.

Mr. Place spoke up with great authority. "We shared everything with the police and the sheriff, too, and I know they looked into it. But until anyone can prove anything different, I guess we have to believe those boys are innocent. I know for a fact that Barry's a good kid. He does a bang-up job as our delivery guy all over town. That's why I've been telling Peri we just might have to install one of those security cameras for the future. Hey, some of the other businesses swear by 'em, so maybe we better get with the program."

Periwinkle was running her fingers nervously through her dyed-blond hair, looking thoroughly disgusted. "Cherico never used to have problems like this. You'd think we were growing like mad and all sorts of new people were moving in that you didn't know a hill a' beans about. But the sad truth is, we're losin' population, and too many businesses have closed up lately. Harlan's closed down the Marina Bar and Grill and left, of course, and I can't say I'm sorry with all I went through with him trying to get back together with me. It's just that some people never really thought they needed a security camera before now. Everybody trusted everybody else to do the right thing. This was an honest, churchgoing community. And now this has happened to change things for the worse. If it's the beginning of a trend, it'll boggle my mind."

"Peri made things right for Lalie, though," Mr. Place added, casting an affectionate glance her way. "She made up the tips for her out of petty cash."

Maura Beth hoisted her wineglass without even thinking about it. "Good for you. But I would have expected nothing less."

"It's not the amount of money, of course. It's the principle of the thing. Plus, that still doesn't solve Cherico's problem," Periwinkle pointed out. "Word's gotten out about those tips, and it has everyone looking over their shoulder and second-guessing every customer who comes into their stores. Is shoplifting gonna be next? I never thought in a million years that Cherico'd be a paranoid place to live and work. That's just what we need with the holidays coming up in a month or two."

"Well, there is something constructive we can all do about it," Maura Beth said after finishing off her wine. "We can attend the special Cherry Cola Book Club meeting I've called this Friday. Sheriff Dreyfus is going to come by and share what he can about crime prevention in the community. He told me over the phone that he wants to set up a gigantic neighborhood watch for the whole town. Sooner or later, whoever did this will make a mistake and get spotted. Nobody was paying much attention before, but that's going to be changing shortly."

Jeremy took a sip of his coffee and screwed up his features. "I'd say they have to be pretty clever. Or desperate."

"But why Cherico?" Periwinkle added with a dramatic sweep of her hand. "We're just a small town in the middle of nowhere. Oh, sure, those of us who live here swear by it. But there's not much of value to write home about. Unless you wanna talk about those expensive homes out at the lake like that lodge your aunt and uncle have, Jeremy. But that's about it. I always think of crime as somethin' that happens in big cities, and stealin' tips from tables is strictly small potatoes, isn't it?"

"Apparently someone doesn't think so," Jeremy said.

"Mama says she wants to come to hear the sheriff tell us all what to do to protect ourselves," Mr. Place announced. "She wants to do her part to keep Cherico safe, bless her heart. Of course, she won't be getting around much since I won't let her drive by herself anymore—even with her new glasses, her eyesight's getting even worse, and then there's her arthritis that's a lot worse than she admits. Lately, I think she's been hiding some new aches and pains from me. I've spotted her catching her breath across the room on the sofa when she doesn't think I'm looking."

"Your mother is a sweetheart, and you know it," Periwinkle said, chucking him on the arm. "Ardenia's really been very understanding about our relationship, Parker. Considering how things were when she was growing up here before the civil rights era, I can see how a white woman and a black man becoming an item might bother her a bit. They say old-school dies hard. But she's been very warm and welcoming to me on my visits to your house."

"Mama just wants me—she wants us—to be happy now."

Maura Beth gave Periwinkle a saucy wink. "Is there an official announcement on the horizon?"

"Not just yet. I think we'll keep things the way they are for a while," Periwinkle told her. "Maybe we'll keep savin' our money for a security camera or two instead of a wedding."

"Well, you just remember now—I want to be in your wedding if and when it happens," Maura Beth continued. "After all, you were in mine, and you never looked more beautiful."

Periwinkle's face lit up. "I have to admit it was pretty special out at the lodge. You and Jeremy did it up right with those original vows that took my breath away—not to mention the sun setting behind you out on the McShays' deck. Y'all just timed it perfectly—right down to the second. And by the way, I still want prints of all of it. You promised me, Maura Beth."

"It's as good as done."

"Oh, wait," Mr. Place added with a little gasp. "Tell 'em all the good news after wading through all this mess about the tips."

Periwinkle lightly clapped her hands several times. "Yes, I almost forgot. It could be huge news for The Twinkle. Maura Beth, do you remember the text I got a good while back from Waddell Mack, the country singer? He said some friends of his had come through Cherico and eaten here and had recommended it highly to him."

"I think I vaguely remember something about it, but to be honest with you, I don't listen to country music."

"Oh, I didn't either—until I married Harlan John Lattimore and kept his books for him all those years before our divorce. I guess I heard more honky-tonk songs than I can count on that jukebox of his out at the Marina Bar and Grill. Honestly, it began to grow on me. Yeah, I know—sometimes it seems a little bit corny. Like, Waddell's latest hit is 'Don't Sell Me Short When I'm Longin' for You.' But it's kinda catchy— you don't forget it."

Maura Beth felt it was her duty to smile at her friend's enthusiasm. It was the least she could do. "Well, to each his own."

"Sure enough. But anyway, I got another text from Waddell Mack himself while you were off in Key West, and he said he would actually be passin' through Cherico on his Christmas tour in early December. Seems he's got two gigs in Mississippi—one in Tupelo at the BancorpSouth Arena and another one in Natchez at the Convention Center down there. Said he's bound and determined to try two places to eat that come highly recommended—The Twinkle right here and Fat Mama's Tamales down in Natchez. I'm so excited!"

"That *is* terrific news," Maura Beth said. "What an opportunity for you and the restaurant!"

"Idd'n it? And he said he'd be glad to tweet about us before and after; and when I asked him if he'd autograph a picture of himself so I could hang it on the wall, he said he'd be more'n happy to do it. It'll be tremendous publicity for not only The Twinkle but Cherico, too. And right now we could use some a' that!"

"You'll have to be sure and keep me posted on the details." Then Maura Beth quickly surveyed the table. "So, display of hands. We're all coming to the meeting at the library Friday, right?"

All hands shot up immediately.

"Excellent. Cherico is nothing if not the little town that could."

3

The Eyes and Ears of Cherico

Sheriff Lon Dreyfus was a man who got right to the point. His frequent talks to civic groups never ran over or caused carefully planned agendas to fall apart—although he made it known that he was always available as a backup should any guest speaker fail to appear. Tall and gangly with an impressive salt-and-pepper mustache that dominated the lower half of his narrow face, he was a towering presence wherever he appeared on or off duty. Few people had ever chosen to "mess" with him, so to speak—not even Councilman Sparks and his City Hall cronies. In fact, the two men and their entourages kept a civil distance from one another, respecting each other's territory in a gentlemen's agreement between those in power in Cherico.

"There are some things I can't tell y'all about because we can't share everything about an ongoing investigation," the sheriff was saying, standing behind the podium in the library lobby. Before him in a semicircle of folding chairs sat most of the members of The Cherry Cola Book Club, hanging on his every word. One or two were even taking notes.

"But I can tell ya what to be on the lookout for in the future to help nip crime of any sort—especially with Christmas shopping not all that far away. I suspect some of you have already done a little bit of it already. When you're in any of our stores, look for groups of two or three people to start with—that is, if they're strangers. Obviously, if you know who they are, chances are there's nothing going on. But be very suspicious if they're strangers and one of 'em is tying up a salesclerk, and the other two are in a different part of the store. What they're up to is creating a distraction so the others can stuff things into their pockets or purses while no one's paying attention. And that's another thing—really big purses or bags can sometimes be a tipoff that somebody's up to no good."

Justin Brachle, who sometimes went by the nickname of "Stout Fella" to his wife and most of the club, was quick to respond, raising his hand. "Sheriff, I don't wanna sound like a typical dumb male here, but there are a whole lotta purses out there. For instance, my wife, Becca, has all sizes that she uses for just about every occasion under the sun. I mean, all I need is one measly wallet. We men aren't fussy about that kinda thing. So, how big is really big?"

That brought a wave of titters from all the members, and the sheriff enjoyed a laugh as well. "Good question. Just use your judgment here. If something seems really outta proportion, it might not be a bad idea to keep an eye on whoever's carrying it around." Then the sheriff's tone grew more serious. "Now don't get me wrong here, folks. Just go about your daily bid'ness and don't get paranoid. We're not innerested in any citizen's arrests here. Most people out there aren't criminals, but we just want y'all to report anything that seems outta the ordinary or suspicious. You just tell us what you saw and then let us handle it from there."

The pregnant Becca "Broccoli" Brachle, as she was known to the fans of her now-defunct radio recipe show, followed up her husband's question. "Can you tell us what some of the most popular stolen items are in general?"

The sheriff briefly squinted while trying to conjure them all up. "Well, we do find that makeup, eyeliner, lipstick, high heels, scarves, and things like that tend to get shoplifted a lot."

Maura Beth sounded a bit skeptical. "So, are you saying that most shoplifters are women?"

The sheriff snickered. "No, men do more than their share. I think crime is an equal opportunity destroyer of the economy."

"What do the men tend to take?" Maura Beth said, somewhat reassured.

"Electronic stuff. Cell phones, watches, laptops, that kinda stuff. There's a lotta fencing that goes on."

Maura Beth continued to press. "Tell us about your most unusual case here in Cherico—that is, if you can."

The sheriff was laughing heartily now. "Sure can. A few years back, we caught a cross-dresser who was puttin' together outfits for himself. Shoplifted a girdle, pantyhose, high heels, and such, and I do believe when we caught him he had just about every one of those items on while he was doing some honest, pay-for-it shopping dressed as a woman. Turns out all he really wanted to do was go buy lotsa girlie things without people lookin' at him like he was crazy. But he told us he needed to get that first round of stuff without all the embarrassment—thus, the shoplifting." The sheriff winked a couple of times as he surveyed the crowd. "Actually, he made a real handsome woman, if you wanna know the truth."

Stout Fella's laugh sounded like a couple of high-pitched hiccups. "Does that cross-dressing fella still live here?"

"Nope, we cut him a break because he was underage. But he still did a little juvie detention center time for all the stuff he stole. By the time he got out, I believe he'd learned his lesson. He and his family moved away shortly after anyway. But before they left, that young man came by my office to tell me he was actually grateful we caught him when they did. Said it gave him the motivation he needed to stop cross-dressing once and for all. At least that was his story."

Mamie Crumpton, the buxom, opinionated half of the town's wealthiest spinster sisters, then spoke up in that imperious manner of hers. "All this talk of cross-dressing impresses me as unseemly. I don't think we have anyone who does that here in Cherico now."

Voncille Nettles Linwood, the town genealogist and Mamie's long-time rival, eyed her with disdain. "And how would you know that, Mamie? Have you been peeking into a few closets around town with a flashlight? You could have passed some woman on the street and not even blinked, never knowing that you were actually looking at a man in drag. Maybe that person even stole the tips from The Twinkle."

"Please, Voncille, don't start anything," Locke Linwood said, gently grabbing his wife's arm.

Mamie bristled, her nose turned up sharply. "Yes. Is this conversation really necessary, Voncille? You always were such a know-it-all. And you run your 'Who's Who in Cherico?' meetings like a mad genealogist. You make things up about our families and think we're all just going to sit there in our seats and take it like we were a bunch of those impressionable students you taught."

"Ladies, please!" Maura Beth said, resuming her customary role as peacemaker. "We're here to let the sheriff guide us, not argue with one another!" Respecting Maura Beth as they did, the two women quickly obeyed and with downcast eyes went thankfully silent. "I appreciate your cooperation very much. Now, Sheriff Dreyfus, will you please continue?"

"I just wanted to emphasize that all of you need to be the eyes and ears of Cherico," he began, a hint of amusement in his voice following the last exchange. "Over the years, Cherico's not had too much of this kinda thing—certainly not anything we couldn't handle. This time, no one seems to have seen or heard anything about the stolen money, and that's un-usual. Yet, those tips just didd'n get up and walk out by them-selves. I assure you, they had help of some kind."

"Did they ever!" Periwinkle cried out impulsively.

The sheriff wrinkled up his nose a couple of times, and his mustache did a passable imitation of a big gray caterpillar wig-gling underneath. "Miz Peri—you knew your two customers who left those tips, and after that, neither you nor your wait-ress were around to see what happened. But we'll get to the bottom of this sooner or later before it escalates into some-thing worse."

Once again, Mamie Crumpton joined the exchange with gusto. "This sounds like it could even end up being a tad bit dangerous. You're certainly right, Sheriff. I don't recall any-thing like this before, and I've lived here all my life, as you all know. Of course, I had no idea about the cross-dressing thing. But maybe being the person who catches this awful person would be exciting."

"Now, Miz Crumpton," the sheriff said, boring into her with his eyes, "we don't want you or anybody else to take any chances, ya hear? I don't think the role of vigilante really suits you. As you said, this could be a dangerous proposition, and we don't want anyone hurt out there. If you or your sister, Marydell, spot something suspicious, you just call us up, and you let that be the end of it."

"Oh, will do," Mamie told him as she clasped her hands with a certain thrill evident in her voice.

Then Mr. Place's mother, Ardenia, waved her hand back and forth. "Sheriff, I just want to say that my son won't let me get out the house without him. Now how am I s'pposed to help out with him drivin' me around like that? Could you do me a big favor and talk some sense into him? When he get the hard head like that, I just throw my hands up in the air. Just like his no-good daddy—and good riddance to him!"

Mr. Place's jaw dropped as a round of snickers and giggles broke out among the members. "Mama, the sheriff doesn't have time for this. It's strictly between you and me."

"I have time for all my constituents," the sheriff declared, rising to the occasion. "And let me just say that you might be in the best position of all of us, ma'am. The driver's the one who has to pay attention to the road and such—and that leaves the passengers free to see a lot more. Why, you can keep an eye out that much better that way!"

Ardenia sat back in her chair, adjusting her thick glasses and then folding her arms with a satisfied grin. "Well, I never looked at it that-a-way. Guess maybe I can do my part after all. When you a certain age, no one seem to pay attention to you. You heard what the sheriff say, son?"

"I heard it, Mama."

The sheriff drew himself up with a great intake of air, adding another few inches to his height. "Well, I'm glad I could help you out, Miz Ardenia. You might be the one who ends up helping us catch the thief." He nodded her way crisply. "Well, I guess that's about it, ladies and gentlemen. We believe the eyes and ears of Cherico will solve this thing and get things back to normal. Better to nip this kinda thing in the bud. Do your part and be smart about it. We're all counting on ya."

No meeting of The Cherry Cola Book Club was ever complete without potluck dishes to sample, and the talk by the sheriff was no exception. In fact, he was the first in line at the buffet table, and soon everyone was digging into the peeled boiled shrimp and cocktail sauce, potato salad with egg and dill, and caramel pie that various members had contributed; and also true to form—everyone was using the occasion to catch up with each other.

"So, your second trimester is going a lot easier for you?" Maura Beth was asking Becca Brachle. The two of them had managed to find a couple of seats next to each other in the midst of the chatting throng.

Becca's face was a study in relief. "Oh, very much easier, thank you. I've been the Queen of Morning Sickness up until now. My mother was like that, too. But thankfully, that's all behind me. I feel like I can get to the end of this now, and believe me, I was doubting that for a while."

"Are you and your Stout Fella still not going to ask your obstetrician about the gender?"

"Justin wants to know in the worst way. I kinda don't, though. So far, I've managed to hold out, but I have to say, he's wearing me down. It would be easier to buy things in coordinated colors, so to speak. I know, I know—in this day and age you'd think people would've moved away from the pink and blue thing. But when you've been waiting to get pregnant as long as Justin and I have, you'd be surprised how traditional our thinking has become all of a sudden."

Maura Beth took a sip of her cherry cola punch and moved on to the inevitable. "What about baby names?"

"Now there, we've made a decision," Becca said, excitement flashing in her eyes. "If it's a boy, he's not going to be a junior. We want something brand-new. So we're going with Mark Grantham Brachle. Grantham was my mother's maiden name, and I want to honor it."

"I like the sound of it, too. And if it's a girl?"

Becca sounded thoroughly resolute. "No Becca, either. I would never tell my mother this, but I've never really liked my name. It always sounded so formal to me. So, we're going to go with Angelica Grantham Brachle, since we just know she'll be our little angel."

"Sounds very original!" Then Maura Beth lowered her voice and leaned in, carefully balancing her plate on her knees. "And what's the latest on the godmother thing, if you don't mind?"

Almost in a whisper, Becca said, "You're still the frontrunner. Just keep it on the down low for now. I don't want your competition to know that I've pretty much made up my mind."

At that point, Jeremy sauntered over with a plate piled high with shrimp. He had been known to tear through a dozen in no time at all. "And what are you two beautiful ladies whispering about? Something about Councilman Sparks, I'm willing to bet anything."

"You'd lose that bet this time, sweetheart," Maura Beth told him. "But please, have a seat."

"Have you spotted something suspicious around town then?" Jeremy continued, pulling up a nearby chair.

"Not me," Becca said. "I don't get out much these days. Justin would be the one—I mean, the way he's all over the place selling real estate to whomever comes down the pike. But I fully intend to pamper myself the bigger I get. You won't see me straying far from the house."

Jeremy speared one of his shrimp and dipped it into the pool of pungent bright red sauce near the edge of his plate. "I'm pretty much like you, Becca. I'm out of the loop teaching all day out at the high school; so unless one of my students is the culprit and confesses, I'm not likely to be of much help."

"Well, I guess that leaves me, then, to help the police and the sheriff out," Maura Beth added. "I think I might start taking little walks along Commerce Street on my lunch hour. Maybe I'll just pop in and out of stores or do some window-shopping. Heaven knows, I always need a break from that dark, windowless office of mine. And who can tell? I could get lucky and see something as it happens. Why, I could even be part of the breaking news of the day."

"Just don't go superhero on us, sweetie. We want you to stay safe and sound. By the way, how's the new library coming along?" Becca said, changing the subject with a smile. "I haven't gotten out to the lake to see it lately."

"It's taking shape quite nicely. Those tall concrete pillars are rising from the slab at last. It's such an exciting time for me, I don't know what to do with myself. Connie and Doug keep me posted on the latest developments, since they're only a hop, skip, and a jump away at the lodge."

Maura Beth sat back for a moment and reflected once again upon the generosity of Jeremy's aunt and uncle. The McShays had sped things up considerably by donating some of their lakefront property for the construction of the new library—thus preventing Councilman Sparks from keeping the project on that infernal backburner of his. She knew only too well that if there was any way he could scuttle the project even at this late stage, he would try his best.

"What's the actual timetable for getting into the building?" Becca continued. "I can hardly wait for my little one to get big enough to sign up for summer reading out there. I looked forward to it so when I was a little girl. Anyone can put a child in front of a television set, but taking a child to the library to learn how to read—now that's some smart parenting and the gift of a lifetime."

Maura Beth paused to count up the months in her head. "My best estimate is next summer—that is, if we don't get too much bad weather during the winter. Of course, once the roof's on, even that won't matter. I'm thinking it would be ideal if we could have a grand opening on or around the Fourth of July. We could even have a fireworks display at dusk to get everyone out to the lake to ooh and aah and carry on in general. I mean, can't you just see it—hot dogs, ice cream, apple pie, sparklers, the works? And people crowded out on the deck of the library to watch it all. It'll be the start of a new era of participation and support!"

"That's a spectacular idea!" Connie McShay added. "I

really hope the timing works out, and you know you can count on me and Douglas to help you with the planning, of course. You could even use our deck for your staging area if you need it."

"Thanks. I look at it this way," Maura Beth said. "If nothing else, the new library will be at least one bright spot on the Cherico horizon."

When the sheriff had finished his second helping of food and finally left smiling and patting his stomach, Maura Beth took her place behind the podium and reminded the club of their upcoming review of *The Member of the Wedding.* "We've got a little more than three weeks to finish our October read, people. It'll be our last of the year since we'll recess for the upcoming holidays. We'll decide what to read next year at that time. And please remember to check with Becca about your potluck assignments, if you're someone we always depend upon."

Becca briefly waved her hand from side to side. "Yes, I haven't heard from some of you on your preferences this time around. As usual, we don't want too many entrées and no desserts—or vice versa."

"I'm halfway through *The Member of the Wedding,* and I just don't see any food theme in the story," Miss Voncille said. "Unless it's a wedding cake. I mean, our *Forrest Gump* review was a natural with the shrimp dishes some people fixed. But that little mixed-up Frankie Addams girl in this one—well, she doesn't eat a thing Berenice Sadie Brown puts in front of her. You can tell Berenice is one of those good, down-home Southern cooks the way she takes the time to shell her peas instead of pouring them out of a can like so many people do these days. She's the sort of help who's fallen by the wayside, unfortunately. I always had a good appetite when I was growing up, and I never went through a period like Frankie did where she didn't fit into anything. And I can't imagine not scrubbing my elbows and then getting all my hair cut so short you look like a boy. What Frankie really needs is the tender, loving care of a mother."

"But she doesn't have one. That's the whole point, Voncille," Mamie Crumpton pointed out with a haughty stare. "Her father is widowed and works hard, so she's on her own all the time. Aren't you paying attention to what you read, or is that too much to ask?"

Maura Beth stepped in once again. "I appreciate your comments, ladies. You're both obviously very involved with the plot, and that's terrific. But maybe we should save these insights for our actual review. And there doesn't have to be a food theme for us to read any work of literature, you know. I realize how important the potluck dishes have become to everyone. They're a big part of the club's success. Today's little feast was a great example. Sheriff Dreyfus raved about everything, and I really thought he was going to help himself to thirds. But references to food are not why we select our books. Anyhow, you can still fix those biscuits of yours if you want, Miss Voncille. I know everyone loves them."

"I sure do, and I've even put on a few pounds eating them since we got married," Locke Linwood added, pointing to his waist.

"I've already told Becca I want to bring my world-famous chocolate pudding this time," Mamie said. "I sprinkle lots of slivered almonds on top for a little change of pace. It was Mother's basic recipe, of course, but I decided to tweak it a little. Isn't that right, Sister?"

For once, the timid, mousy Marydell Crumpton spoke up for herself, surprising everyone. "As I recall, the almonds were my idea."

"Why, they most certainly were not. Now what on earth has gotten into you, Sister dear?"

"I beg to differ. The crunch was my idea, and you know it. One day in the kitchen I commented to you that I thought the pudding had gotten too predictable and needed a little kick. Then I went to the pantry and rummaged through it until I found the almonds."

"I don't remember it that way!" Mamie insisted. "I was the one who poured them on top first!"

Maura Beth's jaw dropped, and everyone else in the club was frowning in disbelief. No one had ever heard Marydell say anything in reply to her dominating sister other than yes. And now here she was, fighting for the floor and respectably holding her own.

The exchange escalated when Miss Voncille joined in with a gleeful expression. "This is rich. The Crumpton sisters arguing over pudding and almonds. I never thought I'd see the day!"

Mamie heaved her chest mightily in Miss Voncille's general direction. "This is none of your all-fired business, Voncille. I claim the slivered almonds, and that's the end of the story!"

Surprisingly, Marydell stood up and sprang to the podium, waving her hands frantically as if fighting off a gnat buzzing around her head. "May I have a word with the club, Maura Beth?"

"Of course. Please go right ahead," Maura Beth replied, stepping aside with ever-widening eyes. What was the world coming to? Marydell Crumpton had finally emerged from the considerable shadow of her overbearing sister. Meanwhile, Mamie was fuming in her seat, but there was no telling when she might explode.

"I just wanted to say," Marydell began while everyone leaned forward in great anticipation, "that being a member of this wonderful club has opened my eyes. I wasn't much of a reader before my sister and I joined, but now I am. There's a world of ideas and characters out there who do more than just sit idly by and watch other people do the talking for them and—"

The fidgeting Mamie finally interrupted. "Really, Marydell, just what are you trying to get at here?"

Marydell gestured toward Nora Duddney in the front row, Councilman Sparks's ex-secretary who had surprised everyone by literally reinventing herself and helping Maura Beth secure the funding for the new library behind the scenes. As a result, she had even acquired a boyfriend in the form of retired stockbroker Wally Denver, who was new in town and more than happy to accompany Nora to her book club meetings. "Miz Duddney was my real inspiration. I saw how she came to our meetings and started asserting herself. She had opinions about the books and everything else. And so, just the other day, as I was reading *The Member of the Wedding,* I said to myself: 'Marydell, you've been acting just like poor Frankie Addams. She's lost, and you're lost. The only way you fit in is to follow your sister around silently like some sort of dummy, and she's the ventriloquist.' " She paused to glare at Mamie, who was aiming daggers at her in return.

"Well, no more. I do have opinions, and at our next review, I'm going to start expressing them. And I'm practicing for it right now by saying to all of you that the idea for sprinkling slivered almonds on Mother's chocolate pudding recipe was mine. All mine. And that's the truth!"

With that, Marydell resumed her seat, looking straight ahead and ignoring the rigid, frowning face of her sister beside her.

"What a nice compliment to pay me," Nora Duddney said, blowing her a kiss from her seat on the end. "I completely agree with you about the book club. Best move I ever made. And Wally here says it's really helped him make friends here in Cherico—yours truly especially."

"It has for a fact, folks," he said, nodding agreeably in that big, teddy-bear fashion of his. "I really do appreciate the warm welcome I've received from everybody here at the library."

But Mamie completely ignored him, turning quickly in her chair and flashing on Nora and Marydell at the same time. "We are not here to drag family quarrels out into the open!"

It was up to Maura Beth to break through the tension gripping the room, as she stood behind the podium once again. "Well, Marydell, I, too, have to applaud your spunk and your honesty. And I have to say that I'm flattered the club has done so much for you. Not only do we get to know the characters in all of the books we review, it's my opinion that we get to know each other as well—and not just on the surface. We've all been there for each other for much more than book reviews and potluck, and I'm quite sure that will continue in the future no matter what happens. So, I'm very much looking forward to your comments on *The Member of the Wedding* when we get together a few weeks from now. Yours, too, Mamie."

"Thank you," Marydell replied, sounding greatly relieved while continuing to avoid her sister's eyes.

"On that note," Maura Beth added quickly before Mamie could say anything further, "I think we should wrap things up. Meanwhile, good reading to everyone, and remember to keep your eyes and ears wide open for anything suspicious around town. And keep on soliciting new members for the club. By the time the new library opens next summer, we want that enormous meeting room I've designed to be jam-packed. I'm talking standing room only for The Cherry Cola Book Club."

4

The Sinkhole

Two weeks out from *The Member of the Wedding* review and potluck, Maura Beth began her front desk clerk interviews in earnest. She certainly wanted the extra staff in place well before Christmas. She'd paid for an ad to run every day on WHYY, and she, Renette, and Emma had tacked posters all over town—including on James Hannigan's bulletin board at The Cherico Market; but she was having serious issues with the selection of candidates who had shown up so far.

"Extremely underqualified and oblivious" was Maura Beth's note to herself after one young housewife offered up the following: "Umm, do you have to have a high-school diploma for this? I'm just kinda bored at home watching TV all the time, but if I got the job, is there a TV here I could watch on my breaks? There are some shows I just wouldn't wanna miss."

"An accident waiting to happen" was her comment on another young female applicant who pressed the envelope in a similar manner: "How many holidays do we get, and if I get pregnant, how much maternity leave? Now, don't get me wrong—I'm not married yet. Not sure I believe in it. But I wanted to check—just in case something happens. Uh, condoms sometimes break, you know."

Then there were a couple of less-than-hopefuls who made even those two look like winners: "Now, would I be greeting everyone as they walk in like they do at Wal-Mart over in Corinth? I think that's such a stupid job, but I could do it if I have to," one particularly vapid young girl in a halter top asked, taking time out from gazing around Maura Beth's office as if she were visiting from another planet and trying her gum-chewing best to get the lay of the land.

"Do we have to stand all the time?" one middle-aged man with greasy-looking, long hair wanted to know. "I have awful feet. You should see my corns. I spend a fortune at the foot doctor's, and I could take my socks off and show ya so you know I'm not just making it up."

"Thank you very much for coming in today," Maura Beth had told them all without a moment's hesitation, always plastering an impossibly wide grin on her face. "We'll call you."

It was beginning to look like there was no one out there in Cherico with the proper qualifications; then a red-eyed, exhausted-looking Emma Frost dragged herself into Maura Beth's office one morning with more bad news.

"Leonard, he definitely has the Alltimer's, Miz Maura Beth," she said, fighting back tears as she took her seat. "Me and my daughter, Cissy—we're gonna have to be lookin' after him all the time now and hire a sitter, too. But you said we could work out my hours here at the library so I could keep my job."

"Of course we can," Maura Beth told her, reaching across to pat her hand. "And I'm so sorry that it's turned out this way."

"They say he'll have to take some kinda medication every day of his life now to slow it down a little," Emma added, sniffling. "But . . . I guess you know there's no cure for it. He's just gonna go even more downhill from here. He's just gonna . . . completely disappear until . . . well, you know how it ends up."

"Yes, I do know, dear. And again, I'm so sorry." Maura Beth handed over a Kleenex from the box atop her cluttered desk and kept a smile on her face. "But don't you worry about your job here. As long as you want some hours to work, I'll see to it that you have them. My idea in hiring two new clerks is that I'll be able to divide up the workload a little better."

Emma blew her nose loudly, crumpled up the tissue, and then exhaled. "You really are the best boss in the world. And if there's ever anything I can do for you, Miz Maura Beth, you just let me know."

Maura Beth thought for a while. "As a matter of fact, if you know anyone at all who might be interested in working here at the front desk, tell them about the openings we have. I've budgeted for two more, but so far, no one's walked in that has the faintest idea of what the job requires. In fact, they've all been downright scary—like something out of one of those reality TV shows. Renette's already asked her circle of girl-friends, but all of them have jobs they really like, so I really do need some help here."

Emma frowned as she considered and then finally bright-ened. "I'll ask around at my next church social. I'm takin' Leonard to the one tomorrow night. Seems like I remember someone sayin' they were lookin' for some part-time work a while back. All the folks at my church, they're good people who'd work real hard for ya. I know I'd vouch for any of 'em."

Maura Beth sat back and tapped her ballpoint pen on the arm of her chair. "At this point, an honest, hardworking, churchgoing front desk clerk sounds like a godsend to me."

"Well, it finally happened at school today, Maurie!" Jer-emy was saying with an edge to his voice as he poured himself a glass of Merlot in the kitchen of their little Painter Street cottage. She had just walked in from her trying day of awkward interviews and consoling Emma Frost at the library to find her husband at the counter looking thoroughly disgusted.

"What did?" She moved to him quickly and pointed to the bottle of wine. "Wait. Before you tell me, pour me a little of that. I can tell I'm going to need it. My day's been edgy, too!"

Despite his bad mood, he gave her a peck on the cheek, retrieved a wineglass, and filled it halfway. "To cut to the chase, I had it out with Obie Hutchinson today about the literary field trip issue for my class. Makes me think he and Yelverton up at New Gallatin Academy have been in cahoots. Hutchinson's been promising me for weeks for a decision on my request to take a bus over to Oxford for a Faulkner field trip, but just like my hardheaded, former headmaster, he's having none of it. So, I'm back to square one."

"You didn't lose your temper, I hope," Maura Beth said between sips of her wine. "Please tell me you didn't."

"No, I managed to hold it together. Last time I lost my temper over the issue, I almost bought the farm in my little Volvo out on the Natchez Trace."

Maura Beth leaned over and gave him a gentle kiss on the lips. "Although something good did come of your little accident with that deer. It brought us together once and for all— we both realized we couldn't make it as a couple with you living up in Nashville and me down here in Cherico." She took another sip of wine, savoring the bouquet for a moment, and then took a deep breath. "So, what's your next move with Hutchinson going to be?"

His exasperated tone suddenly disappeared. "I'm thinking I get the parents all excited about this. Maybe e-mail or even call them all and suggest they each pony up a few bucks so the school can cover the costs. And we'll need chaperones, so I'm thinking I could hook a few of them that way, too. I know,

I've learned my lesson about being patient and not flying off the handle so easily. Now, I won't lie to you—there were a few moments there where I felt like telling him off the way I did Yelverton about his shortsightedness. But the good news is that I didn't. I kept myself under control this time. You would've been proud of me."

She chucked him on the arm playfully. "There you go. Sounds like a plan to me. Oh, and for the record, if you ever do get that trip to Oxford lined up to tour Rowan Oak and have lunch at one of those fantastic restaurants around The Square, you can absolutely count me in. Believe it or not, I haven't made the time to go over there in all the years I've been up here in Mississippi, and I'm a bit ashamed of myself that I haven't."

"Hey, don't be too hard on yourself. Having Councilman Sparks in your face all the time hasn't left you much wiggle room for side trips. I doubt Triple A even has suggestions to keep him at bay." Then he frowned and snapped his fingers. "Oh, I almost forgot to tell you. Johnnie-Dell Crews and I were in the faculty lounge this morning having coffee and doughnuts when she told me some news you're not gonna like too much. She said she'd heard through the grapevine that Cherico Tresses was going to be moving to Corinth in the next month or two. That's where you get your hair fixed up, right?"

Maura Beth quickly put her wineglass down and gave him an incredulous stare. "What? Where did she hear that? She doesn't even get her hair done, Miss Voncille told me once. Last time I kept my appointment, Terra Munrow didn't say a word to me. It was just business as usual. I've been going to her practically since I came up from New Orleans, so I can't believe she wouldn't tell me something like that!"

"I'm just repeating what Johnnie-Dell said. You can call her up if you want. I've got her number."

Maura Beth took her cell phone out of her pocket and punched up a couple of digits. "I'd rather call Terra and get it from the horse's mouth."

But she only got through to Terra's voice mail for her trouble and left a hurried message: "Terra, this is Maura Beth. Please call me as soon as you can and tell me about these awful rumors I've heard that Cherico Tresses is moving away, God forbid. Thanks." Then she put the phone down on the counter and exhaled forcefully. "What next? With all these businesses closing, plant prospects turning us down, and everyone worried to death about thieves running around town, it feels like Cherico has moved to Florida all of a sudden and is slowly being swallowed up by one of those gigantic sinkholes!"

Jeremy put his arm around her shoulder and squeezed it gently. "It's not as bad as all that. You've still got your library going up out at the lake, and I've still got my job teaching."

Maura Beth tried her best to smile but couldn't. "I'm thankful for that, sweetheart. Believe me, I am. But I've got the feeling that things might get worse before they get better."

Mr. Place's drive to his mother's house on Big Hill Lane that evening after work was filled with great anticipation. Once or twice he caught a smirking glimpse of himself in the rearview mirror. Why, the handsome fella he saw there was gonna blow his mama's socks off with what he had to tell her! The two security cameras that had been installed that morning at The Twinkle—one in the dining room and one in the kitchen—were working to perfection, and it was Periwinkle who had put it succinctly: "Just let anyone try anything low-down now. I flat out double-dog dare 'em. We'll catch 'em and put their little behinds in jail!"

They had also decided to treat Ardenia to dinner with all the trimmings sometime during the coming week, showing her the monitors in Periwinkle's office and letting her keep an eye on things for a while after she'd finished her dessert. They even planned to let her keep a log of anything significant she saw. Even if it was nothing but business as usual throughout the restaurant.

"I know Mama'll be impressed, and it'll make her feel like she's helping out with the crime-prevention thing," Mr. Place had added. "She's so adamant about it, but I really do understand. She wants to be a part of everything now. When she was growing up, she couldn't be a part of anything with the Jim Crow laws and all."

In truth, his mother had remained downright crotchety about his decision to take her keys away from her, but he could not in good conscience allow her to drive around by herself any longer. He planned to sell her car, deposit the money in her savings account, and that would be the end of it. They had argued about it more than once, and there had been her outburst at the library when the sheriff had given his crime-prevention lecture. But perhaps letting her come into the restaurant now and then to check things out in the office would keep her frustrations at bay. Besides, she loved watching television and was very possessive of the remote; this way she would have two screens at once to occupy her time. It would be the perfect solution.

As Mr. Place entered his mother's tidy kitchen, which always featured a homemade pie or cake sitting out on the counter under a clear glass dome, he noted for not the first time that she had the volume on the TV set in the living room way up. He had begun to think she was starting to lose her hearing on top of everything else that was wrong with her. After telling her about the security cameras, he was just going to have to work in a suggestion to go to the doctor for a test— diplomatically, of course. There was no way around it— seventy-five had been taking its toll on his beloved mother for some time now, and it was his duty as a good son to protect her as best he could. After all, she had given him a home after the Grand Shelby Hotel up in Memphis had been torn down, and being vigilant was his way of repaying her.

"Mama, I'm home!" he called out as he entered the living room. "Can you turn that down a little bit? I wanna tell you all about the cameras and something else Peri and I think you'll really like doing."

Across the way, he saw that she was propped up in her usual spot on the end of the sofa with her treasured remote resting in her lap, and it brought a smile to his face. Ardenia Bedloe was nothing if not an adorable creature of habit.

"Mama!" he repeated, walking over quickly to take a seat next to her. "That's a little loud, don'tcha think?"

When she did not immediately obey, he snatched up the remote and muted the TV himself. "That's better. Now I can hear myself think."

It was only when he actually focused on her eyes that he grasped the fact she was not watching and listening to the TV at all, and in a further searing flash of emotion that spread from beneath his chest to every nerve in his extremities—one he would remember for the rest of his life—he realized she would never be watching and listening to the TV again. Then the remote fell from his hand onto the carpet below as the room was filled with his primal scream; but despite enduring the worst pain of his life, he was somehow able to compose himself enough to call 911.

Maura Beth and Jeremy had just finished another round of their energetic lovemaking in her brass bed and were cuddling in the afterglow when the phone rang on the nightstand. They weren't going for a record or anything like that, but the honeymoon had continued in their bedroom without a hitch. Yes, it was true that the routine of everyday life had kicked in for both of them and brought them down to earth, but so far, they had kept Key West alive and glowing in their flushed cheeks and throbbing pulses. Their marriage was off to a fast start.

It was Jeremy who reached for the receiver, and playfully said, "The McShay residence. You have reached the party to whom you are speaking." This was followed by a couple of quick snorts and a contortion of his face.

They both chuckled as he listened briefly and continued. "It's Terra Munrow. But I think you'll have to wait until she stops laughing."

"Give me that!" Maura Beth told him, snatching the receiver with a wry smile in place and propping herself up against her pillows. Then she got down to business with her tall, edgy stylist. "Jeremy's thinking of quitting his teaching job and going into stand-up comedy in case you're wondering what that was all about. But please, talk to me about Cherico Tresses and these rumors."

At the other end, Terra's laughter shifted into an even higher gear for a moment. "Your Jeremy is too much, girl. I wish my Ricky had that kinda sense of humor. We went up to Memphis to eat tonight, and that's why I'm so late getting back to you." There was a pause after which Terra's tone changed dramatically. "But to answer your question about the salon—yes, I'm afraid it's true. Miz Shirley Coates—she's our owner—is shutting us down and moving the salon over to Corinth about six weeks from now. Of course, she's letting us all keep our jobs if we want 'em. She says we can make more money over there, and our business has been falling off steadily for over a year now. I know I've lost three of my best ladies in that time, and none of 'em were unhappy with me. They all said their husbands got better jobs somewhere else, and they were leaving Cherico. So, I've been telling all my clients about the move one by one as they come in, and you're scheduled for next week, I believe. I hope you don't think I was ignoring you—because I wasn't."

Maura Beth tried to sound matter-of-fact but fell short. "No, I would never think that, but I sure wish you were kidding about this."

"I wish I was, too, but I'm not."

"But who's going to do my hair now? The Cut-Up is a train wreck. I went there when I first moved up here, and they gave me what I still call the perm from hell. I looked like Little Orphan Annie's big sister and went around for weeks trying to cover it up wearing one of those pretty picture hats. I mean, you would have thought I was getting ready to go to the Kentucky Derby all the time!"

There was more laughter from Terra and then another pregnant pause. "Well, I know the price of gas is through the roof and all, but I'd love it if you drove over so I could keep you as a client. Could you manage it? Ricky and I aren't giving up our place here because of his job, so I'll be commuting, too."

"Sure, I'll drive on over," Maura Beth told her in a tone of resignation. "I can afford it now with the raises we've all gotten from the generous endowment my Cudd'n M'Dear left the library. And now that I know you aren't going to be closing down permanently, I'm not so panicky. I have to admit, those rumors had me going for a while. By the way, are you still going to be calling it Cherico Tresses?"

Terra's chuckle had an ironic edge to it. "Almost. Miz Shirley says she's gonna call it Cherico Tresses of Corinth, so people won't be confused. Uh, well, you could've fooled me. But Miz Shirley said it has to do with name recognition and all. Well, it's her business, so I have to stay out of it."

"Forget about that. Just give me directions and I'll be there."

"Hey, I'll even draw you up a map when you come for your appointment next week so you won't get lost."

"Sounds like a plan to me. Thanks for clearing everything up. As far as I'm concerned, you're the best stylist ever."

After hanging up, Maura Beth brought Jeremy up to date on everything, sounding somewhat reassured. "I guess I can stand change if it's not too drastic," she concluded. "Just don't throw too much at me at once."

Jeremy flashed a devilish grin as he fingered a few locks of her auburn hair like the attentive husband he was. "Hey, I learned how seriously you women take your hairstyles long before I was married to you. Mom wouldn't think of leaving our house in Brentwood and going to her boutique down at Cool Springs without being properly coiffed and made up, and now I see it's definitely not a generational thing. You always show up at the library looking hot."

"Oh, yeah? Well, you men have it easy," she told him, pretending he had said something out of line. But her quick smile gave her away. "You barely run a brush through your hair when you get up in the morning, you glance to the right and then to the left, and that's it."

He inched a little closer and pointed to his crown. "Are you saying you like my cowlick?"

They enjoyed a soft, lingering kiss; then she said, "That's not the only thing I like about you."

The phone rang again, startling them both, and this time it was Maura Beth who answered with a simple, "Hello?"

"Hi, girl. I hope you weren't asleep," Periwinkle said at the other end, sniffling loudly as she spoke.

"No, we were up," Maura Beth replied, eyeing the digital clock on the nightstand. "Is something wrong?" Alerted by the alarm in his wife's voice, Jeremy immediately sat up with a frown.

"I'm afraid so." Periwinkle was clearly choking up now. "I'm . . . sorry. I have some terrible news, and if I sound strange . . . it's because I've been cryin' up a storm. It was all I could do to get myself together to call you."

A spurt of adrenaline coursed through Maura Beth's veins. "For heaven's sake, what is it?!"

"It's Parker's mother, Ardenia," came the constricted reply. "She died tonight. When he got home from work, Parker found her on the sofa—just staring at the TV and stiff as a board. Of course, he's in a state of shock, and I'm not much better. She was the sweetest little woman, once you got to know her."

"Oh my God, what in the world happened?!" The receiver nearly slipped out of Maura Beth's hand, and Jeremy continued to look concerned.

"Parker said they won't know 'til they get her to the medical examiner, but it could have been her heart," Periwinkle continued. "That's what the paramedics told him was most likely after they tried to revive her with those paddle things. He followed the ambulance down to the morgue at Cherico Memorial. He's probably gotten there by now."

"Where are you?"

"Almost there myself. I was halfway home when he called me sobbing, bless his heart."

At that point Jeremy could stand the suspense no longer, vigorously nudging Maura Beth and cocking his head emphatically.

"Periwinkle," she whispered, covering the receiver. "Mr. Place's mother died tonight." The creases across Jeremy's face quickly deepened further.

"Maura Beth, are you still there?" Periwinkle asked, somehow sensing the lack of attention.

"Yes, I'm here. Do you want me to come down there to be with you? I'd be more than happy to."

"No, you get a good night's sleep. I'll call you tomorrow as soon as I know something about the funeral arrangements."

Maura Beth was trying her best to steady herself, reaching out to grasp Jeremy's hand. "Oh, I'm so sorry, Periwinkle. I'm sure you know you'll both be in my prayers. Jeremy's, too— I just whispered to him what happened."

"You and I—we've always been there for each other, girl."

"Yes, we have. I don't think I'd have ever lasted at the library those first few years without your support and advice. I was so naïve about everything. Now you call me in the morning."

After the conversation had ended, Maura sat stunned for a while but eventually was able to tell Jeremy everything further he needed to know.

"That's a terrible break for Mr. Place," he said, shaking his head. "I really like him, and he's one fine pastry chef."

"I'm glad he and Periwinkle have become so close. I definitely know that he helped her through all that trouble she had with Harlan. Now she can do the same for him." She gave Jeremy a bewildered glance. "But I'm about ready to turn off every phone in the house. I've had all I can stand for one night."

Maura Beth was not surprised that she had trouble falling asleep. The image of Mr. Place discovering his mother just would not leave her alone, torturing her every time she became the least bit drowsy. She and Jeremy had talked it all out as best they could, and she had even gone into the bathroom and taken a couple of melatonin tablets; but nothing seemed to be helping.

Finally, she slipped off. But her dreaming attempt to resolve the activities of the day was even worse than being awake and tossing and turning. She was slowly driving down Commerce Street in her little Prius, looking right and left into store windows, hoping to spot criminal activity of some sort but finding none. In fact, she was so absorbed in her detective work that she did not see what was lying in wait for her. Just ahead, a great gaping crater opened up, and she drove her car right to the edge. It teetered there, balancing precariously. Somehow she was able to slide out of the front seat and peer into the abyss below. That sinkhole she had contemplated during the day had arrived and appeared to be spreading outward in all directions.

She had to step back as it pursued her—and then she was on the run. As she looked over her shoulder from time to time, she noticed that buildings on both sides of the street were falling into the bottomless pit below. And then it came to her that if she ran fast enough and far enough, she could seek asylum in Ardenia Bedloe's house on Big Hill Lane.

In a flash she was there, urgently knocking on the front door, and calling out: "Ardenia! Ardenia! Please help me!"

But no one answered even though she kept right on knocking without letup. Would the sinkhole end up devouring them all?

At that point she woke up, her heart pounding. She looked over at Jeremy, who was fast asleep on his side, facing away from her as usual. She decided not to wake him, working through her nightmare by herself. It was then that the faintest beginnings of an idea began to come to her, what with the holidays not all that far away. It was perhaps something that no one would have considered at first to cure what ailed Cherico. And maybe it couldn't solve all of their little town's mounting problems; but it might just be a good start. For the time being, she decided to file it away. She was certain she would know when to trot it out for all the world to see.

5

Yes and No

Visitation for Ardenia Bedloe in the Fellowship Hall of the
Cherico African Methodist Episcopal Church was well under
way when Maura Beth and Jeremy arrived to find a room full
of impeccably dressed people paying their respects against a
backdrop of impressive funeral sprays. More than a few
mourners seemed completely carried away by their emotions
and were standing close to the open casket, sobbing and
moaning with their eyes cast heavenward; others were managing hushed conversations some distance away; and still others—many occasionally wrestling with small, squirming
children in their Sunday best—were sitting in the chairs
against the walls, observing it all in polite silence.

As for the young McShays, they were slightly apprehen-
sive about their appearance, since the only person they knew
for sure was Mr. Place; but they were soon put at ease by the
smiling, prosperous-looking gentleman in black robes with
purple trim who greeted them as they walked in.

"You folks must be Maura Beth and Jeremy McShay," he
said, extending his hand. "Just call me Brother DeLee. I'm the
pastor of our little church, and I want to welcome you."

Handshakes were exchanged all around, and then Maura

Beth added, "How did you know who we were, Brother DeLee?"

"I was just told to be on the lookout for a right pretty redhead, and you do fit the bill and then some," he said, pointing to her hair with an expression of delight. "You know, Sister Ardenia spoke so highly of you all the time. She kept tellin' me I oughtta join that little book club you started at the library because she had such a fine time there. She said between the delicious food and the folks and all the chatter—well, it was all done up just right."

"You should take Ardenia's advice, Brother DeLee," Maura Beth said. "We would love to have you join—and any other church members you think might be interested in reading books and potluck. We're very informal about the whole thing, and we want The Cherry Cola Book Club to include as many Chericoans as possible."

Brother DeLee pointed to a large cork bulletin board just inside the doorway. "Well, you're more than welcome to tack anything up about the club right over there. I'll bring it to the church's attention every Sunday, too."

A sudden commotion across the room at the casket turned their heads, and it was then that Maura Beth spotted Mr. Place consoling a rather heavy woman wearing a navy blue dress and pillbox hat who had apparently broken down and begun wailing with no letup in sight. She had managed to make herself the center of attention. Periwinkle stood nearby in silence holding her hand, very nearly in tears herself at the spectacle.

"Oh, may the good Lord ease her pain. That's our Sister Leola Perkins over there," Brother DeLee explained. "She was Sister Ardenia's best friend. They grew up together here in Cherico and not a day went by when they didn't talk to each other on the phone, I do b'lieve. It'll take her a while to get over Sister Ardenia leavin' out so suddenly the way she did.

The rest of us will take a while, too. Somehow, we thought she would find a way to outlive us all."

"We're so sorry she's gone, Brother DeLee," Maura Beth continued. "She was a dear woman."

Brother DeLee briefly shut his eyes and bowed his head. "But she dearly believed, I can tell you that. She knew she had nothin' to fear in death."

Maura Beth felt herself choking up and took Jeremy's hand to steady herself. "I can see she had lots of people who truly cared for her."

"That's always been our way here at Cherico A.M.E.," Brother DeLee added before gazing across the room and pointing his finger. "Oh, I see Brother Joe Sam headin' over to us right now."

For a moment Maura Beth didn't make the connection. It had been a good while since she'd heard anyone refer to Mr. Parker Place by his given name of Joe Sam Bedloe, but she recovered just in time to give him a hug that expressed all the concern she was feeling.

"I'm so sorry, Parker," she told him, finally pulling back. "I know how close you were to your mother. Whenever I was around the two of you, it was a beautiful thing to behold."

"Thank you. Peri and I are so glad you're here," he said. "You'll never know how much it means to us."

Jeremy offered his hand. "We've had you in our thoughts and prayers since we got the news."

The two men embraced warmly, and Mr. Place said, "Sister Leola needed a little help over there, or I would've been here to greet you at the door like I did the others. Peri's gonna stay with her a bit longer—at least until the service starts. I wanted both of you to know that I'm doing Mama's eulogy. I know she would've wanted that, and I'm not gonna let her down."

Maura Beth was unable to keep the surprise out of her voice. "Are you sure you're up to it, Parker? I know I couldn't deliver eulogies for either of my parents. I'd be too much of a mess."

"You'd be surprised what you can do when you have to," he told her, patting her arm a couple of times. If he was in the midst of the grief of a lifetime, he did not show it on the outside. "This is my moment to show what Mama meant to me all my life, and I want all of Cherico to know."

It was after a lengthy but inspiring rendition by the Cherico A.M.E. choir of "Blest Hour, When Mortal Man Retires" that Mr. Place stepped up to the pulpit to address the congregation with a dignity that radiated from him. Below him at the bottom of the red-carpeted steps rested his mother's closed casket adorned with a breathtaking assortment of flowers, and beyond that—stretching ahead to the front door— were the many pews filled with empathetic faces. There was not an empty seat to be had in this little universe hemmed in by stained glass. Meanwhile, three different worlds—the church of his childhood, The Cherry Cola Book Club, and the staff of The Twinkle—had merged to honor the memory of his mother and bid her farewell.

Of course, Maura Beth and Jeremy were there, but around them sat Connie and Douglas McShay, Voncille and Locke Linwood, Becca and Justin Brachle, Renette Posey, Emma Frost—but without her fragile Leonard, Nora Duddney with Wally Denver tagging along, Marydell Crumpton, James Hannigan of The Cherico Market, and several other club members from various walks of life. The Twinkle was represented by Periwinkle, her waitresses Ruby Varnell, Lalie Bevins, and her son, Barry, and her sous chef, Charlie Marks. Conspicuously absent were Mamie Crumpton and Councilman Sparks.

Mr. Place surveyed his audience with a pervasive calm spreading throughout his body. It was as if his mother were somehow there with him, whispering soothing words the way she had when he was a little boy and the thunder and lightning of summer storms had frightened him, sending him scurrying into her protective arms. The notes he had brought to refer to lay before him on the lectern, but something told him he would not need them on this crisp fall afternoon with so many hearts and minds on his side. He was certain his memory would not fail him.

"Brothers and sisters of the church and honored guests, we are here today to remember my mother, Ardenia Faye Leeds Bedloe. Most of you knew her simply as Sister Ardenia, meaning that she was a sister of the spirit to all of you. Recently, she had made a bundle of new friends at The Cherico Library, where she attended meetings of The Cherry Cola Book Club. It was my mama's opinion that she had come full circle, and I'd like to explain what I mean by that.

"When she was growing up here in Cherico, the public library was not open to her, and also not to some of you sitting out there today in these pews. She was told 'No!' many times over the years when she tried to participate in something or other, or go into this building or that one, or get seated at that restaurant when she wanted to eat out for a change. But she told me more than once that she never took any of it personally, even when those who said no to her surely meant it personally. She said it was about them, not her. That they were the ones who had it all wrong."

Several people cried out, "Amen!" as Mr. Place paused for a deep breath and briefly glanced at his notes.

"I'm not sure Mama ever believed things would change here in Cherico the way they have—or anywhere else in the country for that matter. She hoped they would, of course. We all did. But she never let being told no stop her from living her life the way she saw fit where it counted. Not that things were easy for Mama. My father ran out on us when I was just a little boy. That was his way of saying no to her, too. But once again, she told me when I was old enough to understand about such things that it was about him, not her. He was the one who had it all wrong."

Again, there were cries of "Amen!" and "That's right!" as well as a widespread nodding of heads.

"I held on to that when I went to Cherico High that first year of integration here in Mississippi. I even remember thinking that first day, 'If someone says, *No, you don't belong here,* then they're the one with the problem, not you.' But things were finally beginning to turn around by then. No one ever said no to me at school. And I want to take the time to especially thank my first homeroom teacher, Miss Voncille Nettles she was then—now Mrs. Locke Linwood—for saying yes to me loud and clear from the get-go. She set the example, and all my classmates followed."

He paused to point her out sitting on the front pew, and she accepted his gesture with a wide smile, a gracious nod of her head, and the blowing of a kiss. A round of light applause followed but soon died down.

"When I got outta high school and was thinking about my future plans, I'll never forget the day I told Mama I wanted to be a chef and make all those gooey desserts she whipped up so well. I know some of you out there can just picture it—she put her hands on her hips, rolled her eyes like I was outta my mind, and nearly fell out on the kitchen floor—"

He paused briefly as warm laughter erupted throughout the church, washing over him like something tangible and soaking down to his bones.

"Well, she didn't literally faint, of course," he continued, "but I can still remember what she said to me after all these years: 'Baby, now where did that come from? You never said nothin' to me 'bout that before!' And I told her that I'd been watching her at the stove over the years—the way she'd just put in a half a cup of sugar and half a stick of butter and some eggs and flour and mix everything together, humming all the while like she was in a church choir. I kept it to myself, though. Until I knew that I just had to try my hand at it. I was willing to start at the bottom to learn, too. And that's when Mama told me she'd been 'puttin' aside' for a rainy day from all those years of babysitting and doing housework for white folks. She gave me the money to go to Memphis and find a place to live and get started. And when the time came for me to leave, she stood at the front door of our house on Big Hill Lane and said to me once again, 'Don't let nobody tell you no. You just keep workin' hard as you can for that yes, and I promise you, it'll come, son!' "

The smile on his face conveyed a deep sense of satisfaction as the congregation whispered and buzzed a bit about his last statement. "And it did come," he continued. "I got a job in the kitchen of the Grand Shelby Hotel in Memphis and did anything I was asked to do—bussing tables, doing dishes, then some waiting tables, and finally I reached the promised land of food preparation. I was a sponge. And then I learned how to make sponge cake and took it from there. Before long, I'd turned myself into a pretty good pastry chef, and every time I got compliments from a diner on something I'd made, I'd say 'Yes!' to myself mentally and then pump my fist when I got a moment to myself. Mama knew what she was talking about all along. Her heart may have forgotten how to beat, but her legacy to me—to all of us—will never be forgotten. And so in closing I'd like to thank all of you for coming here today to send Mama off to receive her final 'Yes!' "

He closed his eyes as he wound up his tribute. "I love you, Mama, and I'm proud to be your son."

The congregation rose to their feet, gently applauding as

he stepped down and headed toward his seat on the front row. But it almost felt like he was floating on the way there. He could see tears on some of the faces nearest him—faces both black and white, elderly and young, churchgoers and book club members—and, of course, from The Twinkle where his reputation as a pastry chef had soared to new heights. It occurred to him that his mother might have been surprised by the turnout, but it was one he was positive she richly deserved. She had come full circle, indeed.

6

True Confessions

Maura Beth had practically abandoned all hope of finding even one new qualified front desk clerk. Though she had promised to put out feelers with the members of her church, Emma Frost evidently had nothing positive to report so far from the inquiries she had made.

Then, out of the blue, Marydell Crumpton showed up one morning and plopped herself down in Maura Beth's office. How different the two Crumpton sisters were in every way! Where Marydell was slim, modestly dressed, and all folded in upon herself—at least until now—Mamie was frequently bursting at the seams in her gaudy, sequined gowns and intent on having her status in Cherico duly noted wherever she went and whatever she said.

"I know you're wondering why I'm here," Marydell began, making strong eye contact with Maura Beth as she never had before. "I told that sweet little Renette Posey that I just had to see you immediately, and I'd show myself in, so here I am."

Maura Beth managed to cover her puzzlement with a smile. "Well, I'm happy to see you, Miz Crumpton."

"No, please call me Marydell."

"Marydell, it is, then."

There was an awkward pause during which neither woman said anything, but Maura Beth finally resumed the tentative conversation. "Did you have a question about our upcoming book review, perhaps?"

Marydell fidgeted in her chair for a moment and then leaned forward. "Oh, no, I'm ready to go with lots of comments about *The Member of the Wedding* this coming Friday. It's not that. It's just . . . well, I happened to see your ad for new front desk clerks on the bulletin board at The Cherico Market the last time I went shopping, and I'm . . . I'm here to apply."

Maura Beth tried not to show how flabbergasted she was but failed utterly. This was the last thing in the world she would have expected out of Marydell Crumpton's mouth. "You really want to work here as a front desk clerk?"

"I really do."

"Well, I must say that I'm surprised," Maura Beth began, trying her best to recover her poise. "Not that I'm not happy to have your interest, of course. These positions have been much harder to fill than I thought. But do you have any idea what the job entails? You'd be standing on your feet a lot, and I'm just wondering if that would really suit you. You're an independently wealthy woman, after all."

Marydell raised her chin proudly. "And I'm bored to tears, Maura Beth. All I do is play bridge and eat cocktail peanuts and shuffle around the house putting up with Mamie and her pompous view of the known universe. You have no earthly idea what a trial that is!"

Although Maura Beth wanted to say, "I can well imagine," she restrained herself and settled for, "Well, I'm an only child, so I really don't know what it's like to deal with a sister or brother."

Then it all began to pour out of Marydell like storm water from a gutter spout. "Count yourself lucky. Mamie is a tyrant in public, and she's ten times worse in private. The servants are terrified of her—why, they practically run and hide when they hear her coming, shouting one of her blustery ultimatums from the other side of the house. But at least they get paid for putting up with her. You know, she's had me thinking all these years that she was our official spokesperson and that I had no right to do or say anything that didn't back her up. Well, I got sick and tired of it, and when Sheriff Dreyfus came to speak at the book club meeting, something inside of me just snapped. I knew at that point that I'd had enough!"

"Good for you, then!" Maura Beth said, sounding just the right note.

"I'm glad you understand. So, I realize only too well that I don't need to work. That's not the point. The truth is, I need to get away from Mamie at least part of the time, and I think this library position might just do the trick. You show me what to do and I'll do it. I promise you won't be disappointed in me. You can even skip paying me a salary, since I don't need it."

Maura Beth could not help but appreciate the earnest tone in her voice. "I certainly believe you'd be a quick learner. But I'll have to pay you for your work. There'll be no debate about that."

"I can accept those terms," Marydell said, perking up noticeably.

Maura Beth didn't have to think twice. Here at last was someone with the intelligence and maturity necessary to understand the job description of library front desk clerk. Maybe Emma would come through with a decent candidate for that second position, but even if she didn't, there seemed to be no reason not to give Marydell Crumpton a chance at the first one.

"I'll need you to go ahead and fill this out completely,"

Maura Beth said, handing over an application. "You can pull your chair up to my desk, and here's a nice pen you can use."

A few minutes later Maura Beth scanned Marydell's application, took a deep breath, stood up, and extended her hand. "Congratulations. You are now one of the library's new front desk clerks. When can you start?"

After the handshake, Marydell said, "You mean to tell me that's it? I get the job just like that?"

"Just like that. So, when can you begin?"

"Well, Monday, I guess. Would that be okay? I mean, I do intend to show up Friday for the book review, so I'd like to get that out of the way first."

"Perfect."

"Yes, it will be. It'll give me the weekend to tell Mamie what I've done all by myself without her permission. She won't approve, you know. And I expect she'll try to intimidate me and tell me it's so beneath me to work at the library for practically nothing. But I'm standing up to her for the first time since we were little girls and she told me that she was always going to be the one to name all my dolls. Can you imagine someone being that bossy?"

"Well, knowing your sister—but don't take this the wrong way—yes, I believe I can. Just don't you let her stop you now."

Marydell looked fiercely determined as she sat back down. "Don't worry, I'll handle it. I'm long overdue in that department."

"Glad to hear it."

"You know, Mamie's gotten out of control with her opinions lately," Marydell continued as if she and Maura Beth had been confidantes for decades. "You might have noticed that she didn't come to Ardenia Bedloe's funeral."

"To be honest with you, I most certainly did. And Councilman Sparks wasn't there, either."

"Well, I can't account for him—I mean, who can?—but I do know why Mamie didn't show up. She's decided that she doesn't approve of what's going on between Mr. Place and Periwinkle Lattimore. She says she's well aware it's a free country, but it still offends her sensibilities."

Maura Beth felt the irritation building somewhere behind her eyes, causing her to squint dramatically. "And how does she know what's going on between them? Is she a fly on the wall?"

Marydell momentarily averted her gaze, as if ashamed. "It's the black-white thing, of course. She says she's not going to their wedding, either. That is, if they do decide to take it that far and get married."

"I'm sorry to hear your sister feels that way. But somehow I don't think she'll be missed with that attitude. I know for a fact that Periwinkle wouldn't care one way or another. She's her own woman because of all she's accomplished down there at The Twinkle, and if you don't mind my saying so, you've decided to become one, too. Congratulations!"

Marydell looked exactly like a child who had just been praised by her parents for bringing home a good report card. "Thank you. That means so much to me. And you really need to understand that my joining The Cherry Cola Book Club was the smartest thing I've ever done, even if it was Mamie who made the initial decision. It not only got me out of the house for something more stimulating than Miss Voncille's 'Who's Who in Cherico?' meetings, but it also made me realize that I didn't have to settle for being one of Mamie's appendages. You've done a world of good by starting up the club, and you should pat yourself on the back."

Now it was Maura Beth's turn to beam. "Well, I realize it's a cliché, but necessity really is the mother of invention. I had to come up with something quick to keep the library afloat and Councilman Sparks from completely shutting us down.

He had me so intimidated those first few years, saying no to everything I proposed, that I didn't think it was going to be possible to improve the library in any way. I was on the verge of giving up."

"Well, Durden Sparks really is a mixed bag when you get right down to it," Marydell observed. "He's done some good things for Cherico, but he's always been too full of himself. Our families have been connected for generations, of course, and Mamie continues to give him the benefit of the doubt all the time. And generous contributions to all his campaigns, by the way. I'm just glad that you've been able to handle him, and he didn't run you out of town."

"Believe me, it wasn't for lack of trying," Maura Beth told her with a shrug. "But the contribution that you and Mamie made to the new library campaign fund pretty much put it over the top. It enabled us to go ahead with the plans a lot sooner than we'd projected. You came through for us big-time, and I'll always be indebted."

Marydell suddenly blushed and took a while to find the right words. "I . . . uh, have a confession to make now that's it all over and done with and the new library is going up out at the lake. Mamie . . . didn't want to make the contribution at first. It's true that there's oodles and oodles of money in the trust fund our parents left us, but you'd think we were on welfare the way Mamie nickels and dimes people to death for whatever we order and buy. But I appealed to that ego of hers that's as big as her bosom. I told her that this was our big chance to put our family name on a building that would be around a lot longer than we'd be. We both have used the library all our lives, so for one of the few times in my life I can recall, I won an argument with my big sister—and the rest is history."

Maura Beth shot her a skeptical glance and giggled. "Don't forget about the slivered almonds on the chocolate pudding argument. I think we'll all remember that as the time you came out of your shell."

Both women were laughing now, and Marydell said, "I have something else to share with you that's pretty funny. When we got home from the sheriff's talk that day, Mamie was fit to be tied, just strutting around the room mumbling things. Then the first thing she screamed at me was 'Nuts!' "

"As in almonds?"

"Well, that was her opening gambit. From there she went on to say that I was crazy to air our family's dirty laundry out in the open that way in front of all those people. So she repeated, 'Nuts! You are nuts!' "

"Slivered almonds are dirty laundry?"

"I know," Marydell added with a smile. "All I have to say is that it's a good thing Mamie has never had to work a day in her life because she couldn't survive in the real world with her pampered priorities."

Maura Beth picked up Marydell's application again and gave it a gentle thumping with her finger. "Well, this is proof that you're not afraid to do an honest day's work. I can't wait for you to start working with us here. I'm sure you'll like it. And now that I know the truth, I want to thank you again for making my dream of a new library come true."

"You're very welcome, and I'm excited to become an integral part of it on a daily basis."

Maura Beth and Emma Frost were getting ready to open up the library the morning of *The Member of the Wedding* potluck and review. There was a biting, late-October chill hanging over Greater Cherico—one that required bringing winter coats out of closets and urgently fumbling with keys at front doors to escape it later on. But once they were inside, Emma spoke up with a noticeable tension in her voice.

"Miz Maura Beth . . . I have somethin' I need to tell

ya . . . and give to ya, too. Could we go into your office for just a minute? It's really very important you hear what I have to say."

As no one had entered the library yet, Maura Beth pointed the way, but Emma did not take a seat, obviously pre-occupied by something. Then she pulled $120 in cash from her purse and placed the bills atop the considerable paperwork scattered around Maura Beth's desk.

"There!" she exclaimed, gesturing emphatically toward the money. "Take it off my hands!"

Maura Beth's eyes widened. "What's this?"

"It's the money I stole from The Twinkle."

"*You* stole?"

"Yes, I was the one who did it. My conscience, well, it wouldn't let me keep it no longer. Not with everybody all over town keepin' an eye out the way they've been. And that's the reason there hasn't been more stealin'. I've learned my lesson, and I've gotta give the money back now."

"Let's both sit," Maura Beth said, looking incredulous. She said nothing more at first, trying to take it all in. "First, let me understand this. You're telling me that you sneaked in and out of The Twinkle and stole those tips from Lalie Bevins? You— my loyal, trustworthy, churchgoing Emma Frost—you actually did that? Excuse me if I find that close to being absurd."

Emma's head was bowed, and she began tearing up. "I know it's hard to believe, but I did it. And even though I'll be givin' it back, I know I'll be punished for it when the time comes for me to meet my Maker. But . . . I was hopin' maybe you could help me out, Miz Maura Beth—you bein' such good friends with Miz Periwinkle and all. Maybe if you could return it for me and ask her to keep the police out of it and not press charges? I know what I did was wrong, but I just cain't be away from my Leonard now. I cain't go to jail. He'd be lost without me, and I don't wanna put it all on my Cissy or some sitter, neither. I have to do my part at home."

"But why on earth would you do something like that, Emma? I still can't believe what you're telling me."

Emma continued to avert her eyes as the tears began to stream down her face. "I know it's hard for you to believe. I thought it would come in handy to help pay for a sitter for Leonard if we needed us one down the line. It happened on my lunch hour that day, and I walked down to The Twinkle with my heart set on some vegetable soup or maybe just one a' Miz Periwinkle's salads, and then I saw the money on the tables just lyin' around. There was nobody in the dining room, so I just snatched it up real quick and put it in my purse and walked as fast as I could back to the library. My heart was beatin' a mile a minute. Of course, since I didn't eat my lunch, my stomach growled all the rest of my shift that day. Served me right."

An alarm had gone off in Maura Beth's head and wouldn't stop scrambling her brains with all the noise it was making. Something seemed completely out of kilter. "But why didn't you say anything to me about this when I first got back from my honeymoon? We had that long talk about Leonard and how worried you were about his possible Alzheimer's diagnosis. You let your hair down that day, and I was happy to listen to your concerns. It seems to me you could have reached out and asked for my help back then. Why did you wait all this time?"

"The guilt—it got to me. With the sheriff and everybody so concerned and upset about everything, I just couldn't keep it bottled up no longer. Please—could you explain everything to Miz Periwinkle and keep me outta trouble? Maybe she could find it in her heart to forgive me—with Christmas comin' up and all."

Maura Beth was beginning to feel a headache creeping up

on her. She wasn't an expert in such matters, but she even wondered if she had now become an accessory to a crime after the fact. Stealing tips seemed more like a misdemeanor, of course, but in any case, where did she go from here? "I'm going to have to think it over, Emma. Maybe ask my husband for his advice first. I can't make a decision like this on the spur of the moment."

"I want you to take this money no matter what you decide," Emma told her, still sniffling. "I don't want stolen money in my house no more. It just eats at me so, I cain't hardly sleep at night. Take it off my hands, please, Miz Maura Beth. Then maybe I can start to atone for my sins."

"Yes, I suppose that's the least I can do right now." Maura Beth scooped up the bills, shaking her head in bewilderment. "One hundred and twenty dollars, just like Periwinkle said went missing. Well, for the time being, I can lock up the money in my bottom desk drawer for you, and then I'll decide what to do about all this over the weekend."

"Thank you, thank you, thank you. I guess I better get to my job. I still have one, don't I?"

"Of course you do."

"Even if I have to go to jail?"

Maura Beth dismissed the idea with a wave of her hand. "I think I can say with some confidence that that's not going to happen. Trust me on that much. I'm sure we can work something out."

Neither woman said anything as Emma nodded, rose, and headed toward the door. Then Maura Beth remembered, snapping her fingers.

"Oh, I forgot to tell you. Miz Marydell Crumpton is coming to work as one of our new front desk clerks. She starts Monday."

The news turned Emma's head, her expression one of complete disbelief. "You mean you hired one a' *the* Crumpton sisters to do what Renette and I do? One a' the Perry Street Crumpton sisters that have all that money and live in that fine old house with all the servants?"

"I did. And please keep in mind that Marydell is not her sister, Mamie. They're like night and day."

A smile broke across Emma's face for the first time all morning. "That may be. But I hope Miz Marydell's got her a boatload a' patience and some sensible shoes to wear. She's gonna need 'em both."

Maura Beth spent the rest of the day trying her best to focus on the evening review and potluck for *The Member of the Wedding*. After all, she and Emma had posters to place around the lobby—one each of Julie Harris as Frankie Addams and Ethel Waters as Berenice Sadie Brown from the 1952 film, and a third of the author herself—the sad-eyed but wildly Southern Carson McCullers. They also had to position and drape the buffet table just so and make doubly sure there were enough paper plates, punch cups, and silverware to go around for the potluck—always the big draw.

But Emma's startling confession continued to weigh heavily upon Maura Beth. At times she thought she might explode, especially being in such close proximity to Emma. She could imagine herself shaking the woman and scolding her like a naughty schoolgirl: "What on earth were you thinking, Emma? Are you planning to stand up on Sunday and tell all your fellow churchgoers about this? Do you think they'll believe it any more than I do?"

On breaks from all the decorating, Maura Beth only half-heartedly reviewed the critical notes she'd made while rereading the novel. Her heart wasn't in her upcoming critical role of moderator—and even peacekeeper at times. What she really wanted to do was call up Jeremy, but she decided it wasn't the sort of thing to discuss while he was in the teacher's lounge and unable to speak freely. She wouldn't even be able to talk to him about it during the book club meeting with so many people milling around, and she didn't plan to leave the library in the interim. It would just have to wait until they both got home late that night. Jeremy would give her his best advice; then she would know exactly the right thing to do.

At some point she realized she needed to draw up new schedules for front desk duty now that Marydell Crumpton was coming onboard on Monday. It would be a great relief not to have to spell someone quite so often when lunch hours rolled around. So she pulled out the old work schedule from her desk drawer and scanned it quickly. She decided she would continue to let Emma and Renette—and now Marydell—take the early lunch slot from eleven to twelve, while she would again reserve the noon-to-one slot for herself.

But as she was filling out the new schedule, something began to gnaw at her, simmering just below the surface of her consciousness. It was trying hard to push through but couldn't quite make it to the top. Was there anything more annoying than having a name, or date, or something else of crucial importance on the tip of your tongue and being totally unable to retrieve it? To be sure, a flash of it would entice her now and then, making her think the rest of it would soon emerge and unburden her, but the clever little tidbit always ran away and hid every time she wrinkled up her forehead. Once, she even stuck her tongue out at the schedule she was manipulating so diligently. Somehow, she knew the answer was looking up at her from the paper below. Perhaps whatever it was that was taunting her would return when she wasn't trying so hard to wrestle it to the ground. She would probably be in the middle of something totally unrelated, and then one of those gasps of revelation would come out of her like a hiccup. Wasn't that always the way?

7

The Downside of Shelling Peas

The phone call from Periwinkle about an hour before the review and potluck was no big surprise to Maura Beth. They were all not very far removed from Ardenia Bedloe's funeral and the raw, churning emotions that went with it.

"Parker's just not up to comin'," Periwinkle began. "And I'm not sure I am, either. I hope you'll understand, girl."

Maura Beth was properly consoling and did not make a big deal out of it. "Oh, I do. Friday's one of your biggest nights at The Twinkle anyway. Of course, we'll miss you, and Mr. Place, too. Both of you always add so much to our discussions. It makes the club the melting pot it really is."

"Oh, I don't know about that part. I try my best to contribute. But I do appreciate you understanding how we feel right now. We're both just gonna have to pass this time around."

Then Maura Beth realized how much Emma's confession was affecting her perspective on the very mention of The Twinkle itself. The image of those stolen tips had suddenly heated things up on the front burner of her brain. It was very difficult keeping secrets from her best girlfriend in all of

Greater Cherico. Almost as a reflex action, a question popped out of Maura Beth's mouth.

"Those security cameras working okay for you?"

Periwinkle sounded a bit caught off guard. "Uh . . . oh, that. Yes, we've had no problems so far. They'd better work—as expensive as they were."

"So, no more stolen tips to report, I hope?"

Periwinkle's hearty laugh quickly dissolved the awkwardness of the moment. "Oh, girl, you woudda heard from me long before now if somethin' like that had happened again. And I b'lieve we woudda had us an arrest, too. Nothin' says guilty like bein' caught on camera."

"You're so right. Maybe the worry is all over for you," Maura Beth added, carefully testing the waters. "If whoever did this knows about the cameras, surely they wouldn't even think of trying it again."

Maura Beth clearly detected the concern in Periwinkle's sigh. "But that's not the point, girl. I want justice to be done. I can't let go until this is solved. There's no way anyone who works for me did this, so the culprit's still out there somewhere. Sure, I made up Lalie's tips to her, but as I said before, it's the principle of the thing. I mean, people can't just come into my restaurant on their lunch hour or whenever and think they can get away with somethin' like that. You know what I mean?"

And that was when Maura Beth had her "Aha!" moment. That little gasp of recognition she had been pursuing did indeed float up out of her and register audibly over the line. "Of course I do," she managed. But what she needed most was to hang up and work it all out in her head. So she quickly made her manners to get on with it. Why, she even realized just how Miss Marple felt when she had stumbled onto a revelation of some sort! "Please give Mr. Place my best and tell him I'm still thinking about him. Jeremy is, too. I'm sure we'll see you both soon."

After the call had ended, Maura Beth took a deep breath, pulled out the new front desk schedule she had just made, and nodded her head as everything finally fell into place. Nice detective work, she was telling herself. Now she wouldn't even have to tell Jeremy about Emma's confession. She no longer needed his advice about anything. She would be able to handle it by herself.

Maura Beth glanced at her watch. Emma wasn't going to be at the potluck and review—she had already left for home to go look after her beloved Leonard; so the matter would just have to be put on hold for now. Even though she could hardly wait to get a rational explanation from Emma. Could there even be one?

At the moment, the potluck buffet table offering up shrimp, chicken, veggies of all sorts, two kinds of fruit pies, and chocolate pudding with slivered almonds seemed to have inspired a curious debate among some of those seated in the lobby semicircle and already digging in with gusto. The crux of the matter was whether or not shelling peas was the true mark of a good Southern cook, and it was Mamie Crumpton who was insisting that there could be no doubt that the answer was a decided yes.

"After all," she was saying in that officious way of hers, as if her folding chair were her throne, "cooking from scratch is time-honored. Pouring things out of cans is simply common. Removing lids is the lazy way to cook."

"So you're saying you take the time to shell your peas?" Becca Brachle responded, after swallowing some of the very peas with fresh dill and caramelized onions that she herself had contributed to the evening's fare. "I just don't have the time these days with my pregnancy and everything. I know it would work on my last nerve. Except that even when I wasn't expecting, I didn't bother to do it. Matter-of-fact, I made the dish we're eating tonight using a package of frozen peas, and I think they worked out just as well. I really don't think you can taste the difference."

"Oh, they're delicious. Everything you make is, Miss Becca Broccoli," Connie told her.

Mamie produced a smile that was obviously forced and all too brief. "Well, our cook, Jellica, does all our veggies from scratch. We have this little garden in the backyard beyond the gazebo that she tends for us, and she brings in the most delicious tomatoes and okra and beans and peas every year— everything you can imagine. Fresh and from scratch is the way to go."

The new, aggressive Marydell Crumpton entered the fray with a smirk on her face. "But you have to admit that Jellica doesn't do our meat from scratch. I have yet to see her wring a chicken's neck on our behalf. She's more than happy to buy it frozen from James Hannigan at The Cherico Market."

Mamie flashed on her sister. "I am totally unimpressed with your graphic descriptions and grasp of the obvious, Sister dear. That will be enough out of you in front of everyone and God."

"Oh, I don't think so," Marydell told her, refusing to be intimidated. "And furthermore, I'll have plenty to say about *The Member of the Wedding* as we move along."

Maura Beth had been watching the little drama unfold nearby, happily munching on the baked chicken that Connie McShay had prepared. She decided to fly by the seat of her pants and open up the book discussion right then and there.

"I'm just curious, Miz Crumpton. Did you get the idea for the shelled peas comment from the novel? If I'm not mistaken, I believe you mentioned it when the sheriff dropped by for his crime-prevention talk here at the library."

That took the heat off Marydell for the time being, and Mamie said, "Well, of course I did. There was that long sequence where Berenice Sadie Brown was shelling peas and telling Frankie and little John Henry all about her Honey Camden Brown, I believe. I just thought the whole thing was very Southern with Berenice being the housekeeper, cook, and mother to those two children. Berenice was the ultimate help—just like our Jellica is."

"Are we starting the review now?" Miss Voncille put in from the end of the row, sounding annoyed. "Locke and I haven't finished eating yet. Don't you have to get behind the podium first, Maura Beth?"

"Well, I thought we might go ahead since certain subjects have come up in the course of conversation," Maura Beth said. "Just keep in mind that our outside-the-box theme this time was to relate Frankie's experience to our own at that age. But by all means, those of you who're still eating, please continue. Informality is always our trademark here at The Cherry Cola Book Club."

"Well, I'm almost through," Locke Linwood added. "But even if I weren't, I do believe I can chew and listen at the same time."

There was scattered laughter, and then Connie took Maura Beth's cue and continued the book discussion. "I was touched by Frankie's predicament. I mean, there she is—a twelve-year-old tomboy without a mother, and then a father who's always at work. My goodness, twelve is a terrible age for anyone to be—much less someone who's missing two parents. I remember how desperate I was to lose some weight when I was that age. I thought if I didn't slim down, I wouldn't fit in—I wouldn't belong. My weight and I have always been at odds, to be honest with you. We've declared a truce at best—an uneasy one and—"

"Listen, I like you just the way you are, sweetie," Douglas McShay interrupted, nudging his wife affectionately. "Always have."

"That's because you're my wonderful husband."

"And I've got thirty-eight years on my résumé to prove it, too."

"What about you, Douglas? What was being twelve like for you?" Maura Beth continued, smiling his way.

Douglas finished off the shrimp he'd been working on, looking thoughtful as he wiped his fingers on his napkin. "It was typical for a boy, I think. My interest in girls hadn't kicked in all the way yet. I read *Mad Magazine* all the time and even thought I might like to write for it when I grew up. I still thought The Three Stooges ruled, and I made all the stupid noises and did all the crazy stunts they pulled off with my buddies. But mostly I remember looking into the bathroom mirror while insisting I needed to shave—and actually liking myself. I mean, what can I say? You can't punish a guy for that, can you?"

Becca raised her hand as if asking a teacher for permission. "You were one of the lucky ones, then. In general I think girls worry about themselves more than boys do at that age. Your mirror comment was interesting, Douglas. I used to fret constantly about my looks. Would I be pretty enough? Would I be too tall? Would I—" Becca broke off and blushed. "Well, would I actually grow a pair of breasts that the boys would gawk at? Would I ever need a bra?"

There was an outburst of laughter and then Becca continued. "I loved Frankie's description of herself as an *unjoined* person. I love that made-up word. Haven't we all been there at one time or another?"

Nora Duddney, who had blossomed like an exquisite orchard only after joining the book club, responded immediately. "Frankie had it easy as far as I'm concerned. When I was her age, my parents were downright ashamed of me. I wasn't making good grades, I was the very definition of antisocial, and as most of you know by now, it was all because my dyslexia went undiagnosed all those years. I was wandering in the desert all that time. At least Frankie could read and write the way she was supposed to. I felt like I was living on another planet. So I'd definitely agree that I wasn't connected to anyone. The novel hit home with me. It's real easy for me to dredge up all those old icky feelings with a snap of my fingers."

"Well, I did like the book for the most part, but I think it was a bit overdone—even contrived at times," Mamie declared, puffing herself up as usual. "I've always known exactly who I was and where I belonged!"

"Good for you!" Miss Voncille snapped back, dropping her fork to her plate for emphasis. "I'm sure you arrived at the hospital ready to hit the ground running and deliver the valedictorian speech at Cherico High!"

Mamie's expression indicated that she was about to go on the attack when James Hannigan spoke up emphatically to steal her thunder. "Well, I sure didn't know where I fit in. I was the youngest of six Irish Catholic brothers, so I was the one who everybody picked on. It was also a 'take a number' situation for me most of the time. Stand in line for the bathroom, wear my older brothers' hand-me-downs, fight for time to get a word in with either my mother or father when I had a problem, and on and on. I remember feeling overwhelmed long before I was twelve and wondering if I would ever amount to anything."

"Frankie Addams wonders that, too," Maura Beth pointed out, falling back on the notes in her head. "Finding your place in the world isn't easy for anyone—that is, if we're honest with ourselves."

Unexpectedly, Mamie switched from bombastic to defensive. "Was that meant for me, Maura Beth? Are you implying that I was fibbing about my confidence at the tender age of twelve?"

But it was Marydell who stepped in and answered quickly. "But you *were* fibbing, Sister. You were a nervous wreck all the time about your piano and voice lessons back then. You told me you wanted to have the sweetest voice in the church choir, but as it turned out, you had a voice like a bullfrog. If they'd given out awards, you would've won something like . . . oh, Best on a Lily Pad."

"You think you're so clever, don't you, Marydell? My teacher, Miz Lola Clinton, couldn't coax it out of me, that's all!" Mamie protested, nearly coming out of her seat. "I had one of those difficult alto voices!"

"Ha! Off-key is more like it. Everybody in town swore by Miz Clinton, and you know it, Sister. She wasn't the one at fault."

"When you don't carry the melody, sometimes you don't think you can carry any tune. I had to learn that the hard way!"

"Let's try to stay on the subject of our review, ladies," Maura Beth said as calmly as possible.

"Very well," Marydell replied, looking suddenly impish. "Frankie Addams had dirty elbows, and my sister, Mamie Eloise Crumpton, had the voice of a frog, and that is why she is about to croak."

Gasps and titters simultaneously filled the room. For her part, Maura Beth suddenly came to the realization that Marydell Crumpton was now overflowing with opinions just like her sister always had been. The sleeping dog had been awakened and was now enjoying hearing itself bark, making up for lost time. All the more reason for Maura Beth to keep this latest meeting of The Cherry Cola Book Club under control and not let it get away from her as she had too often in the past.

"Enough about frogs and elbows, ladies. We need to chill out a bit here. May I suggest you resolve this in the privacy of your own home?"

Mamie seemed somewhat chastised but still maintained her haughty posture as she continued. "Oh, the words people use these days! Chilling is for food in the refrigerator, my dear. But anyway, what about going back to the significance of shelling peas? That was my original comment, and I think it was a good one."

"Yes, it was," Maura Beth added, clearly seeing the way to keeping the peace. "Let's examine it a little further. I do think Mamie has a valid point to make here. It's my opinion that shelling peas for the Addams household to eat is Berenice's way of displaying her affection for the family—actually one of many ways she does it. Anyone care to comment on that?"

It was Becca who ran with the request. "Well, if you think about it, shelling peas takes a lot of patience. And Berenice needed boatloads of patience to deal with Frankie's fantasies and threats to run away from home—not to mention little John Henry's constant whining and complaints."

"Yeah, but that Berenice didn't have the patience when it counted," Justin Brachle pointed out. "She didn't listen to John Henry when he said his head hurt that time. She didn't believe him is the way I read it. And then the poor little kid ended up dying from meningitis."

"He cried wolf once too often," Connie continued. "She had tuned him out over the years, and it ended in tragedy. But it was sweet the way Berenice had that cute nickname for John Henry, calling him Candy."

"Shelling peas can be fatal sometimes," Miss Voncille observed. "Didn't Idella in *Driving Miss Daisy* keel over while doing just that?"

"Now you know good and well that that wasn't what did her in, Voncille!" Mamie added. "It was just her time to go. She could just as easily have been washing the dishes!"

Maura Beth allowed herself a moment of rare satisfaction where the book club was concerned. Everyone was pitching in and doing the book justice, even if some of the exchanges were a bit trivial and heated. The notes in her head were serving her well now.

"So how did y'all view Frankie's attempt to go on the honeymoon with her brother and his bride?"

"It's the heart of the story, of course," Jeremy said, entering the discussion for the first time. "Frankie so desperately wants intimacy of some kind in her life that she obsessively attaches herself to her brother's wedding. The concept of a third wheel hasn't occurred to her yet. None of us likes to think of ourselves that way, but it happens. It sneaks up on you most of the time. That part of the novel is very painful to read—imagine if you were witness to a twelve-year-old being pulled out of the backseat of a honeymoon getaway car. At that point she's just a lot of background noise and clatter—like the tin cans that have probably been attached to the back bumper."

"Calling someone background noise is rather cruel, I think," Mamie said, eyeing Jeremy with skepticism.

"You should know, Sister," Marydell added. "You've called people much worse than that over the years."

Finally, Mamie shot up from her seat, dropping her paper plate with its half-eaten chicken breast to the floor with a muffled thud. But instead of taking on her sister any further, she directed her hostility toward Maura Beth. "I think I've had just about enough of The Cherry Cola Book Club. I'm positive my sister wouldn't have turned into such a loose cannon but for all this outside-the-box prodding you've done, Maura Beth. Marydell simply won't shut up around the house anymore. She's driving me crazy, and it's all your fault. You've created a monster!"

"Tit for tat, Sister!" Marydell replied, wagging her finger as Mamie grabbed her purse and headed for the door.

"Oh, let her go, Maura Beth," Miss Voncille said, barely able to suppress her amusement. "She's stormed out of a few of my 'Who's Who in Cherico?' meetings just like that. She'll be back as if nothing ever happened. You just wait and see. She craves the spotlight too much."

Mamie turned on her heels, staring down her rival. "I most certainly will not be back. Y'all can eat all the picnic food and review all the books you want until there's nothing left to cook and read, but you'll do it without me!"

And then, over Maura Beth's sincerest protests, Mamie was gone.

"Well, I certainly didn't see that coming," Maura Beth said, as everyone else sat stupefied.

"I didn't either," Marydell added. "And I'm truly sorry to have caused such a big row."

At the moment Becca was glancing at the second helping of her own green pea recipe on her plate. "Who knew veggies could be so controversial? Maybe this wouldn't have happened if I hadn't fixed them. But the truth is, I've had this incredible craving for them lately, haven't I, Stout Fella?"

Justin smirked. "She's tellin' y'all the truth. Our freezer has practically nothing in it but those plastic packages of frozen green peas. I halfway think we've cleaned out The Cherico Market. I betcha anything Mr. Hannigan over there has had to reorder out the wazoo. Well, at least Becca doesn't put them on her chocolate ice cream and baked custard when her sweet tooth kicks in."

"But I wouldn't hesitate to if that's what the baby needed. They say that's how those cravings work, you know."

A wave of much-needed laughter swept across the room, and then Maura Beth said, "I hope no one else is going to walk out like that. I'll say this much. Mamie Crumpton is just about as headstrong as Frankie Addams was when it comes to making impulsive decisions."

"Trust me. She'll be back," Marydell insisted. "Probably not tonight. But eventually. She won't want to miss the opportunity to let everyone know what she thinks about everything under the sun—which she thinks rises and sets on her. Why, what would we all do without that?"

But Maura Beth was determined not to let it happen again. Another Cherry Cola Book Club meeting was simply not going to be derailed by something unfortunate and unforeseen. No heart attack, thunderstorm, or people storming out incensed—none of those would send the rest of the members to the exits early. This time, her ace in the hole was the idea that had been intriguing her for so long. She was convinced that not only the club but also the entire town needed it very much.

"With or without your sister, we'll continue to be a force to reckon with," Maura Beth began, putting her plate on her chair and taking the podium at last. "We'll continue our discussion of *The Member of the Wedding* in a few more minutes. But first, I wanted to run something else by all of you. I've been thinking about mentioning it before now. We know that our little town is going through a rough patch. We thought we had the Spurs 'R' Us factory coming to the new industrial park, but it looks as if that's going to fall through. Some more of our stores and businesses are closing downtown and all around, and some of our citizens are moving away to find better jobs. We've even had a bit of criminal activity that we haven't been able to figure out yet, and it's got us all wondering what'll happen next to disturb our peace of mind."

Here, Maura Beth couldn't help but pause, remembering what she now suspected to be true. But it was only for an instant, since she had not yet had the showdown with Emma to prove it.

"So, what would y'all think about holding a special meeting of our club in December to buck up our spirits? My idea right now is that we don't actually review a book. We would still bring our potluck dishes, of course, but this time, we'd all exchange inspirational and spiritual stories. Something to lift us up and get us all on the same page and pulling together. They say there's power in that kind of group effort. Now, don't misunderstand. I'm not talking about holding a religious service here at the library. Our churches can do that quite well. This would be an ecumenical exchange of anecdotes and stories that would make us feel good about ourselves and Cherico as we wind up this year and move into another one. Any reactions?"

Becca was the first to clasp her hands together. "Oh, I love the idea. You have my vote!"

"Mine, too!" Connie cried out.

"Are you asking for any spooky experiences we've had?" Miss Voncille said. "I'm not sure I've seen any apparitions."

Maura Beth maintained her good-natured tone. "Oh, no. We're not going to be telling ghost stories like we were sitting around a campfire roasting marshmallows at summer camp or anything like that. I meant that we should share experiences that have perhaps changed our lives in some way. Things that have enabled us to glimpse the big picture, so to speak."

Miss Voncille cocked her head smartly. "And what is the big picture, Maura Beth? Sometimes I wish I knew what it was for certain. But I can tell you that I distrust people who walk around saying they have all the answers while looking down their noses at you because you don't believe as they do. I started out life as a Presbyterian, but I'm not sure where or what I am now. I don't feel bad about that, either. Live and let live is pretty spiritual in my book."

"We don't have to come to any definite conclusions on our spiritual views. There are so many to choose from. It's one of our greatest freedoms. That's the American way, isn't it?"

"Well, do you want any outright denominational experiences?" James Hannigan added. "I mean, I have a funny story I can tell about my First Communion after trudging through catechism. It's not exactly uplifting, but it definitely is funny. At least it is now in retrospect."

"Save it for our meeting, then," Maura Beth told him, nodding approvingly. "I just think we should have a free-form get-together where everyone's insights are welcome. I'd be willing to bet the time of the year will bring out the best in all of us. We could even think of it as our very own Cherry Cola Christmas party—but without the foolishness that usually happens on such occasions."

"That's refreshing—an intellectual, inspirational, spiritual Christmas party. I'm all for it," Marydell said. "And when I tell Sister about it, I can guarantee you she won't want to miss it."

"Then how about a display of hands?" asked Maura Beth. "Those in favor, raise 'em up high."

Everyone present followed through, and there were no dissenters when Maura Beth asked for them.

"Good deal. So the next thing we need to do is pick out a date. I've been looking at the calendar, and I think we need to go with something in early December so as not to conflict with any organized church activities later in the month."

Nora Duddney raised her hand again. "Don't forget about December 7th. Pearl Harbor Day. We don't want to conflict with that, either—just in case there's some veterans' celebration or something."

"Good catch, Nora."

When it was all over and done with, December 6th had won the vote for the meeting date, and Maura Beth said, "Becca, I want you to be honest with us. Are you still feeling up to coordinating the food assignments for us?"

Becca rubbed her growing belly gently, something she never tired of doing. There were times she could have sworn she could feel the baby's life force flowing into the palm of her hand. "Oh, I believe so. All I think about these days is food,

food, and more food. Stout Fella knows where to find me when he gets home from the real-estate office. Tell 'em, honey."

Justin snickered, nodding agreeably. "She's always hypnotized in front of the refrigerator, lettin' all the cold air escape. No tellin' how long she's been there when I walk in and bring her outta the trance."

"I can't make up my mind, that's all. I just know the baby needs this vitamin or that one, and I hunt and peck on the shelves until I find it."

"And if we don't have it, I have to go jump in the car and get it," Justin added. "I think that's the time-honored way for all husbands."

"That's the way it worked out for me," Douglas added, enjoying a chuckle. "With Connie, she just had to have those little pearl onions you put in martinis. I have no idea what that was about."

Connie perked up considerably. "The sodium, maybe? I remember I put salt on everything when I was carrying Lindy. Even on desserts."

"She was just ahead of her time," Douglas said, gently squeezing his wife's arm. "Now, they put a dash of sea salt on just about everything sweet—even ice cream. They get away with calling it gourmet, too. I think what happened was, somebody spilled some salt while they were whipping up a dessert somewhere and tried to make the best of it."

"Well, if somebody's pregnancy cravings have led them to an 'Aha!' moment or some other insights worth sharing, we'll be happy to hear about them on December 6th. And be sure and spread the word—this could very well attract new members who weren't interested before."

Maura Beth felt a tremendous sense of accomplishment as *The Member of the Wedding* review continued and the evening began to wind down. Now that Mamie Crumpton was no

longer there to stir things up, everyone was able to contribute
their insights in a friendly manner. The give-and-take was
completely under control. Maura Beth also noted with some
relief that this was the first Cherry Cola Book Club meeting
that had not been dismissed early as the result of some contro-
versy caused by such culprits as Councilman Sparks, the mysterious Sarah Key Darwin, and even Maura Beth's meddling
mother, Cara Lynn Mayhew. Or a medical crisis in the case of
Justin Brachle. Even so, Cherico and many of its citizens were
hurting and needed to feel better about themselves as the holiday season approached.

Would the December 6th meeting be just the balm they
all needed?

8

A Short Walk to the Truth

It was one of those autumn days in the northeast corner of Mississippi that couldn't decide where it belonged: just enough warmth to imitate spring or summer, but not nearly enough chill in the air to pull off genuine winter weather. Halloween had come and gone uneventfully, and November would be staging its big Thanksgiving number in a couple of weeks. Meanwhile—and only after carefully considering any number of face-saving alternatives—Maura Beth believed it was past time for the truth to emerge. Not that the neighborhood watch posters Sheriff Dreyfus and his deputies had posted all over town were necessarily a bad thing. But her best instincts had been telling her for quite some time now that a genuine crime spree was not something Cherico needed to worry about at all.

"Come walk with me. Let's go get some exercise together. Miz Marydell will continue to watch the front desk for us," Maura Beth told Emma after the two of them had eaten their lunchtime homemade sandwiches in the library's cramped little break room. Maura Beth had brought tuna on wheat, while Emma had fixed ham and cheese on white.

As for the break room itself—it summed up everything

that was wrong with Cherico's woefully outdated library. It consisted of nothing more than an old refrigerator that made terrifying humming noises off and on, a microwave oven whose bell no longer rang when the food was ready, a small wooden table with salt and pepper shakers and a bottle of ketchup in the middle, and a couple of patio furniture chairs for the final mix and mismatch touch! Maura Beth could hardly wait until they moved into the spacious kitchen with its state-of-the-art appliances that she had designed for the new library out at the lake. But that would just have to wait until next summer and the projected Fourth of July grand opening.

Emma looked somewhat surprised by the request as she wiped her mouth with her paper napkin and then threw it into the plastic trash can. "Well, where do you wanna walk?"

"Oh, just up and down Commerce Street. I've been doing it a lot lately, trying to keep an eye on things like the sheriff asked us to. Haven't spotted anything yet, though. Have you?"

Emma's expression went from surprised to uncomfortable. "Uh . . . no. But I always go home to Leonard straight from work to see how he's doin'. I really don't have time for much else."

"Anything new to report from home?"

"Wish there was. But things are about the same. Leonard, he's doin' the best he can, I guess."

"And I'm sure you are, too. But come on now. A little walk in the fresh air will do us both good," Maura Beth added, leading the way out of the break room. She stopped briefly at the front desk to inform Marydell of their plans, and soon they were out on the sidewalk, facing a light, "sweater weather" breeze as they headed down Shadow Alley toward Commerce Street.

"It's such a shame we're going to be losing more of these

downtown stores," Maura Beth observed, as Cherico's busiest street came into view. Even though it didn't look that way at the moment. Perhaps it was just a random snapshot, but no one else was out on the sidewalk on their lunch hour, and there was nothing approaching traffic congestion in the street. "Things really are dead in Cherico these days. Somehow, we've got to turn it around. During all my wedding hoopla, I finally got my mother to understand why I care so much about Cherico the way I do, but no matter what, Jeremy and I intend to stay for the long haul."

Emma turned her head with a grateful smile. "That's nice to hear. Of course, me and Leonard, we was born here, so we never had a choice. It's our home, and I guess we're just stuck with it."

They had reached the cozy wooden bench in front of Audra Neely's antique store, and it was there that Maura Beth stopped and gestured. "Let's sit here for a moment, why don't we? I have something important I want to discuss with you."

The alarm clearly registered in Emma's voice. "You're not gonna fire me, are ya, Miz Maura Beth? Is that why we're on this walk? I figured somethin' was up 'cause you've never asked me to do it before."

"No, indeed. Nothing is up, Emma. At least not the way you mean it. I hope I've made it clear that you have job security. Whatever gave you that idea?" Maura Beth quickly took her seat and Emma followed her lead, nervously rubbing her fingertips together.

"I don't know exactly why I said it. Guess you could say I was just followin' my instincts."

Maura Beth reassuringly patted Emma's arm a couple of times as she continued. "I'm so glad you put it that way. I like to follow my instincts, too. Of course, they told me from the very beginning that you weren't telling me the truth about stealing those tips from The Twinkle. It was just too out of character for you with the way you feel about going to your Church of Christ every Wednesday and Sunday. And now, I know for sure you didn't take that money, Emma. You couldn't have."

"But I did, Miz Maura Beth!" Emma insisted, fidgeting in her seat. "Why would I lie?"

"That's what you need to tell me now. I promise you that whatever you say, I'll handle things with Miz Periwinkle and Lalie Bevins. I just want you to tell me the truth so I can put my instincts to bed and things can get back to normal in my brain. I can't help it, you know. Being so detail-oriented comes with being a librarian. We're natural-born processors of books and just about everything else."

"But why do you say I couldn't have took the money? You sound pretty sure of yourself."

Maura Beth drew herself up, even looking smug about it all. "Because there was something about your little confession that bothered me from the beginning, but I could never quite put my finger on it. Then I went back later and confirmed things with Periwinkle about the timeline that day. I remembered she said those tips were stolen at the end of the lunch service—close to two o'clock—and you said you walked down to The Twinkle on your lunch hour. You know as well as I do that you always take it from eleven to twelve—just like the two of us did together today. So there's no way you could have taken that money like you said you did. It's time for you to tell me why you made up that story and where that money you gave me came from. I'm assuming it didn't come out of your own pocket."

Maura Beth had not expected Emma to break down, but she did—tearing up as she turned her head away. Then she started sobbing quietly, and Maura Beth had to wait until Emma had gotten it all out of her system.

"Take your time, dear. I'm not going anywhere."

"I didn't know about the money at first," Emma began while sniffling. "I mean, I heard people talkin' about it, but that's all I knew. Then one day I was puttin' Leonard's sock drawer in some kinda order—it was just too messy for my taste and you know how organized I am at the front desk—and there the money was just as plain as could be. So I went to Leonard, and said, 'Where did this come from, honey?' And he says to me, 'That was supposed ta be a surprise. It's my birthday money for you. I'm gonna spend it all on your party.'"

Maura Beth was squinting now, trying her best to follow along. "Your birthday party?"

Emma exhaled with a great deal of force and continued patiently. "Don't you remember I told you how Leonard was carryin' on about my sixty-fifth birthday and singin' to me all the time?"

"Oh, yes, now I do. You said he was driving you crazy."

Emma managed an odd little chuckle as she glanced at the overcast sky. "You don't know the half of it. Anyhow, I asked Leonard where the money come from, and he says, 'It was left behind.' 'Left behind where?' I says to him. And that's when it all come out. Oh, Miz Maura Beth, he's so confused all the time—I can't blame him for what happened. But I wudd'n gonna let him take the blame for it, neither. It was one of those times Leonard got out of the house and wandered around without a thought in his head. He told me he walked all the way down to Commerce Street and back, and at one point he just happened to look in the window at The Twinkle, and that's when he saw that money just settin' around on the tables. 'I'll just go in and take it for my Emma's birthday party,' he says to me."

Emma briefly broke down again but steadied herself more

quickly this time. "He didn't really know what he was doin,' Miz Maura Beth. He told me he figured no one needed the money since they just left it there. It's his brain, ya know. It's just on the blink, and there's nothin' the doctors nor anyone else can do about it. I sure wish I could snap my fingers and make it go away."

"I understand," Maura Beth said as soothingly as possible, putting her arm around Emma's shoulder. "Although I have to say that this wasn't the explanation I was expecting. Well, to be perfectly honest, I don't know what I was expecting, but I would never have guessed you were covering for your Leonard. I just knew you weren't telling me the truth."

"But you believe me now, don'tcha? I swear I'm not makin' any of it up. It took me by surprise as much as I bet it did you just now."

"Of course, I believe you. Now that I think it through, it's the only explanation that makes any sense."

"Well, that's why me and Cissy have been keepin' such an eye on him now. He's liable to wander off anywhere and do anything if we don't. But I hope you see why I didn't say nothin' to you about Leonard when you first come back from your honeymoon. I didn't know he'd done it then. I found out later, and that's when I decided to give you the money and take the blame and ask you to help me out with Miz Periwinkle. No way was I gonna let my Leonard go through havin' to deal with the law. He's no criminal—no way. So, no—I didn't steal nothin'. But I did break me another commandment when I lied. I hope you don't think I'm a bad person doin' what I did. It weighed heavy on my heart."

Maura Beth took her arm from around Emma's shoulder and then gently squeezed her hand. "There's no way I could ever think that about you. A good wife and mother always protects her own."

"I'm glad you put it that-a-way. That's exactly why I did it. I've always been fierce as a lion when it comes to my family." There was a thoughtful pause. "So, are you gonna tell Miz Periwinkle everything?"

"I'll handle it, and I'm sure she and Lalie Bevins will understand about what Leonard did. Nobody would ever hold that against him."

"But whadda we do about the law? Won't the sheriff and the police keep tryin' to solve it?"

Maura Beth's expression was determined, her voice brimming with confidence. "I know Periwinkle will explain what happened to the sheriff, and that should be the end of it. It was one of those quirky things that no one could ever foresee. I'm even inclined to think your Leonard wasn't caught doing it because he didn't have any malice in his heart. Who knows what his world is really like on a daily basis? He's bound to see and hear things differently than the rest of us."

"Oh, you're an angel from heaven, Miz Maura Beth!" Emma declared, leaning in for a spontaneous hug. "Leonard's doctors, they've given me all these brochures to read about what to expect and how to deal with it, and you sound just like what I've been readin'."

"I'm glad to help in any way I can. And I have a great suggestion for you. I want you and Leonard to come to the December book club meeting where we'll all share some inspirational stories with each other. It'll do him good to get out, and this time you won't have a problem keeping an eye on him."

Emma hung her head and didn't speak for a while, and for a moment, Maura Beth thought she was going to be turned down. "I've been wonderin' if I'd be able to get in the Christmas spirit this year with all I've been goin' through. This was about the time last year that Leonard really began actin' up, and I think I was in denial for too long. So I believe I'll take you up on your invitation. I know Leonard won't mind—I'll just tell him we're goin' to a Christmas party at the library."

"Well, it is, actually. Maybe a little fancier than most, but we need something out of the ordinary with everything that's been happening."

Just then the front door to the antique store opened and out stepped Audra Neely herself, looking perfectly coiffed and stylishly attired, but also perplexed. "What on earth are you two discussing out here so intently? Are you trying to solve all the world's problems or what?"

Maura Beth laughed and stood up quickly. "How are you, Audra? No, we weren't tackling the world—just a few odds and ends that needed a little attention here in Cherico."

The two women embraced warmly, and then Audra and Emma exchanged pleasantries as well.

"I've been meaning to come by and tell you how sorry I am that you'll be closing your wonderful shop soon," Maura Beth said, gesturing toward the window display that featured vintage lamps, vases, and even a Chinese cloisonné sideboard. "I think it added so much to downtown, and I kept telling myself that when I could afford it, I'd come down and actually buy something from you. But now that I can finally do that, I find you're taking off for greener pastures."

"No one's more disappointed than I am, but I've been sticking it out as long as I can," Audra explained. "I thought things might get a little better when there was talk of that cowboy boot manufacturer moving to town. New jobs would bring new blood, and maybe some of it would plunk down their money with me. But that didn't happen, and I've discovered the hard way that this is the wrong market for my antiques. Maybe any antiques. Believe me, I went to every estate sale in Mississippi trying to find a variety of pieces that would fit into every budget. Whenever some antebellum home would go by the wayside in Natchez or somewhere else historic, I was there, ready to bid with a vengeance. But Chericoans just weren't buying what I was selling. I may try again over in Corinth, but only after I take a little vacation from the business to get my spirits back up."

That gave Maura Beth another opportunity to promote her December meeting, and she lost no time explaining everything in detail to Audra. "You absolutely must come. The more the merrier. I've just gotten Emma here to agree and bring along her husband, too. If you've got any relatives in town, bring them, by all means."

Audra brightened considerably while fiddling with the fashionable aqua–colored scarf tied loosely around her neck. "I just might do that. I'm not moving away until after the first of the year anyway. It sounds like a great format for me to say good-bye to all of you."

"Oh, I hate the sound of that," Maura Beth said, pouting slightly. "But if you do open up again in Corinth, I promise Jeremy and I will drive over and check things out. If you hadn't heard, we've moved into Miss Voncille's old house on Painter Street, and I've told Jeremy I think it needs a bit of updating."

Audra looked amused. "And I always say nothing updates better than a classic antique."

"Couldn't have said it better myself."

"Well, I better get back inside in case the phone decides to shock me and ring," Audra said with a wink, heading for the door.

"I'm looking forward to seeing you on December 6th at the library." Then Maura Beth turned to Emma. "Why don't you go on back to the library, and I'll take care of everything at The Twinkle. You don't need to explain anything to Miz Marydell, either. Just tell her I'll be back soon."

"I just cain't thank you enough, Miz Maura Beth," Emma

said, embracing her boss once again. "And I promise, me and Leonard'll be there for the December to-do. Maybe I can even come up with a story if I think hard enough."

"Don't worry about it. The two of you being there is all that matters."

Maura Beth's intention had been to tell Periwinkle all about the missing money and then hand it over, but she wasn't able to get a word in edgewise because of her best girl-friend's unprecedented excitement. "Can you even believe it?" Periwinkle was saying as the two of them sat across from each other in her office. "I couldn't possibly pay for that kinda publicity, and now it's just fallen into my lap. Now, I know you don't particularly like country music, but I definitely want you to be right here at The Twinkle on December 7th. Bring Jeremy along, too. It'll help me keep my feet on the ground. If you need an extra incentive, dinner's on me."

Maura Beth knew immediately she would have to put it on her calendar. After all, it was nothing short of a coup for The Twinkle. To have a major recording star like Waddell Mack rent out the entire restaurant to feed his band and crew that evening on the way to their concert the next day in Tupelo was the sort of "happening" that sometimes made *People* magazine. Sure, it would be all fluff and photo ops, but lots of people would scan it in doctors' and dentists' offices—not to mention hair salons all over the country. "We'll be there. I promise you. Maybe I'll even listen to one of your Mr. Mack's CDs to psych myself up."

"Oh, I could lend you one if you want. And when he's here, he'll prob'ly tweet all the time about the food and the good time they're all havin'. We could even be a regular stop for country music people when they're on the road and headed this way. Girl, I can't stop thinkin' of all the possibilities!"

"Well, you're already a huge success story here in Cherico. There's no reason why the rest of the world shouldn't know about it."

Periwinkle gave her a double thumbs-up. "There ya go. I don't know when I've been so pumped!"

Maura Beth let it all sink in. It would indeed be a big week for Cherico. She had high hopes for her special inspirational book club meeting on December 6th, the evening before the Waddell Mack invasion. There might even be television coverage from the Memphis and Tupelo stations just because everybody liked stories about celebrities in their hometowns or anywhere nearby. Maybe if she played her cards just right, some field reporter might even get interested in doing a piece on the construction of the new library. Why, she could even go to Councilman Sparks and enlist his help in that department since she believed their relationship had morphed from constant manipulation into semi-cooperation of late! Suddenly, she was the one with all the possibilities swirling around in her head.

Then a more sobering thought brought her back down to reality: She still had to explain the missing tips to Periwinkle—and hand over the money besides. So she decided not to mince words, straightforwardly recounting everything that had happened from start to finish. "So there never was any threat of a crime spree, you see," she concluded. "It was just an unfortunate series of events, and Emma hopes you'll understand and forgive her dear Leonard."

Periwinkle reached across her desk and briefly took Maura Beth's hand. "Oh, of course I do. And I know Lalie will, too, when I explain everything to her." She paused for a thoughtful little frown that was quickly replaced with a smile. "But I never would have guessed that that was the solution. That poor man. What he must be goin' through!"

"I know. Everything I've read on the subject says Alzheimer's is a frightening journey for everyone concerned. But I've told Emma that she can think of me and the library as another family member when it comes to support. In any case, she doesn't have to worry the least little bit about her job."

Periwinkle sat back in her chair, her face almost glowing with approval. "I've said it before and I'll say it again: You were, are, and always will be a wonderful addition to Cherico. This town wouldn't be in the least bit a' trouble if more of our people were like you. I mean, you really do think outside the box about your library and what it's for and what it means to our little community."

The testimonial caught Maura Beth by surprise, but she managed a bright little smile. "You are too kind. But I do agree that Cherico's in trouble. That's why I've come up with my inspirational get-together at the library in December. Then, if everything goes right, those country music stars will order everything on the menu, right?"

"Right! Those twangin' boys in jeans and cowboy boots have big appetites, ya know. Waddell Mack texted that he's right partial to cornmeal-fried catfish, so Parker and I'll be sure to whip up a batch a' that for certain!"

Maura Beth eyed her intently. "Oh, he'll be crazy about everything, I'm sure. But I suppose you know I expect you and Mr. Place to attend the book club meeting. Could you let your assistant chef run things for a couple of hours? I really want y'all there as much as you want me at The Twinkle when you feed Mr. Mack and all his people."

Periwinkle did not dawdle, waving her off. "Oh, I expect I can trust ole Charlie Marks to get the job done up right. He's done it for me before when I've needed to be off elsewhere."

"Good. The Twinkle won't even miss a beat, then. We'll definitely be there for each other's big event." Then Maura Beth dug into her purse and handed over the $120 Emma had entrusted to her. "And here you go. That should settle things up nicely."

"It definitely does, and I'll just put it back in the petty cash drawer where it came from."

"By the way, how is Mr. Place getting along? I know he must miss his mother terribly."

Periwinkle looked off to the side, her expression one of concern. "Oh, the shock has worn off, of course. Now, the grief just comes and goes without rhyme or reason. One day Parker'll walk in and say he had a good night's sleep, and the next he'll tell me he stayed wide awake thinkin' about the things he never told his sweet mama that he might should have. Of course, the only way to avoid that is to tell people how you feel about 'em while they're still alive. I try my best to do that with my mother, bless her difficult little heart."

Both women laughed as Maura Beth said, "Same with my mother. Except things have gotten much better with her since my wedding. We managed to work out a ton of stuff right there at the finish line—just before Jeremy and I said our 'I do's' out on Connie and Doug's deck. And when I told her over the phone recently about my special meeting of the book club in December, she just raved about the idea. She said she thought it was perfectly brilliant, very much in keeping with the season, and she was very proud of me for thinking of it. Hey, she's gone from one extreme to the other, but I'm not complaining."

Then Maura Beth took a square of white scratch paper from a nearby stack, plucked a pen from a ceramic coffee cup filled with half a dozen of them, and quickly wrote something down, handing the note over.

Periwinkle glanced at it and recited the words in emotion-less fashion: "Sheriff Dreyfus."

"Yes, don't forget to go by his office and explain everything about the tips to him so he'll call off his dragnet. Although there's nothing wrong with his neighborhood watch program. I trust that'll continue. He just needs to understand that this particular case is closed."

"Thanks for the reminder, girl," Periwinkle said in that disarming, down-home way of hers. "Loose ends are just the pits!"

9

Be Careful What You Wish For

Jeremy had warned Maura Beth that it might not be the best idea to enlist the help of Councilman Sparks in publicizing anything dear to her heart—such as progress on the new library construction. "You ought to think twice about putting him in the loop about your special inspirational meeting, too," he had continued one November evening over a dinner of shrimp and grits they were enjoying in their Painter Street cottage kitchen. "I don't need to remind you he's found ways to mess up many of your Cherry Cola Book Club outings before. His presence has been about as welcome as a python in a chicken coop."

But Maura Beth had been too full of herself to listen to his advice back then. "Oh, things have changed between us now. He practically considers me one of his own these days."

Jeremy had dared to pursue his line of thinking and risk his wife's displeasure. "I'm not so sure that's a compliment, Maurie."

"That's not a very nice thing to say to me," she had answered. "I thought you above all people would understand how much plenty of media coverage would mean to me. It would validate everything I've been working toward since I took over the library here in Cherico. Councilman Sparks has beaucoup contacts all over the state, so why not take advantage of that?"

At that point Jeremy had backed off and let her do as she pleased. But by the time they had sat down to a traditional Thanksgiving dinner a couple of weeks later, Maura Beth realized her mistake in going over to City Hall to gush effusively with a man she knew better than to trust, and now she was pleading with her husband for ideas on damage control.

"This isn't working out the way I thought it would. Councilman Sparks is actually interfering with the construction crew. They've already gotten behind because of all the rain we've had, and now he's got them constantly staging things so he can get lots of photo ops out of it and create some sort of documentary. He claims it's to promote Cherico to new industry in the park, but I'd be willing to bet it's probably for his next reelection campaign. Yesterday I was out there on my lunch break, and Kyle Hoskins, the foreman, told me that he's hired this camera crew from Tupelo to follow the crew around no matter what they do—even going into and coming out of the port-a-potties. That's just too much information. It's all very distracting and way too much to deal with. I can tell Mr. Hoskins is intimidated by Councilman Sparks and doesn't want to tell him no. Hey, I've been there myself, so I know exactly what he's going through."

Jeremy said nothing at first, and Maura Beth was hoping he wouldn't dare say anything to her as predictable as, "I told you so!" or "Be careful what you wish for!" Fortunately—and even though he was just a newlywed—he had better sense than that. "Well, I'm sorry to hear he's up to his usual tricks."

Maura Beth skillfully added a bit of cranberry sauce to the slice of turkey on her fork and began munching thoughtfully. "He's also driving Periwinkle crazy about Waddell Mack's gang reservation at The Twinkle. He wants that camera crew to go in and film the band while they're all sitting around eating dinner—as part of that same documentary, of course."

Jeremy took a sip of the good Merlot they were enjoying and frowned. "I hope she's telling him and his crew where to go."

"She's tried in so many words, but he keeps trying to wear her down. She even texted Waddell Mack and asked him if he would mind that kind of intrusion, and he texted back that he'd mind very much. He told her that the last thing the band wants to do is 'be on,' as he put it, at a private dinner. They want to be the ones to control their own publicity. I can certainly understand how they feel about it. I'm sure they don't have that many chances to relax on a road tour like the one they're doing."

Jeremy put down his wineglass and devilishly raised an eyebrow. "You have to fight fire with fire. Periwinkle ought to put the fear of God into Councilman Sparks for starters."

"How?"

"I'd tell her to add a little something to that text she got from Waddell Mack. She's a strong woman—she can pull it off. How would Councilman Sparks know the difference anyway? Just tell her to say that the dinner's off and the band won't even stop in Cherico unless they can be guaranteed complete privacy. That would include people out on the sidewalk pressing their noses to the glass. Bring Sheriff Dreyfus in on it, too. Ask him to block access to The Twinkle that evening. Commerce Street would be easy enough to rope off. It's not like you'd have cars backed up to Corinth and people honking like mad. When was Cherico ever like that? Just make it clear that there will be no media circus allowed this time around."

Maura Beth's eyes widened dramatically, as if Jeremy had invented the wheel. "Why didn't either one of us think of that?"

"Too close to the situation, I'd imagine. But remember, I'm used to dealing with devious people, too. Headmasters and principals from hell, I like to call them. First, Yelverton at New Gallatin and now Hutchinson here in Cherico. All I've ever wanted was a little respect for the English department and classic American literature versus the Deep South obsession with football, and I intend to get it before I die."

Maura Beth managed a little shiver as she put down her fork and frowned. "Let's not bring up all that again. The last time we argued about it, you nearly *did* die out on the Natchez Trace, thanks to that deer scrambling across the road."

"But you have to admit it did eventually bring us together. I lost a Volvo but got you. Something good really did come of it."

"Another toast to us, then," she said, hoisting her wineglass and clinking rims. "But what do I do about all these construction delays?"

Jeremy thought for a while and finally shook his head. "That foreman has to grow a pair and stand up to Councilman Sparks. It's in his best interest, of course. That construction company has a deadline to meet, as you well know. They can't do that and allow this documentary or whatever it is to interfere with their schedule. Just how far behind are they, by the way?"

"Mr. Hoskins says almost a month, but he thinks they can catch up if they can get that film crew and Councilman Sparks to stop bothering them and staging things. The big problem is that if the library's not ready on time, we'll miss our Fourth of July grand opening window next summer. That's when we'll actually need all the media coverage—not now. But in Cherico, too often it's been Councilman Sparks's priorities or nothing."

"Pass me some more of that yummy sweet-potato casserole you made," Jeremy said, reaching over to take the bowl. "I'm still brainstorming." He scooped another generous helping onto his plate and sat with everything for a while as he enjoyed his food. "How about this?" he continued finally. "Have Periwinkle go to Councilman Sparks and invite him to the dinner at The Twinkle, but without the film crew. Periwinkle would be okay with that, wouldn't she?"

"I assume she would."

"Well, have her play to his ego and remind him of how important it'll be to have the Charles Durden Sparks and Company Library completed in time for the big Fourth of July event. I'd close the deal by telling Councilman Sparks to personally invite Waddell Mack and his band to play at the grand opening next summer during the dinner at The Twinkle. What band doesn't want to book more gigs? The way I see it, everybody would go home with big smiles and full bellies. Whaddaya think, Maurie?"

Maura Beth realized just how much she had to be thankful for on this crisp Thanksgiving day in Cherico and had no trouble expressing herself. "I think I married a brilliant man who is eventually going to defeat the local educational bureaucrats and bring 'Living the Classics in the Real World' to life. I think there's nothing you can't do when you put your mind to it. You're even going to get rid of that writer's block you've been having with your novel. You're as determined as I am, and I think our children are going to be trailblazers, whatever they decide to become."

Jeremy enjoyed a hearty laugh. "Wow! A simple 'I like it!' would've sufficed, but I'll take the rave reviews."

"And I'll share your suggestions with Periwinkle after the holiday weekend is over. The important thing is that we keep Councilman Sparks from screwing the pooch, and I think you've given us a plan that'll do just that."

★   ★   ★

Across town on Big Hill Lane, Periwinkle and Mr. Place were finishing up the Thanksgiving dinner he had lovingly prepared for them in the cozy little house he had inherited from his mother; although the food was delicious—from the first course of duck gumbo to one of Mr. Place's signature desserts—Periwinkle felt Ardenia Bedloe's presence everywhere. Not that it was a bad or intimidating thing she was feeling, for in the last few weeks before her death, Ardenia had truly warmed to her son's new love interest over a couple of down-home dinners she had fixed for them. She had opened up her house as well as her heart.

Periwinkle had treasured those first tentative conversations, pressing the gist of them into her scrapbook of memories.

"I hope you like my cookin', Miz Periwinkle," Ardenia had said after loading up the dining room table with her roasted pork tenderloin, seasoned collard greens, and rice with onion gravy.

"Please. Call me Peri just like Parker does."

"All these names I got to get right. I'm still tryin' to get used to Joe Sam changin' his to Mr. Parker Place back in the day once he got up to Memphis. But once a chile is all grown up, a mother got to let go and let him live his life."

Periwinkle had sensed Ardenia's genuine interest in getting to know her as a person—perhaps even as a future daughter-in-law—even if she was a white woman who had never experienced what it was like to grow up "Colored" in the Jim Crow Deep South as Ardenia had. Then that promising dialogue that eventually would have bridged their two different worlds had been cruelly cut short by death itself. Her task now was to be there as her Parker worked through his terrible, ongoing grief—helping him toward the closure he desperately needed.

"It's so ironic, Peri," he was saying to her as they lingered at the table after dessert. "You won't believe how ironic."

When he didn't elaborate further, Periwinkle gently pressed on. "What's ironic, Parker?"

He avoided her gaze, looking down at his half-eaten piece of grasshopper pie. "I used to come home every night from The Twinkle, and I could count on it like clockwork. Mama'd have that TV blaring so loud, you could hear it outside in the carport as soon as you shut off the engine. But it was reassuring, you know. Every time I heard all that noise, I knew Mama was still up, waiting for me like the sweetheart she was. 'How was work today?' she'd always say as soon as I walked in. 'Y'all had a lotta people down there, I hope?' And I'd tell her how many desserts we'd sold, or how many people came in just for a piece a' cake or some of my cookies to carry out, and she'd just light up like a sparkler on New Year's Eve. 'That's my son!' she'd say to me. 'You got you a gift, and Miz Periwinkle lucky to have you!' "

"She was sure right about that part," Periwinkle told him. "But I still don't get the irony."

Some barely heard sound caught in his throat as he continued. "There were also times when I heard that noise and wished Mama wouldn't be watching TV at all. Maybe you can understand me when I tell you that while it was reassuring, it was also annoying because it really hurt my ears and got on my nerves at times, and now I'm feeling so damned guilty that I got what I wished for. Man, did I ever!"

"Come with me," Periwinkle said, rising from the table. "Forget about the dishes. We'll do them together later. Let's go over to the sofa and sit, and you'll talk and get this all the way off your chest."

He got to his feet and shook his head. "Not over there. I can't bear to sit there anymore because that's where I found her. I can't even watch TV anymore because it reminds me of her. I'm even thinking of selling it. Nothin' on I like to watch anyway these days."

She moved to him quickly, and they embraced tenderly. "We can sit wherever you want to. I'm here to listen."

They ended up on a couch on the screened-in back porch that ran the length of the house. It faced a small backyard dominated by two mature fig trees that were always prolific during the summer months. "Mama put up her famous fig conserve every year from those trees. They were saplings same time as when I was a sapling—we grew up together— and I've been meaning to give you a jar to try," Mr. Place pointed out as they settled in comfortably, holding hands.

"I'm sure it'll be delicious just like everything else your mother fixed. I can vouch for the fact she knew her way around the kitchen and then some—it takes a good chef to know one."

Soon enough, he picked up where they had left off in the dining room. "I know I'm probably being too hard on myself about Mama and the TV up so loud, but I can't seem to get it outta my head. Why did I ever allow myself to think anything like that? You got any advice for me?"

"I believe I do. You wishin' away all that noise was just one of those careless thoughts we all have from time to time," Periwinkle began. "I can't tell you how many times I wished my Harlan John Lattimore would stay outta my life this past year or so with his foolish stalkin' and all. And now he's gone to Texas where I hope he'll finally find him some true happiness. But that was all on him, not me. So, it was just time for your mother to leave, and you know in your heart that nothin' you coudda thought or said or done woudda stopped it. They say the acceptance part a' sayin' good-bye to someone is the hardest. You just remember that I'm here to help you through it, Parker. I know that woudda made your mother happy, too."

Mr. Place sighed while staring out at the bare fig trees of late autumn. "Yeah, I know you're right—and you're helping by just being you. I'm just wondering . . ." He couldn't seem to get the rest of it out, however.

"What, Parker? What are you wondering?"

"Well, it's not just the TV and the sofa that bother me. Being in the house bothers me now. It's so empty without her. The silence seems like my enemy. I'm just wondering if I can live here any longer, even though it's mine, free and clear."

"You wanna sell it?"

"Thinking about it. All the memories—well, they're turning on me now, if you know what I mean."

"Where would you live?"

The intensity of his stare told her exactly what he was going to say. "Well . . . could we live together in your house? We've slept together there, and everything worked out just fine. Or we could buy a new place anywhere you'd like if you don't like the sound of that."

Her tone managed to be both tentative and expectant. "We could worry about that later. Meanwhile, is that a proposal?"

For the first time since they had sat down to dinner, he smiled. "I guess it is. To tell you the truth, I hadn't intended to go there—at least not this afternoon. But I know it's been in my heart all along."

Periwinkle's face was suddenly transformed by his words. She wondered if she looked as pretty as she felt. Inside, she was full of youthful excitement the way she had enjoyed when Harlan Lattimore had first proposed marriage to her over two decades ago. Somehow—despite years of his philandering and a divorce that had dragged on longer than it should have—she had managed to hang on to just enough of that innocent little country girl to bring her out of hiding once again.

"I think we should prob'ly do this engagement up right with rings and all at a later date, but I really do think the next step for us is to get married." Then she reminded him of

Maura Beth's upcoming inspirational book club meeting. "She wants us both to come, and I sorta promised her we would. Charlie'll take over the restaurant for us that night, of course." Then she drew back slightly and giggled. "Oh, and I suppose I should make it sound more official. So, yes, I'll marry you, Mr. Parker Place."

"And I'll marry you, Miz Periwinkle Violet Kohlmeyer Lattimore."

They embraced again, this time adding a lingering kiss— another in a long line they had enjoyed in recent months.

"Maybe moving to a new place will help us put what's happened so far in perspective. It wouldn't be a matter of your place or mine. It would just be ours," he added.

"We'll work something out," she told him, looking very pleased. "I do have to ask you, though. Will you worry very much about what people will think of us? Have things changed enough so that no one will bat an eyelash?"

He didn't answer her for a while as he thought everything over carefully. "Mama saw it all in her lifetime, you know. A lot of hatred that was out in the open, some that was cleverly hidden and much more difficult to deal with. The opportunities she didn't have. How hard she had to work for her money but still managed to save and make the mortgage payments on this little house. But she was mostly happy with her lot and didn't ask anybody to do her any special favors. I'll take my cue from her and go on with my life not expecting bad things to happen. I guess I've rambled on a bit, but does that answer your question?"

Periwinkle nudged him gently. "It sure does. When do you think we should announce this to everybody?"

"Let's think about that carefully, okay? Maybe we should just let one or two people know in the beginning and see how it goes. Maybe Maura Beth and Jeremy? Can we trust them to keep it a secret for a while?"

Periwinkle sounded emphatic. "Maura Beth and I have been best girlfriends for years, as you know. I'd trust her with my life. I'll phone her up tomorrow and tell her to keep it under her hat. It'll be just fine."

"Sounds good to me. Meanwhile, I'm glad we had this talk," he continued. "I don't feel nearly as depressed as I did before."

"That's what I'm here for." They kissed again; then she pulled away slightly. "And don't you forget to give me that jar of your mother's fig conserve. At the very least I'll do my best to guess all of the ingredients she used and then try to duplicate it for The Twinkle. That is, unless you just happen to have the recipe lying around here somewhere."

"Afraid not. Mama cooked with a pinch a' that and a dash a' that, and she tasted every fifteen seconds, it seemed like. Nothin' was gonna sneak up on her. It was pretty unscientific, and it's also pretty much a lost art these days." Mr. Place teared up briefly and wiped his eyes with the back of his hand. Then he looked out over the backyard with a wistful grin. "Guess there won't be anyone to pick the figs next summer."

10

Dinner Guests

Connie and Douglas McShay were relaxing on the deck of their lodge with sweaters around their shoulders and glasses of Chardonnay in their hands while a plate of pepper jack cheese slices sat out on the small wooden table between their chairs. A Cherico mid-afternoon in early December often required a bit of flexibility when it came to "dressing for the occasion," and today was no exception. In truth, Douglas would have roughed it in just a long-sleeve flannel shirt had Connie not kept at him about the nip in the air, and both of them wondered in amazement that there was actually someone out on the lake in a bass boat at this time of the year. At the moment, however, the weather was the last thing on their minds.

"I'm still a little bit nervous about all this," Connie was saying as she glanced at her watch for the umpteenth time in the last half hour. "They'll be here soon, and I just don't know how Maura Beth will react when she finds out what we've done. Some people really don't like surprises, you know."

Douglas shrugged. "You worry way too much about everything. It all worked out last time. Didn't Maura Beth tell you that she and her mother were getting along just fine now?"

"Yes, but that's been entirely over the phone since she and

Jeremy came back from Key West. You have to admit there were some tense moments during the wedding weekend. And then the image of Cara Lynn Mayhew storming out of that Cherry Cola Book Club meeting the other time sticks with me, too. I know for certain that Maura Beth would be very upset if her mother did anything close to that during the meeting at the library tomorrow."

Douglas put his glass down on the table and gave her a stern look. "It's just not gonna happen. We're all going tomorrow to share inspirational stories and get into the Christmas spirit and all the feel-good stuff that comes with the end of the year. No way would Cara Lynn and William Mayhew call us up and ask to stay here again if they intended to come up here and cause trouble. They would have just stayed down there in New Orleans."

"I know you're right, of course," Connie admitted. "I just wish Cara Lynn hadn't made us promise to keep it a surprise. I'd feel better about it if we could've told Maura Beth up front that they were coming. It just feels wrong getting into the middle of it this way."

Douglas snickered and then returned to his wine, taking a big swig. "We're not getting into the middle of anything. We're just giving the Mayhews a place to sleep." He paused to pick up a slice of cheese and make short work of it. "I know what you're really worried about. You should just come right out and say it instead of beating around the bush."

"Okay, okay. I'll say it, then. Everything would've been fine if Cara Lynn hadn't opened her big mouth in front of that Cudd'n M'Dear person and let her know about their surprise trip. The Mayhews by themselves would've been perfectly okay, but I'm leery of that cousin of theirs coming up with them. What kind of story do you think she plans to tell tomorrow? And remember, we didn't have to host her for the wedding—but now we're stuck with her for the weekend."

"What's the big deal? This is a huge house. We've got enough bedrooms. Everyone can come and go as they please. Unless the woman sleepwalks, it shouldn't be a problem."

"It's not that. It's just that she is so unpredictable. Maura Beth happened to tell me a little while back that Cudd'n M'Dear has been on the warpath down there in New Orleans for months because—get this—the television stations won't let her organize a telethon to eliminate static cling and static electricity. It's hard for me to fathom the brain of someone with priorities like that."

Douglas remained unperturbed. "Maybe she isn't really serious. Doesn't she have more money than she knows what to do with?"

"I believe Maura Beth said something to that effect. The woman has pretty much guaranteed that The Cherico Library will never want for anything as long as it's up and running. But what's your point?"

"My point is that sometimes an independently wealthy person has time on their hands and doesn't know what to do with themselves. Maybe this telethon thing is just a case of her throwing nonsense against the wall and seeing if it'll stick. If by some bizarre quirk of fate, it actually does, she'll run with it because she can. But I'll bet she's just after a little attention to relieve her boredom."

"I never looked at it that way," Connie said with a thoughtful frown. "So there's a method behind the madness, after all."

"Probably. But everything's going to be fine, honey," Douglas added. "In a perfect world, maybe the Mayhews wouldn't have wanted Cudd'n Whozit's to tag along, but that's the way it turned out. So let's just get out the welcome mat and trust that everyone'll get into the spirit of the season. That's the whole point of this 'tell stories' to-do tomorrow, isn't it?"

She turned and gave him a peculiar stare. "You know, I believe retirement is finally agreeing with you in the right way. All that guilt you like to whine about because of your illustrious career as a trial lawyer is finally beginning to fade. It's not just all the fishing you do out on the lake, either."

He nodded slowly with a smile that involved every handsome feature of his face. "No, but all that time fishing and drifting and thinking was how I got the idea of donating some of our land so Maura Beth could build her new library next door. Maybe I wasn't all that generous when I was practicing—hey, I know damned well I wasn't—but I truly see the virtue of it now. And I've put my money—well, our money—where my mouth is."

"That could be your story tomorrow," Connie added, enjoying the buzz from her wine. "Or do you just plan to listen to the others?"

"I think I'll just sit back and take it all in. I've spent enough time running my mouth over the years. What're you gonna do?"

She didn't have to think twice about her answer. "Right this minute, I'm leaning toward being quiet, too—unless the spirit moves me between now and then, and I have some sort of epiphany."

At the moment, Maura Beth was handling everything with her usual public service demeanor leading the way. Every now and then, she would catch Jeremy's eye across Connie's dining room table and wag her brows as if they were sharing some wicked secret; but the shock of walking into the lodge a half hour earlier and finding her parents and Cudd'n M'Dear waiting for her with open arms had worn off sufficiently. She was now enjoying her portion of Connie's baked chicken, sugar snap peas, and twice-baked potatoes topped with cheddar cheese and effortlessly contributing to the conversation as well.

"So, is that Councilman Sparks of yours going to be there tomorrow night?" Cudd'n M'Dear was asking her with a mischievous grin. "I truly enjoyed tweaking that smug face of his last time. He looked like I'd pulled his pants down or something worse, he was so embarrassed."

"He knows about the meeting well enough. There are posters all over town," Maura Beth answered, remembering Cudd'n M'Dear's performance fondly. "But I never exactly picked up the phone and invited him. Not this time around. My gut feeling is that he'll stay away, but if he figures there's some political gain in coming, he may show up with the usual ulterior motives."

Cudd'n M'Dear's homely face brightened. "Oh, I do look forward to bedeviling him if he does. It was such fun—practically the highlight of my year so far. I thought that little wife of his was going to have a stroke when I started squeezing his lips together the way I did."

"Yes, you were definitely his puppet master, and I could picture him turning on his heels and hightailing it out of the library lickety-split if he spots you when he walks in," Maura Beth added with a smirk. "So I halfway hope he does decide to put in an appearance."

Cara Lynn Mayhew put down her fork, chuckling under her breath. "Did I mention that William and I got in early enough to take a brief little tour of the construction site next door? We're very impressed with the progress. The library is really starting to take shape, and we're so happy and proud for you. It was just a concrete slab last time we were up here."

William Mayhew beamed at his daughter. "And your mother says you're aiming for a Fourth of July grand opening next summer. We'll have to circle our calendars and come up for that for sure."

"Well, the truth is, we're running behind thanks to some bad weather and also some foolishness on the part of Councilman Sparks. He's trying to turn the library construction into a documentary on his political accomplishments. I never would've dreamed he'd come up with something like that."

Cudd'n M'Dear quickly swallowed a bite of her potato and drew herself up with every inch of importance she could muster. "Do you need me to go to City Hall and mess with his head? You know I can do it."

The entire table erupted in laughter, and Maura Beth said, "It's nice to know I'll have that as a backup plan."

Cudd'n M'Dear snapped her fingers smartly. "You must let me know if you need me front and center."

"I promise."

Then Connie spoke up. "Does everyone have their stories ready? Douglas and I have decided we'll just listen."

"I do have something I've been preparing," Cara Lynn said, giving Maura Beth an affectionate glance. "I hope it won't be overly sentimental, but William can tell you how long I've been working on it. When Maura Beth told me about her special idea, I just knew I had to come up and be a part of it. I like to think of it as a sort of early Christmas present."

With a tilt of his head William gave his daughter a wink. "Your mother has been talking about nothing else for over a month now, and then she came up with the idea of surprising you."

"Oh, I was definitely surprised, wasn't I, Jeremy?"

"Maurie's right. We both were. And now I halfway keep expecting Mom and Dad to pop in from Brentwood any minute. We McShays have a way of doing things a bit differently," he said, giving his aunt and uncle an admiring nod. "I assume this is it for the guest list tonight, Aunt Connie."

"It is, sweetie. Just the five of us. Actually, I did invite the Brachles on the spur of the moment, but Becca wasn't having one of her better pregnancy days when I called—so they regretfully declined. She said she definitely wanted to rest up so they didn't miss the library event tomorrow evening."

"Could I trouble everyone around the table to come up with some fresh ideas for a telethon?" Cudd'n M'Dear asked, abruptly changing the subject in that inimitable manner of hers.

"Oh, dear," Connie muttered out of the side of her mouth, exchanging glances with Douglas.

Cara Lynn eyed Cudd'n M'Dear sharply. "Now, you promised me driving up in the car you weren't going to bring that up while we were here, cousin dear. We're here for Maura Beth and the library, remember?"

"There are so many good causes that are going begging. Surely among all of us here we can come up with something timely and appropriate," Cudd'n M'Dear answered, completely ignoring Cara Lynn's rebuff.

"I'll bet all the inspirational stories we'll hear tomorrow will suggest a few ideas," Maura Beth added, thinking on her feet. "Why don't we wait until then and see what comes to mind?"

"Brilliant!" Connie exclaimed, bringing her hands together dramatically and then running as quickly as she could with the opening. "Why burden ourselves now while we're enjoying our dinner? We haven't even had our dessert yet. By the way, does everyone have everything they need? More water, perhaps?"

A couple of hands shot up, giving Connie the chance to make the rounds with a pitcher of ice water and momentarily diffuse the situation. "You know, this is not bottled water I'm pouring for y'all. We get it from our well right here on our property, don't we, Douglas?"

"Yep, we opted not to connect with the county water system. There's nothing like deep well water in my book. I grew up with it in Middle Tennessee, and it had this almost sweet, mineral taste that was so refreshing—especially when it was ice-cold on a hot summer day. I think it has something to do with all the rocks deep down in the ground, I'll bet."

Cudd'n M'Dear suddenly sat up in her chair as if someone had just pricked her with a needle several times in a row. "Well, what do y'all think about water quality, then? I believe that would make an excellent telethon. Everyone's concerned about it these days with all the pollution around."

Connie sounded like all the air had gone out of her very being as she returned to her seat. "Yes . . . I . . . suppose . . . it would."

For her part, Maura Beth began to wonder seriously if Cudd'n M'Dear was going to be a problem at the library the following evening. Would she interrupt people with non se- quiturs and try to dominate the proceedings with her trade- mark foolishness? Who knew what her idea of inspirational or spiritual was? Maura Beth couldn't really blame her mother for bringing the woman along, though. No one in the known universe had ever been able to tell her "No!" or "You can't come within a five-hundred mile radius of us!" or anything close to that.

Then Maura Beth realized that her experience conducting meetings of The Cherry Cola Book Club certainly counted for something. She had faced a myriad of disruptions and chal- lenges every time out since its founding, and somehow the group had stayed together, getting to know each other better and better, their bond growing even stronger with each crisis that had confronted them all.

Tomorrow evening, she concluded, would be their finest hour!

11

Hanging by a Thread

With her inspirational club meeting just a few hours away, the last thing Maura Beth needed was any sort of confrontation with Councilman Sparks. Yet it appeared she was going to have to deal with precisely that. She absolutely hated it whenever he called her up and demanded that she traipse over to City Hall to hear his latest pronouncement, threat, or demand. Jeremy had been right. Getting too chummy with the man was not good news, as well as an illusion in all likelihood.

"What's wrong?" Marydell Crumpton wanted to know after Maura Beth emerged from her office following the private phone conversation she had just endured. "You look very upset."

"Film at eleven," Maura Beth mumbled as she hurriedly approached the front desk. "Which means I won't know what Councilman Sparks is up to until I get there. You just hold down the fort here—I know you're up to it—and I'll just hope for the best on my little visit to City Hall."

A look of sudden panic overtook Marydell. "You've never left me in charge before. Do you think I'm ready?"

"If you have any doubts about your abilities, just picture your sister, Mamie, barging in and demanding that you drop everything you're doing to round up six or seven books for her—pronto. That should get your juices flowing."

Marydell laughed softly. "You really are the perfect mentor."

"Thanks. Believe me, I've earned my stripes."

"Good luck," Marydell called out as Maura Beth reached the front door, visibly upset that she was having to put her busy agenda on hold.

She had tried in vain to discuss whatever it was Councilman Sparks wanted after he had initially issued her marching orders. "But can't you tell me what you want with me now, please? My schedule really is insane today. I'm sure you know about the special meeting of The Cherry Cola Book Club this evening. I've got tables and chairs to arrange, food to put out later, and lots of other things to attend to. So many people are counting on me."

But he had raised his voice a couple of decibels and repeated his request that she come over right away for one of their one-on-one encounters. "Put all that stuff on the back burner, please!" Even the tone of his "please" had sounded rude.

As she made her way briskly along the Commerce Street sidewalk in the December chill, Maura Beth's mood ranged from cantankerous to livid. No matter what happened between them, it always seemed to come down to Councilman Sparks insisting on holding the upper hand. She was about ready to send Jeremy to City Hall to read the riot act to her nemesis. Instead, she trudged up the steps of Cherico's most elaborate building for yet another time, dreading what awaited her inside.

"Go right on in," Lottie Howard told her, gesturing toward the inner sanctum from her desk outside. "He's expecting you."

Maura Beth managed a smile as she headed in with a perfunctory nod—even though she felt like frowning. Now that was downright peculiar. Lottie's tone was decidedly pleasant, and there was a wide grin on her face that didn't seem plastered on for once. Funny how a secretary frequently took on the officious behavior of her boss! But such was not the case today.

"Thanks for your promptness, Maura Beth," Councilman Sparks told her as he closed the office door behind her. A moment later, they were seated across from each other on either side of his desk as usual. But from that point forward, the resemblance to their many other difficult private sessions ended. The harshness and impatience he had exhibited only a few minutes ago over the phone completely vanished, replaced with a tone that came off as almost humble.

"I know you must think I've been interfering with the construction crew out at the lake," he began, getting right to the point. "I know you've also been talking to the foreman, but I wanted you to understand the whole story. It's slightly ironic that tomorrow is Pearl Harbor Day, since Cherico may not recover from all the hits it's taken recently."

Maura Beth had never been more interested in what the man had to say; she sat up further in her chair and gave him her undivided attention. "Please continue. I'm not sure where you're going with this, but I'm all ears."

"Yes, it's true that I'm making a little promotional film out at the lake and around town in general," he continued, making genuine eye contact instead of looking past her as he usually did. "But it's not about me. It's about Cherico. I'm trying to put it together as fast as I can to show that this town is progressive and deserves good things to happen to it. Here's a news flash for you: It's come to my attention that Dillard Mills, the CEO of Spurs 'R' Us, hasn't signed on the dotted line yet to build their new boot plant in Nashville. It's true that he yanked it from us at the last minute—and I could wring his neck for that alone—but maybe there's time for us to yank it back. The core of my film is the new library construction because I thought that would impress this man the most, showing him that we understand how important a state-of-the-art library is to the entire community. Maybe he'll think long and hard about the type of educational facilities Cherico could provide to his employees and their families. Maybe we could get him to become as enthusiastic about Cherico as he once was."

Maura Beth felt like pinching herself. Who was this talking pod-person in front of her? Somehow, she managed to form words that made sense. "You are . . . preaching to the choir, of course."

"Glad you feel that way. Because things are much worse here in Cherico than I've let on to the public—and even you. We're headed for a budget disaster because we're literally hanging by a thread. Just since we talked when you got back from your honeymoon, things have unraveled even more. Both our sales and property tax revenue are so far behind last year that we may have no other choice than to lay people off in various departments—across the board. That means police, fire protection, City Hall staff—actually every department except the library." He paused for a breath, and it came to Maura Beth that she had never seen him look so defeated.

"How things have changed in such a short time!" he continued. "You're covered until the end of time, thanks to all that money your cousin from New Orleans gave you as a wedding present. The trouble is, every cent of that money is dedicated specifically to the library and all the new people you'll be hiring soon. The City of Cherico can't touch it for any other reason. But it's one helluva lot of money and could keep the general municipal budget afloat if my last-ditch efforts to impress Dillard Mills fail and Spurs 'R' Us definitely decides to locate in Nashville."

Maura Beth knew what was coming next but said nothing

as Councilman Sparks finally got to the bottom line. "Do you think there's any way you could talk to your cousin and get her to allow us to tap into that library fund temporarily so all of our employees can keep their jobs? The last thing I want to do is give people pink slips a couple of weeks before Christmas. Yeah, I know—you probably think I'm a latter-day Scrooge anyway. But a long time ago, my father and Nora Duddney's father charged me with overseeing the well-being of Cherico for the foreseeable future, and I've taken my role seriously. Maybe some people haven't always seen me in that light, but I've never shrunk from the task."

"Those are all noble sentiments for sure," Maura Beth said, unable to keep the skepticism out of her voice. "And it will probably tantalize you to hear that my Cudd'n M'Dear is even in town for the library event tonight. But I think it would be worse than useless for you to approach her with your little proposal. She's not about to let go of the purse strings, and I'm sure it wouldn't shock you to hear that she's not exactly a fan of yours."

Councilman Sparks offered up a sigh of resignation. "I did get that message loud and clear with the way she made silly putty out of my face during your wedding festivities. Maybe tonight wouldn't be the right time, but is she staying over for the Waddell Mack dinner at The Twinkle? As you probably know, Evie and I have been invited to that by your friend, Periwinkle. Who, by the way, laid down the law to me about bringing my film crew into The Twinkle no matter how much I begged her. 'When Hell freezes over!' she said. The little lady does have a way with words, but did you possibly have anything to do with that?"

"Now, Durden, you know as well as I do that Periwinkle Lattimore is her own woman."

"I'll take that as a no, although I suspect you did. But what about your cousin staying over?"

Maura Beth was trying to picture Cudd'n M'Dear and Waddell Mack in close proximity to anything other than an alternate universe and struggled mightily to suppress outright laughter. "I believe my parents and my cousin are going back to New Orleans sometime tomorrow. Their coming up in the first place was a big surprise to me, but I'll deal with that at the library tonight. So, will you and Evie be popping into the library or not?"

"Your posters all over town say we have to come and share inspirational stories with each other, right?"

Maura Beth leaned in, considering her words carefully. "What you've just told me about Cherico's dire financial straits convinces me more than ever that I've done the right thing creating this special event. Since you've been leveling with me, just do me a favor and don't show up tonight and start your usual special brand of trouble. If you have a genuine story to share, then fine. Otherwise, please just listen respectfully and enjoy the food."

"Fair enough."

Maura Beth's tone veered slightly into the realm of disbelief as she cocked her head. "Really?"

"Really. And I guess the only way to show you that I mean what I say is to finally apologize for all the grief I've given you over the years about the library. And, yes, it's absolutely true that I had a crush on you and thought I might be able to get you to come work for me, and then one thing would lead to another and so forth." He paused briefly and hung his head. "But I guess you figured all that out because you were having none of it."

"Yes, I did, and no, I wasn't."

They both chuckled. "I'll have to ask Evie if she really wants to come tonight," he added. "I'm not sure I deserve to be there."

"Wow! I don't think I've ever seen you like this before!"

Councilman Sparks put his elbows on the table, resting his hands under his chin. "The fact is, for the first time in my life, I'm really scared for our little town. The statistics don't lie. People are leaving Cherico in droves for Corinth or Tupelo or Memphis because they just can't find decent jobs here, or they've lost the ones they had. And the few people who try to bring something upscale to the table like Audra Neely haven't been able to find a profitable niche here, either. She even dropped by one day to tell me why she was leaving, and I could tell she was heartbroken. Hell, Evie's hair salon is moving away, too. I never can remember the name, though. Always makes me think of long hair and Lady Godiva riding on that horse naked."

"Tresses. Cherico Tresses," Maura Beth told him, thoroughly amused. "I go there, too. They're moving to Corinth."

He nodded and snapped his fingers. "Which illustrates my point perfectly. Anyway, I've always been deadly serious about trying to bring jobs in, and our new industrial park really is the key to our future. It's not just some folly of mine. If we can just get that first big plant to locate here—like Spurs 'R' Us—we could use that for a possible domino effect and maybe stop the bleeding. Our little Cherico would have a decent chance again."

Instinctively, Maura Beth leaned forward and extended her hand. "Well, all I can say is I feel like I'm meeting the real Charles Durden Sparks for the first time. Could we shake on it?"

"You always were overly dramatic about everything," he said, gripping her hand firmly and then sinking back into his chair once again. "But you have a tremendous stake in all this now that the new library is well under way. Imagine if we hold that grand opening we're aiming for next summer, and it's the biggest head-scratcher in the history of the state! Can't you just hear people all over Mississippi saying things like,

'Everybody knows that little town of Cherico up there on the lake is dying on the vine, but at least they got themselves a brand-new library out there in the middle of the weeds!?' "

Maura Beth had to admit that the thought had occurred to her, but she had preferred to keep it buried deep within her brain. "You have a point. But it's also possible that the library will be the first step we take toward a greater vision and prosperity. I'm glad you explained what you're really trying to accomplish with the film crew, too. I hope you can put your presentation together in time to persuade the Spurs 'R' Us head honcho, and it's not too late."

"Thanks for understanding my urgency, although too little, too late is not a very good legacy."

Then another idea suddenly flashed into Maura Beth's head. Maybe Councilman Sparks wouldn't go for it, but she couldn't remember a time when they had been this open and relaxed with each other. Now was the moment to strike. So she put it all out there for his consideration and patiently waited for his reaction.

"I guess it would be one way to go," he told her finally.

" 'Tis the season, as they say."

"It sure seems like you're determined to turn me into Santa Claus. How about I give you my decision tonight at the library?"

Maura Beth's surprise was genuine. How far had she come in their checkered relationship that she actually felt she had the upper hand for good now? "So you'll definitely be there?"

"Yes—even if Evie decides not to come. And I promise I won't spoil things for you like I've done in the past. You've definitely made me a believer in the worth of the library with all that's happened."

She smiled, feeling as if she'd won the lottery. "And that's all I've ever asked of you."

12

Story Hour

It was remarkable how different the atmosphere was for this particular meeting of The Cherry Cola Book Club. It had nothing to do with the cold temperature outside—typical of the first week in December in northeast Mississippi. At first, Maura Beth was puzzled by the heightened level of chatter and laughter around the lobby hung with big red and green bows and a small cedar that had been turned into a Christmas tree complete with bubble lights and a bright, blinking star at the top; but she finally figured it out when Stout Fella sidled up to her in the buffet line, and said, "I don't know about the rest of 'em, but I'm relieved I don't have to do a book report here tonight. For all the others I've been to—even *Forrest Gump*—I always felt like I was being graded."

Maura Beth frowned right in the middle of helping herself to a large slice of the mouth-watering glazed ham James Hannigan had contributed. "Well, Justin, I can assure you I didn't mean to come off as a high-school teacher assigning too much homework over the weekend. I've tried not to be too structured—instead, I've stayed outside-the-box, as you know."

"Oh, I didn't mean it to sound like criticism, Maura

Beth," he answered as he hungrily scanned all the food in front of him on the bright red tablecloth, choosing a baked chicken breast and a couple of deviled eggs for starters. "Matter-of-fact, both Becca and I are counting on this meeting to put us in the Christmas spirit. Maybe that big bowl a' eggnog and those sugar cookies with all the red and green sprinkles on 'em over there on the end will help. Fact is, I haven't sold a single house or a plot a' ground in months now, and the bigger Becca gets, the more uncomfortable she gets. We're a pair, aren't we?"

Maura Beth turned and briefly glanced at the former Becca Broccoli, who was already seated in the semicircle of folding chairs, balancing her paper plate on her protruding belly as a makeshift table. At the moment she had just finished spearing two grapes with her fork and was carefully maneuvering them to her mouth. Anyone with any insight and a grasp of the obvious could see that dropping them on the floor and then trying to bend over and retrieve them would have been an utterly lost cause.

"She almost decided to stay home with the cranky way she's been feelin' lately," Justin continued. "But she said she was determined to overcome the trials and tribulations of pregnancy—as she put it—and put things in perspective, and your idea of 'big picture' stories really sounded like something she needed to hear at this time in her life. In both our lives when you get right down to it. Once the baby comes, we know things'll be changed forever."

They moved along the line and continued to help themselves to other goodies as Maura Beth said, "So, are either one of you planning to share a memorable story with us tonight?"

"Becca is. That's provided she can waddle up to the podium."

Maura Beth stole another glimpse of the greatly inflated Becca and chuckled under her breath. "Oh, I expect we'll let her speak from her seat if she has any trouble getting up when the time comes."

Then Justin turned and waved to his wife across the way as he spoke. "I know she'll appreciate that."

"So, I keep forgetting. When is the baby due again? February?"

"Middle a' January or thereabouts, which sure can't get here soon enough for the both of us."

Maura Beth gave him a gentle, playful nudge. "For the record, that makes three of us. Don't forget about your baby's godmother standing right here debating what to put on her plate next."

Justin lowered his chin and his voice at the same time. "Really, Maura Beth, you were the only person we seriously considered. And we felt the same way about ole Doug Mc-Shay for godfather. Doug and I really got to know each other pretty well over beers out at the Marina Bar and Grill before it closed. He's good folks, and so is his wife. This baby sure is gonna have a lot a' special people in his life."

"His? Then you definitely know it's a boy?"

Justin screwed up his face for an instant, looking slightly guilty. "Nah, could be a her for all we know. I still haven't caught on to all this politically correct his and her stuff you're supposed to use in every sentence these days."

Maura Beth was greatly amused and flashed a wide grin. "Well, if that's your worst fault, Justin Brachle, Becca is one lucky woman!"

"Hey, I'm one really lucky man, too. Becca's stayed on me pretty good about my diet and my weight, and she's gotten me to slow down for real. That heart attack I had was my wake-up call, and now I've got a child on the way I need to hang around for. I've got something to live for besides making money. If I had a speech to make tonight, that'd be it in a nutshell."

"Then why don't you get up and say it? It's right to the point and pretty inspiring in my book."

He stayed quiet for a while but finally produced one of his big smiles. "I've got a lot a' competition tonight from some folks who know how to make fine speeches, but I'll give it some serious consideration."

Maura Beth made a point of visiting with practically everyone who had shown up as they all settled into their seats with their plates of chicken, ham, deviled eggs, green bean casserole, and Miss Voncille's reliable biscuits. She was happiest to see Emma Frost had kept her word and brought her Leonard with her, even though the conversation with him was strained.

"And are you enjoying all that good food, Mr. Leonard?" Maura Beth was saying, noting that he and Emma were indeed a good match. The man was as plain and ordinary-looking as she was, but the blank look on his face told the tale of his ailment.

"I . . . uh . . . believe so," he said, staring at her and then down at his plate as if it were about to speak to him.

"He really likes the green bean casserole," Emma put in. "I really favor it myself. Who fixed it? Do ya know?"

"That would be Nora Duddney's contribution, I do believe. You'll have to tell her how much you like it when you get the chance. It's her first time to bring anything, so I know she'd appreciate the compliment. She's sitting back there with her gentleman friend, Wally Denver."

Then Leonard spoke up after finishing off his helping of casserole. "Coudda . . . have some more?"

"Have all you want," Maura Beth told him, gesturing toward the buffet table. "I could go get it for you."

"No, I'll do it, Miz Maura Beth," Emma added. "I was headed back for a second helping myself."

Maura Beth connected with Periwinkle and Mr. Place next. "I guess you're both getting excited about Waddell Mack and his band having dinner at The Twinkle tomorrow night. What a great opportunity for you!"

"You bet we are!" Periwinkle told her. "Except Waddell Mack and his band are one and the same."

Maura Beth's eyes shifted back and forth. "Beg pardon?"

"That's the name of his band—Waddell Mack. He named it after himself."

"Ah, I see."

"You should really download his latest album and listen to some of the songs between now and tomorrow night. You and Jeremy are still coming, right?"

"We're planning on it. By the way, what's on the menu?"

Mr. Place spoke up. "We were planning on our baked chicken and roasted asparagus until Mr. Mack texted us that he was in the mood for some fried catfish and coleslaw."

"Well, I'm sure he'll love anything you fix him."

A few minutes later Maura Beth found herself chatting with Marydell Crumpton and Renette Posey, who were sitting together in the back row. "Where's Mamie tonight? She's not sick, is she?"

"No, indeed, Maura Beth. She's still mad about my working here at the library. So she's boycotting the meeting tonight," Marydell began, after sipping her cup of eggnog. "I know how her brain works. She's sitting at home right now, all dressed up with no place to go—imagining that everything is falling apart without her and that any minute now, we'll all be banging at the door and practically begging her to grace us with her presence. Ha!"

They all laughed, and Renette said, "Miz Marydell is such fun to work with. I get to hear all about the things Miz Mamie does."

"I'm afraid my sister doesn't like sharing the spotlight with anyone, least of all me," Marydell continued. "I know we're all better off not having her here anyway. I can't think of anything remotely inspirational she might have to say. She's good at nitpicking but not much else."

Then Maura Beth continued making the rounds. "Tonight, I feel like I imagine a children's librarian feels all the time," she was saying at one point to Miss Voncille and Locke Linwood, who were seated to her right while enjoying their potluck spread. By then, she found herself very much in her professional mission mode and was enjoying herself thoroughly.

"In about fifteen minutes I'll be presiding over our little story hour—if you want to call it that. We librarians like to say the traditional kind is the first real opportunity to get young brains hooked on reading. Of course, I haven't been able to do story hour as often as I would have liked over the years, since I've worn way too many hats with not enough money to buy a one of them. But somehow I've still managed to find time to throw together a makeshift summer reading program for at least a couple of weeks. I'll start interviewing candidates for the position of children's librarian in January, and let me tell you—I can't wait to delegate that responsibility once and for all."

"This truly is a thrilling time for you and the library," Miss Voncille said, finishing up a deviled egg. "And I can't wait to hold my 'Who's Who in Cherico?' meetings in that new genealogy room you keep telling me about. Maybe we'll finally attract some new members for the first time in years."

"You'll have more room than you ever dreamed of, and we'll keep on expanding the genealogy collection and buy some genealogy software for you that's all the rage now. When the drywall is up next year, you and Locke must come out and I'll give you a little tour so you can get the feel of your new stomping grounds." Maura Beth took a generous bite of her ham and a sip of her eggnog before she continued. "So, I'll ask you the same question I asked Justin Brachle a few minutes ago. Will either of you be sharing a story with us tonight?"

"We both will," Locke told her with a noticeable excitement in his voice. "I think everyone will be moved by what we have to say."

Miss Voncille took Locke's hand and squeezed it, but Maura Beth sensed the gesture was more for courage than affection. "I'm . . . well, I'm going to read one of my Frank's letters that he wrote to me from Vietnam a little before he went MIA. This was a very difficult decision for me. I've never shared any of them with anyone before—not even my Locke since we got married—but I think this is the time and place to do it. If we're supposed to talk about the 'big picture' and inspire each other here tonight, then I know what I'll be reading will do the trick."

"And I'll be sharing something Pamela wrote in her journal, which she turned over to me a few days before she died," Locke added. "I really don't think I could have kept on going after her death if she hadn't left me with those words. They've been guideposts for me. I debated whether to share that or a letter she instructed me to open on the two-year anniversary of her death, but I decided on the journal. It's one of those short but sweet gems that will never leave you."

"I know it will be full of Pamela's special insights," Miss Voncille told him, still holding on to her husband's hand tightly. "She was a remarkable woman and a wonderful wife to you all those years." Then she turned to Maura Beth. "Locke asked me if I wanted to read any of her journal, same as I asked him if he wanted to read this letter of Frank's before tonight, but in the end, we both decided to keep things fresh and surprise each other."

"I'm very impressed," Maura Beth said. "You two understand perfectly what I want to achieve here this evening. I'm convinced Cherico is going to bottom out of this spiral it's been in for a while, and I hope everyone leaves here resolving to help our little town do just that."

"If you don't mind my asking, do you know how many others will be speaking?" Miss Voncille added.

Maura Beth put down her fork and began concentrating with a thoughtful squint, moving her lips as she counted up. "Well, so far, we have the two of you, Becca Brachle, Connie McShay, James Hannigan, Mr. Parker Place; and then, my parents are here from New Orleans, as you know by now, and my mother told me last night at dinner out at the McShays that she had something she wanted to contribute."

"Please don't take this the wrong way," Miss Voncille continued with a lighthearted flick of her wrist, "but I truly hope we're not here inspiring each other until Christmas Day."

"I appreciate the humor," Maura Beth said, smiling pleasantly. "But I did request that everyone keep their presentations to under ten minutes or so. The last thing I want to inspire here tonight is boredom and yawning."

Miss Voncille quickly scanned the library lobby and lowered her voice. "What about that cousin of yours sitting next to your parents and your husband at the other end? She cornered me when I first got here, and I thought she'd never stop running on about how she was going to discuss the importance of telethons for good causes when it was her turn at the podium. I don't want to come off as catty here, but I really could envision her going on for days like an actual telethon would. She could end up putting a real damper on the evening."

In fact, Maura Beth and Jeremy had discussed the problem of Cudd'n M'Dear before leaving the house earlier and had agreed that the way to handle it would be to make sure that the family loose cannon from New Orleans went on last. That way, Maura Beth could interrupt politely if things started getting out of hand and declare that they had unfortunately run out of time and the meeting was over. It was strange but true—Cudd'n M'Dear always required significant advance planning, or anything under the sun might happen.

"You have to trust me. I have a game plan that I'm positive will work," Maura Beth explained, checking the clock at the front desk. It was nearly time for the story hour to begin.

Yet it was more than troubling that despite his promise earlier in the day, Councilman Sparks had not made an appearance. Perhaps her bold suggestion that he make up the budget shortfall out of his own deep pockets this year to avoid those layoffs had been too much for him to stomach. She and Nora Duddney had already forced him to part company with some of the fortune his father had embezzled from library funds when the twentieth century was still young. Perhaps he just didn't have it in him to shell out even more. Still, it was disappointing to accept; she had imagined that Councilman Sparks would deliver his generous decision in his customary grandiose fashion in front of the group to their vigorous applause and then take a bow. She could just envision all the excitement that would create.

Now what could be more inspirational than that?

13

Charles Durden Sparks— Step One

As story hour was beginning at the library, Councilman Sparks was sitting at his dining room table in his gracious Perry Street home. He was in the process of defusing Evie's concern over the way he had pushed his food around his plate over her delicious dinner of pot roast with new potatoes and carrots. Perhaps he should have forced himself to eat something more than he had, but he didn't think he could keep it down. Not at a time like this.

"I had a big late lunch today at The Twinkle," he told her without batting an eyelash, but also avoiding eye contact. "Even had a piece of one of Mr. Place's pies. I should've known better, but my appetite hasn't recovered yet."

"Then I'll put it all up for you in case you get hungry later. No need to let this much food go to waste," she replied as she cleared the table, fretting just a tad bit. "You aren't coming down with something, I hope."

"No, no. I'm just fine, sweetie. Go right ahead and put up a plate for me. That'd be just great. For now, I think I'm going to work on a few municipal budget items in the den," he continued. "I'm way behind in ironing out a few things, so I don't want to be disturbed."

"Well, I'm glad you didn't drag us to that lovefest over at the library tonight. There are just so many people in that club I simply don't care for—from Maura Beth on down," she added. "Plus, you said that awful woman from New Orleans that played with your face at Maura Beth's wedding is going to be there. I might just haul off and slap her upside the head if she tried anything like that again. The very idea!"

He couldn't hold back his laughter. "Now that would be worth the price of admission. Almost."

"Yeah, almost is right."

And that was the end of the exchange.

True to his word, he promptly went into the den and sat down at the handsome plantation desk Evie had bought for him on their tenth anniversary. That was the year he had told her he thought she should cut her hair short, and she had worn it that way ever since. But he must stop letting his mind wander.

He had begun Step One: Go to the den. Lock the door. Write the note. The blank piece of paper was staring him in the face, daring him to find the words. It was unseemly at such a time, but he almost laughed out loud at his predicament.

So this is how writer's block feels!

Momentarily, Evie knocked at the door somewhat insistently, interrupting whatever weak train of thought he had going. "Sorry to bother you, but I'm taking Bonjour Cheri for her poopsies, sweetheart. Be back soon."

"Take your time!" he called out.

"Oh, we always do. My little darling sniffs at everything under the sun before she finally goes."

Inappropriately, he chuckled at the image, and said under his breath, "What will dogs think of next?"

He returned to the paper and the pen in his hand. Not a syllable was forthcoming. He hadn't thought it would be this hard. Everything in his charmed life had always come so easy for him. But this? He leaned back in his comfortable armchair and took a deep breath. He thought again of Evie and her poodle, padding along the sidewalk without a care in the world. How wondrous to live the life of a pampered pet—and that applied to both his wife and her dog!

Finally, he was able to eke out the first sentence: *Evie, I hope you'll find it in your heart to forgive me for what I've done.*

He picked up the paper and read it over before crumpling it up and throwing it in the wicker trash can under the desk. No, it was too trite, too predictable. Well, there was no need to rush. Evie was out on her walk, and she already had orders not to disturb him when she returned. So it was back to the drawing board to strike just the right tone, find those perfect words that kept eluding him.

Then he would proceed methodically to Step Two.

14

Frank Gibbons

Mr. Parker Place had just finished reading his mother's eulogy that he had written and then first spoken at the Cherico African Methodist Episcopal Church not all that long ago. It was the first presentation in the library's story hour and was well-received by the gathering. There were even a few eyes welling up with tears at the end as he stepped away from the podium and returned to his seat next to Periwinkle.

"Thank you for sharing that with us, Parker. Some of you did not get to hear his tribute to his mother at the funeral," Maura Beth said as she took his place in front of the crowd. "But I can assure you, it was even more moving for those of us who attended the service."

"And I just wanted to say again how much it meant to me to see so many of you who are here tonight at the church that day," Mr. Place added. "It has definitely helped me heal."

Then, even before she could be introduced, Miss Voncille rose from her seat and approached the podium. "Closure in life is so important to everyone," she said along the way.

"Ladies and gentlemen," Maura Beth added, gesturing graciously. "A lady who needs no introduction, Voncille Nettles Linwood."

Miss Voncille waited for the light applause to die down before she pointed to the letter in her hands and began. "Thank you for that. I'm not sure I would ever have shared this with anyone—not even my dear husband, Locke—were it not for Maura Beth and The Cherry Cola Book Club. I like to say that it opened me up for good after I shut down many decades ago when I received the news that my Frank Gibbons was officially MIA in Vietnam. As most of you know by now, Frank and I were engaged to be married before he was deployed around January of 1968. The Tet Offensive. It's part of history now. But then, it was just wartime jargon to me. A term I'd never heard of that was repeated over and over by Walter Cronkite and Huntley and Brinkley on the evening news at dinnertime. I kept hoping and praying it wouldn't affect me since it was so far away, but I knew better. Frank was in the middle of it, so how could it not affect me? I was certainly in denial. What I'm going to read to you tonight will show you what a fool I was to try and wish it away. Now, if you don't mind, I'll skip a few very personal parts in the beginning that would only mean something to me. So, bear with me, please, while I catch my breath."

Miss Voncille was as good as her word and then began.

And I believe I've been plunged into the worst of it, along with my company. The Cong are relentless, and I'm not sure we can match their intensity. But the truth is, this is a civil war, and I wonder if we're going to do any better here than the French did when it was called Indochina. No, I'm not having second thoughts about being here and being a soldier. It's what I've chosen to do with my life—at least, this part of it. My choice showed up early.

I played with plastic toy soldiers from the time I was five or six years old. I took sand from the sand-

*box and put it on top of an old wooden table with
peeling paint out in the backyard. Then I put my little soldiers through their paces. I created good territory
and bad territory on the surface of that table, and I
don't know where that came from. Who knows?
Maybe it was the South and North Vietnam to come.
Did I somehow know that? Do we somehow know
what we've chosen even before we've chosen it? By
the end of my playtime, some of my soldiers had
keeled over and died, while others lived. I guess you
could say I played God with them.*

*Do I believe in God? That was such an easy
question to answer when I was little. I did what I
was told, went to church and Sunday school, and
never doubted anything. I'd never been tested. But
now, the napalm takes my breath away—the fireballs
and the booming sounds in the distance, burning the
tops off the palms and leaving nothing but the black-
ened trunks. I want to keep believing in the goodness
of the world, but here I am—a real, flesh-and-blood
soldier in bad territory—and now I feel I'm the one
who's being toyed with somehow on the surface of
something larger than myself that I'll never fully understand.*

*I would never go AWOL, though. It would be
easy to disappear in these jungles, but none of my toy
soldiers ever did anything like that. They stuck it out
because that's the way they were wired. At the end of
one of the many battles I staged, I would always
count up my casualties and smile. "Good job, fellas!"
I would say. "You've served your country well."*

*So I have to be at least as brave as they always
were, even though I'm beginning to wish I was made
out of plastic. Then I wouldn't bleed. I couldn't die.*

*Like some of my buddies have already. This is no
game played by a child on top of a backyard table. It's
way bigger than I am, which leads me back to the notion of God. I don't want the role I took on as a
boy—it doesn't feel good anymore. I'm not capable of
handling it. So that in itself is a form of belief. I ac-
knowledge my mortality as I see others dying around
me. I know that doesn't seem like much to go on, but
it works for me. Anyone who tells you that they
aren't frightened to the bone when they play this
game of war for real is lying through his teeth.*

*Now I find myself on my knees at times, and I
flash back to my childhood in church. That was easy.
This is not. I do the best I can to imagine something
greater than myself, presiding over all of this, and it
sees me through. I can feel myself changing in a way I
never expected, though. You will see it in me when I
come home to you. Maybe you can have some potted
palms waiting for me, and the fronds will be green
without the tops burned away. Will you do that for
me? It will be nice to see something rooted and thriv-
ing like that without a care in the world as it grows.
Just some water now and then, and lots of light all
the time, of course.*

Miss Voncille broke off, and for a moment it was difficult
to tell if she had finished or if she couldn't continue because
of the emotional toll the words were taking on her. Then she
said, "I think that's all I'll read of this tonight. But what I'm
always left with is that Frank had come away with the idea
that there were no easy answers to anything. In some of his
other letters, he expressed the notion that it was more spiritual to stop insisting on certainty and to question things instead. Were answers in life possible—especially when things

were so difficult and traumatic? I believe he still thought so—but only after people were sorely tested and then not found wanting. That was his notion of something greater than himself, and I have to tell you, it's mine, too. Thank you for listening to me."

The gathering applauded politely as Miss Voncille returned to her seat and took Locke's hand. He leaned over, taking the time to rub her arm gently several times, and appeared to be whispering something soothing to her.

"And we thank you for sharing that with us," Maura Beth said. "I almost felt like I was there with your Frank."

For the first time, however, she understood clearly why Miss Voncille had fallen in love so deeply with Frank Gibbons. And why it had been so difficult to forget him and go on with her life. But go on, she had, teaching history to decades of Cherico's schoolchildren and making a name for herself doing so; and Frank's letters had obviously encouraged her not to give up and shown her how to endure the years of loneliness to come.

15

Charles Durden Sparks— Step Two

Cutty Sark had always been a friend to Councilman Sparks. He didn't particularly like the taste, which had driven him to dilute it with soda. The hangovers the stuff had caused him over the years were off-the-charts nasty and head throbbing. But scotch and soda was such a glamorous drink. It was in lots of Hollywood scripts, A-list, B-list, and particularly the film noir genre, and he enjoyed the fantasy that he was one of those razor-sharp detectives or playboys who were always guzzling it while eyeing the sexy, buxom girls. It never failed to deliver the buzz he needed to feel he was on top of the world even when he wasn't.

Tonight, he wasn't. Having finished his note to Evie, he felt like he was staring up at the sky from the bottom of a deep well. How had he fallen so far in his own mind? Well, no matter. Three, maybe even four scotch and sodas would take him where he needed to go. So he went over to the wet bar and retrieved the bottle of Cutty he had been working on for a month or so. Only tonight he intended to finish it off.

"Do your thing," he muttered to the bottle as he poured the first drink into one of the crystal tumblers Evie had bought for him. It was no accident that he chose not to include the soda. It would be scotch on the rocks this time.

He returned to his favorite armchair and took a big swig. "Just . . . do your thing," he mumbled again.

Of course the liquor did not answer him as he swallowed more of it, making a lot of noise rattling the ice cubes. When he had drained the first drink, he poured another one and then started in on it. This time, he chugged. That buzz could not overtake him fast enough, but his nearly empty stomach would serve him well here.

"That's . . . better," he said out loud, hoisting the tumbler as if someone else were in the room with him making a toast.

But he was still not satisfied. He got up again, a little less steady than before, and poured out a good, stiff third round. He had to do Step Two up right. There must be no mistakes. He wanted no messes.

By the time the third one had begun circulating throughout his veins, he was nearly where he wanted to be. He was in control by losing control. He even laughed at the irony of it.

"I call the shots," he said to the empty room where he always liked to retreat to brainstorm his political moves. "I . . . always have to call the shots."

He was manifestly drunk. He knew it. He felt it. It had come faster because he wanted it. Once again, he liked where his beloved Cutty Sark had taken him. But he had one more step before he arrived at his destination. Step Three was in the pocket of his shirt. He reached up with the fingers of his free hand and palpated them through the fabric. They were still there, waiting for him. Waiting to do their mischief.

Just a few minutes longer to enjoy the buzz from the alcohol. Just a few blissful moments. Then he would proceed.

16

Pamela Linwood

Locke Linwood had just taken his place at the podium. Dressed in his three-piece gray suit with silver tie, his skin a healthy pink and his full head of white hair meticulously brushed in place, he looked as bright and shiny as tinsel on a Christmas tree. Only when Miss Voncille nodded his way, however, did he open the small brown journal he had brought with him for his inspirational presentation.

"Ladies and gentlemen, tonight I am going to read a selection from my late wife's diary that she kept from the day she was diagnosed with breast cancer to a few days before she left me. I never really knew just how strong Pamela was until she entrusted me with these writings and I finally worked up the courage to read them all. It took me a while to let her leaving really sink in. But once I began reading, I was sorry I hadn't done so sooner. I think you'll see why when I proudly share the following passages with you."

I can't pretend I'm happy that I've been told that not only do I have this aggressive cancer, but that it has also metastasized. That will only make it that much harder to treat and greatly reduce my chances for survival. But something began to happen to me when I took a deep breath and looked at this diagnosis as the elephant in the room. My mortality kicked in big-time. Did I actually think I was going to live forever? When I was very young, I thought so. Several of my girlfriends and I thought so every time we stayed up all night at slumber parties talking about boys and love and what we wanted to be when we grew up. I even think I continued to believe in immortality well into middle age. Could anything touch the privileged life I've led all these happy years with my dear Locke? Could saying good-bye to it really happen to me?

Well, something relentless has touched me now, and I have to face the strong possibility that I may have to leave my wonderful Locke behind. I have to prepare him for that eventuality with my ongoing attitude.

Do I have the right to fall apart? Yes.

Do I want to do that? No.

I've been considering that age-old question: What comes next? We all think of it now and then, even if we never admit it. I've come up with three possibilities. The first is that I will simply go to sleep. There is nothing to fear in that. My good friend, Beverly Norris, is an atheist, and she insists that that is what will happen to all of us. She doesn't say it out of anger or certainty, and when I asked her one time if she thought she could be wrong about it, she said quite calmly, "Of course." I liked the fact that she spoke to me out of her own comfort zone. She wasn't proselytizing or anything close to that. So, she didn't end up turning me off of the possibility that quiet, peaceful sleep could be an end result.

The second possibility is that I will encounter something along the lines of the traditional religious teachings I have embraced more or less throughout the years. I have no quarrel with the Episcopal Church. I have taken communion all these years, and I know what that is supposed to prepare us for. There isn't much more to say here, except that I have never re-belled against traditional teachings.

Because the third possibility is the one that really intrigues me. Suppose it's not the first two. Instead, it's something completely amazing, and at the same time, surprising beyond words. Not Heaven. Not Hell. Not Purgatory. Not Limbo. Suppose it's some-thing no one ever thought of because we are all bound by these finite bodies that wear out? And only until they completely wear out or we are thrown out of them under disastrous circumstances do we see the universe as it really is. Suddenly, we are on a differ-ent wavelength. The projector shows us something that's never been advertised in the theaters. There was no trailer to intrigue us. Not everything is meant to be seen or heard or felt. Does that mean it does not exist?

So, I return to the premise that while I don't have certainty in this life, there is likely some benefit to fighting until the end. Whatever else life is, it is most certainly not to be thrown away. I steadfastly refuse to say, "Why me?" I say instead, "I am worth fighting for, no matter what comes next."

I will undergo this dreadful chemo and await the outcome. If it turns out I am unable to keep this jour-nal any longer, I will tell Locke that I want him to read it when he feels up to it. That I want him to re-turn to it whenever he misses me, which I know he

*will. Our life together has been like a long-run
Broadway hit. It's just that there are no understudies
for us. Yes, we have Carla and Locke Jr. to show for
it, but they have their own roles to play in their own
lives. All we did was bring them to the auditions.*

*I do know that I feel better when I write down
these ramblings of mine. Some would say I am talking
to myself. Others would say I am talking to God.
Whatever the case, I am not going to give up. I am
going to fight and fight hard until the end. Because I
believe life matters.*

Locke closed the journal and nodded graciously. "And that, ladies and gentlemen, is the contribution of Pamela Alden Linwood to our little gathering here tonight. Her words are her presence, and I feel it strongly."

"And I feel it, too," Miss Voncille added, her voice as soft and soothing as anyone had ever heard. "I'll always be eternally grateful to this remarkable woman for helping Locke let go by showing us how she was going to do it herself."

The emotion clearly registered in Locke's face as he made his way back to his seat to the applause of the group. "Thank you, one and all," he managed as he and Miss Voncille hugged warmly.

"Oh, my," Maura Beth said, returning to the podium and fanning her face quickly a few times as a beauty pageant contestant who had just won it all might have. "I do believe we're getting our money's worth tonight. These presentations are just what the doctor ordered. I don't know about the rest of you, but I'm feeling better about our problems here in Cherico already. I knew there would be strength in numbers."

17

Charles Durden Sparks— Step Three

The little round yellow Valium tablets Councilman Sparks had stolen from Evie's medicine cabinet were burning a hole in his shirt pocket as he sat soaked in scotch, feeling sorry for himself. He put down his crystal tumbler on a nearby end table and retrieved them, one by one, until he had all five of them in the palm of his hand. As he had done before with the bottle of scotch, he began speaking to his wife's drug of choice as if they were old friends.

"And now . . . you little high-dosage devils will do your job."

Then he realized he had completely drained his last drink and had nothing to use as a chaser. So he rose, this time even more unsteady on his feet, made his way to the wet bar with his glass, and poured a small amount of soda into it. Just enough to swallow the pills.

He didn't swallow them all together. Instead, he made an elaborate ritual of downing them one at a time. He placed each pill on the tip of his tongue and let it linger there for a few seconds. He decided to count to ten silently before bringing the soda into play. Wasn't this a countdown?

When the last little devil had been sent to his stomach, he

decided to pick up the note he had written to Evie and read it one last time. While he still could. But he didn't start at the beginning. Instead, his eyes landed on certain phrases:

> *. . . and I was entrusted with the care and feed-*
> *ing of Cherico by my father and Layton*
> *Duddney . . . I have failed miserably in that . . . and*
> *perhaps you have forgiven me for not being able to*
> *provide us with children, but I haven't been able to*
> *forget . . . you get more comfort from Bonjour*
> *Cheri . . . our poodle is a better companion to*
> *you . . . I like to pretend I've accomplished some-*
> *thing, but all I've done is boss people around . . . I*
> *should have kept the Spurs 'R' Us CEO on a*
> *shorter leash, too . . . We really needed those*
> *jobs . . . I really blew that, I guess . . . I know in*
> *my heart what I am . . . and I believe you and all of*
> *Cherico will be better off without me . . .*

Oddly, as his faculties began to fade, one particular insight stuck out. Miss Voncille had been right about him all along. She had as much as told him that he was a different kind of bully, lording it over people intellectually and not wanting them to have even a brief second of the limelight in the class-room. She had finally taken him aside one afternoon after the bell had rung, and her harsh words were still branded on his brain as if she had spoken them to him yesterday.

"There are many other students sitting around you, Dur-den Sparks. You have no sense of fairness the way you fret and fume and squint at me. I simply can't call on you every time your hand goes up, and you should know that by now. You'd better learn it right now—the universe doesn't revolve around you!"

He had called her a bitch mentally, and then as soon as he

was out in the hallway, he had actually uttered the word several times over with ferocity: "Bitch, bitch, bitch!"

A couple of students walking by had even turned their heads and wondered what in the world could be bothering the school's most accomplished student so much that he would have such a public tantrum.

But Miss Voncille had nailed it. He wanted to shine every second, and he knew even then that he would be capable of doing anything to make sure that happened. What kind of legacy was that? Oh, sure, his name would be on that library Maura Beth and Nora Duddney had forced him to build, and he had taken full credit for it. But he still didn't believe in libraries, even though he had recently told Maura Beth something along those lines. He had also told her that she was now a member of his team. But he was lying both times. He wanted to get rid of her, or conquer her, or subdue her, but he had been unable to do any of those things. She was her own woman, and he just didn't know what to do with someone like that.

More importantly, she had rejected him—the first woman to do so in his life of conquests. How could she have failed to fall for his charms? She obviously took her idealism to heart. He had abandoned his a long time ago, if he had ever had any to begin with. Perhaps it was missing from his DNA.

He thought of Nora's father, Layton Duddney, propped up in bed out at the nursing home, essentially waiting to die. But Layton was not forcing the issue. He was simply waiting patiently for the inevitable.

Step Three was now complete. Charles Durden Sparks put the note down on the end table next to his glass and closed his eyes.

18

James Hannigan

Everyone's favorite grocer briskly stepped to the podium and scanned the library gathering with flushed, pudgy cheeks and a warm smile. His Cherico Market continued to be a mainstay of the town, and James Patrick Hannigan—Mr. Hannigan to his many customers—was the main reason for it. While other businesses were moving away or had failed outright—including one of the big, impersonal, national grocery chains out on the bypass—The Cherico Market was *the* place to shop, meet up with friends for a chat, and post notices and flyers on the cork bulletin board.

Yes, it was true that everyone had to buy groceries, but Mr. Hannigan went the extra mile and treated his customers as family, and he had helped Maura Beth immeasurably by making announcements over the PA system during her petition campaign to keep the library open. He had provided her with an enormous chunk of signatures that had kept Councilman Sparks and his machinations at bay.

"I believe I know every single one of you in the audience tonight," Mr. Hannigan began. "I see y'all in the store at least once a week. Some of you, maybe more. Hey, you know what kinda diet you're on better'n I do."

Heads nodded as a wave of polite laughter erupted.

"I had thought I'd maybe start off tonight with a little anecdote about me trying to wrestle the communion chalice away from Father O'Beirne at St. Mary's down in Natchez where I grew up," he continued. "But I realized there wasn't much to the story—I just loved the taste of that wine so much, I wanted more than what everybody else was getting. That little sip just wasn't enough. Father was okay with it in the end, but my mother grounded me for two whole weeks and made me say about a thousand Hail Marys."

There was more laughter, and then Mr. Hannigan's face grew solemn as he took a deep breath. "What I really wanted to tell y'all about was something that happened to me after my mother died a few years back, and I'd been living up here in Cherico for over twenty years. First, a little background for those of you who may not know: I am the youngest of six brothers, and we were and still are a close-knit, Irish Catholic family. My mother, Theresa, was very strict with all of us, and she needed to be. We were a rowdy bunch, and she really had her hands full. But we knew she loved us, and we all loved her in return.

"The summer she died unexpectedly in her sleep shortly after Maura Beth took over the library here, I hadn't seen Mother in several years. It was one of those things where you have every intention of visiting, but something always comes up that gets in the way. Of course, I'd sent birthday and Christmas cards and talked on the phone now and then, but I hadn't taken the time to visit her face-to-face. My brothers all got married and had loads of grands to show off, plus they stayed to make a living in Natchez. Me, I set off on my own and just never found anyone, and my mother was always on me to find a nice Catholic girl like all my brothers had—"

He broke off and appeared to be smirking about something. "Do any of you know of a catalog where I can order one?"

This time, it took a while for the laughter to die down.

"Well, Mother was almost that bad about it. I don't know—maybe I was tired of every visit being dominated by why I hadn't gotten married yet. But anyhow, she died in her sleep, and no one got to say good-bye the way we'd all like to when a loved one leaves us. Even my brothers. But at least they had all seen and talked to her recently. I was the odd man out and completely without closure. I can relate to what Miss Voncille said earlier. It's tough to make your peace when you don't have it."

"Amen," Miss Voncille called out, smiling at him affectionately.

"I remember that Maura Beth helped me find some books on grief at the library, and I read them all. They did give me some comfort. But I'm now going to share something I've never told anyone before. I was—well, I was afraid of ridicule and that people would say I'd just made it all up because I was hurting so much. I changed my mind when Maura Beth came up with this exchange of inspirational stories.

"I need to backtrack just a tad bit, though. When my brothers and I were very young, Mother and our aunt Margaret came up with a delightful little trick to keep the magic in our lives. Or at least that's what they told us later on. What they did was to buy two large, silver-plated birds with long tails, but we weren't told there were two of them. Mother kept one on the fireplace mantel, and Aunt Margaret did the same at her house. Mother called it The Magic Bird and told us that it was capable of coming to life and flying to Aunt Margaret's house to greet us when we got there. And that's what we believed had happened when we saw The Magic Bird on Aunt Margaret's mantel. Eventually, both of the birds got broken and couldn't be repaired. But the fond memories continued and—"

"What an adorable story!" Miss Voncille interrupted.

"Thank you, but I haven't quite gotten to the point yet, Miss Voncille."

"There's more? Well, how delightful!"

"Yes, well, now comes the part that I've never told anyone about before, and it involves this matter of closure. I was beside myself at the funeral, even though everyone did everything they could to console me. But then, something happened to give me that closure, and it involved the idea of The Magic Bird coming to life. I wasn't looking forward to Christmas that year, but I dutifully decorated the house as I always had. I put up a tree in the living room, put a wreath on the front door, and was in the midst of stringing some small white lights throughout the azaleas that lined the walk leading up to my front porch.

"And that's when something remarkable happened. I heard a knocking noise coming from behind me as I faced the street with my lights. When I turned around, a large bird with a long tail was pecking at one of my front window panes. I immediately dropped the lights and approached this bird—if that was indeed what it was. Finally, I was less than six inches away, but the bird did not take flight as I would have expected it to do. Instead, it hopped down from the window, and without even thinking about it, I said, 'Mother?'

"The bird followed me halfway down the path to where I had dropped the lights and stood there watching me string them. I continued to talk to it. 'You see? I'm going to have Christmas just like I always have.'

"That bird did not fly away until I had completed all of my yard decorations, but when it finally did, I knew I had closure. I don't pretend to understand exactly what happened

that day, but I can tell you that I fully recovered that childhood sense of magic Mother and Aunt Margaret gave to us
when they created The Magic Bird. Was this Mother's way of
letting me know everything was fine so that I could go on
with my life? I know there are those who will say that I was
just guilty of wishful thinking and that there had to be a sci-
entific explanation for what happened. Maybe there was, but
I don't care. All I know is that I definitely had the closure I
desperately needed, and the beliefs I was brought up with
were only strengthened in a quiet, internal way. I was content
with those, but it didn't matter if no one else in the world understood. That bird was meant for me, and the message was
received."

Connie McShay raised her hand. "Did you ever see the
bird again?"

"Never. Just that once. But that was all I needed. I guess
you could say—mission accomplished."

"Well, anyway, I'm glad you chose to share the story with
us tonight," Connie continued. "We take a lot of things on
faith in this life, but the notion that birds can be messengers of
some kind is not out of left field to me. I don't think we fully
understand the role that some animals can play in our lives.
Do they see and hear versions of reality that we don't? Do
they share their special gifts with us? As our pets, it's well-doc-
umented that they cheer us up and even warn us from time
to time. Is it so unreasonable to think that they know things
we don't know?"

Mr. Hannigan seemed relieved and nodded with a grateful smile. "Thank you for saying that, and I hope my story
helps all of you in some way." And with that, he returned to
his seat to the applause of the club.

"I'm convinced my cats hold the secrets to the universe,"
Audra Neely said, subtly waving her hand. "I wish I could tap
into their brains. Maybe they could tell me how to keep my

store open." She paused for a little giggle as she stood up in the front row and turned to face the group. "I'm only kidding about my cats, of course, but I would like to take this opportunity to wish everyone a Merry Christmas. I've loved being here in Cherico and making so many good friends."

"Will you stay in touch with us after you get settled?" Maura Beth added.

"Of course I will. You're all exceptional people."

"Audra, I'll miss your special lobster orders every now and then," Mr. Hannigan said.

"What can I say? I have extravagant tastes, but I guess you could say my antique store wasn't keeping me in lobsters."

Everyone laughed, and then Maura Beth resumed her duties as moderator. "All I can say is that each new story seems to top the previous one. Now, who would like to go next?"

Connie raised her hand again. "I would, if you don't mind. In a strange way I think my story and Mr. Hannigan's might be first cousins in the take-it-on-faith department; and it has something in common with the moving words Locke read from his late wife's journal."

Maura Beth smiled and gestured to her invitingly. "Then by all means, come on up and don't keep us in suspense."

19

Bonjour Cheri

Evie Sparks noticed that her beloved poodle, Bonjour Cheri, was acting strangely on their evening walk along fashionable Perry Street. The dog was dawdling and whimpering where before she had always been straightforward about doing her business. She had already passed up two of her favorite spots on the sidewalk median strip close to the edge of the curb where Evie would always clean up after her with her pooper scooper and doggie bag. As Cherico's perennial First Lady, she had continued to be the impetus behind a beautification program that included dog-walking responsibilities and protocol, among many other trivial things.

"What's the matter, girl?" Evie had said more than once. "I know you have to go, so why don't you?"

But Bonjour Cheri continued to delay the inevitable, occasionally looking up at her mommy with sad eyes while refusing to sniff and circle.

"Come on, now, sweetie, you have to go. It's really cold out here tonight. No more nonsense, okay?"

Finally, Bonjour Cheri complied in a spot she had never chosen before. But the puzzling drama was far from over. All the way back home, she continued to whimper, going faster and faster and pulling on her leash as if driven by some powerful but unseen force.

"Slow down, girl! Stop it, now!"

But all of Evie's commands were completely ignored.

Once the two of them walked into the kitchen, Bonjour Cheri's agitation only increased, and Evie struggled mightily to unhook the leash from her collar as her pampered pet refused to sit still for a second. It was almost as if the ordinarily calm and well-mannered poodle was possessed.

"What in the world is the matter with you, sweetie pie? Mommy has never seen you like this."

Bonjour Cheri started barking the way dogs bark when they spot a squirrel in the yard and then give chase. Next, she sprinted straight for the door to the den where she began pawing at it frantically. The sound of the dog's claws scratching the wood grated on Evie's nerves like the fabled fingernails across a chalkboard. It was almost too much to bear.

"My goodness, sweetie, I almost feel like we're in one of those *Lassie* rescue episodes," Evie said, trailing after, as Bonjour Cheri continued acting completely out of character.

But Evie's fleeting moment of humor was quickly replaced by more troubling thoughts. She could not forget that her Durden had toyed with his food and then excused himself to do some work after hours. But she had never known him to bring the office home with him over the many years of his political reign in Cherico. She tried the doorknob and found that he had locked himself in. Meanwhile, Bonjour Cheri took her constant barking and whimpering and pawing to yet another decibel, another level of frantic activity.

"Durden! Durden!" Evie cried out, continuing to work the doorknob with one hand while she knocked insistently with the other. "Open up, please! Durden, you've got to open up!"

But there was no answer. The silence behind the door was frightening, causing her pulse to quicken even more.

"If you're playing some kind of joke, it isn't funny!"

The duet of urgency from both dog and wife was at a fever pitch now. It was difficult to tell who was more agitated.

"Durden! Can you hear me, sweetheart? Please, Durden, open up! What's going on in there?"

Finally, Evie broke away from the door while Bonjour Cheri remained at her post like the good, loyal dog she was. At that point Evie had only one thing on her mind—calling 911. Something bad was going on in her house, and she sensed that there was no time to lose.

20

Connie McShay and Cara Lynn Mayhew

To say that everyone in the library lobby was intrigued by the opening statement of Connie's presentation was an understatement. "I'm here tonight to tell you all a remarkable story of unfinished business that resulted in saving someone's life," she had already told them all. She was careful to let everyone sit with that for a few moments before speaking again.

"Of course, I've seen my share of people leaving us, being the retired ICU nurse that I am. But this is about someone who stayed with us. I was always overjoyed when that happened, of course, and this particular recovery is one I was given permission to share a long time ago. Lucianne Connor was a patient of mine the one year I was transferred to the oncology wing of my hospital up in Nashville. I saw her during the period of time she was undergoing chemo, and, of course, it was difficult for her, as it is for everyone. Lucianne was an active, beautiful mother of two young boys and had just turned forty when she first got her diagnosis of ovarian cancer; and I was with her as she lost her lush brunette hair and the drugs began to distort her good looks.

"But despite all the nausea and everything else she went through, she never complained. I mean, not even once. Instead, she told me all the time how grateful she was that her cancer was being treated before it advanced to stage four, which gave her a fighting chance for the remission she eventually achieved. Ovarian cancer is extremely difficult to detect until it's gotten out of hand, but it's how hers was caught in time that makes her story so remarkable."

Connie paused once again to let her last statement sink in, and she could easily see that she continued to have the entire gathering on the edge of their seats.

"At any rate, Lucianne was from New Canaan, a little town about halfway between Nashville and Clarksville. She was a regular library user there, which turned out to end up saving her life. Lucianne told me that the previous librarian who had worked there for many years—a sweet, dedicated lady who everyone simply called Miz Trilby—had the misfortune of waiting too late to go to the doctor when she discovered a lump in her breast; and when she finally did go, her cancer had metastasized, and unfortunately, she didn't make it."

There were soft, sympathetic murmurings from the audience, and then Connie continued.

"But Lucianne visited the library quite often to check out the latest best-sellers. As it happened, she had to walk along a row of nonfiction on her way to the 'new releases' display. The first time several books practically jumped off the shelf and landed in front of her feet, she said she picked them up quickly and stacked them neatly at the end of a row that had a little room. I guess she was just like me—always obeying those signs about letting the staff do the reshelving. That's sometimes a problem for you, isn't it, Maura Beth?"

"More than you know," Maura Beth said. "We find our books in the strangest places all the time. But we just shrug and do our jobs. Emma and Renette can vouch for that, can't you, ladies?"

Both women nodded in agreement, and Renette said,

"Even on our slowest days, someone always seems to come in and rearrange things."

"I'm sure," Connie added. "So, anyway, the next time Lucianne walked that way and those same books fell off the shelf at her feet, she was more than puzzled. This time, she paid more than passing attention to those titles as she picked them up. To her astonishment, they were all about some aspect of ovarian cancer. Lucianne said that one was even about the importance of early detection. It was then that she began to put two and two together, for lack of a better way to put it. She already knew what had happened to Miz Trilby, and this poltergeist effect that kept happening to her was just too weird for her to ignore. I imagine all of you can guess what happened next. She went to the doctor, told him what had happened at the library, and asked to undergo a battery of tests, and that was when they detected her ovarian cancer in the nick of time. It was one of those things that everyone around her called a miracle."

Maura Beth was the first to sigh in astonishment. "Is Lucianne still with us, I hope and pray?"

Connie sounded as proud as a grandmother talking about her grandchildren. "She sure is. I just got a beautiful, newsy Christmas card from her yesterday. I thought to myself, 'How perfect, since I'm going to be telling her story to everyone at the library tomorrow night!' More than anything else has, it has really put me in the Christmas spirit. Because no matter how hard we try, there are just some things that can't be explained in conventional terms, and I know I'm okay with that. I firmly believe we aren't meant to know the answers to everything."

This time, it was Jeremy who spoke up, nodding approvingly. "You'll have to excuse me for being the English teacher that I am, but as William Shakespeare once put it: 'There are more things in heaven and earth, Horatio, than are dreamt of in your philosophy.' That old chestnut from *Hamlet* just seemed to fit in well here, don't you think?"

Connie flashed Jeremy her warmest smile. "I couldn't agree more, and Lucianne also mentioned in her Christmas card that she was thinking of trying to write a memoir called *Miz Trilby Saves the Day.* She said she's just not sure she can get the words down the way she wants, though. She has absolutely no experience writing anything more than a note to her sons' teachers, but she believes her story could help promote cancer awareness and prevention."

"I'd like to offer to help her, then," Jeremy continued, feeling suddenly inspired and generous. "I haven't made much progress on the novel I've been trying to write. Maybe she and I could collaborate on her concept. Do you think you could possibly put me in touch with her?"

"Well, I could tell her all about you, see what she says, and then get back to you, Jeremy."

"That would be wonderful. The worst that could happen is that she'll say she's not interested, but maybe something great will come of this."

Maura Beth shot her husband an understanding gaze. Only she knew how much he had been struggling with the manuscript he had unwisely tried to begin on their honeymoon. The newlywed distractions had been way too much for him, and perhaps he should have anticipated that. But, ah, to be young and very much in love! "Who knows what all we'll set in motion because of getting together and sharing these stories with each other?"

"All I can say is, I got the chills listening to Connie's story," Nora Duddney added. "Actually, all the stories have made me think outside the box about my life. Sounds just like a typical Cherry Cola Book Club meeting, doesn't it? I'm practically addicted to our get-togethers."

Maura Beth might have come up with something along

those lines herself but was pleased that someone else had actually said it. It might have sounded too boastful coming from her. "This one is turning out to be even more special. Does anyone else have anything to say about Connie's story before we move on?"

Becca raised her hand, her voice suddenly stressed. "I did a few seconds ago . . . and I hate to interrupt this wonderful exchange . . . but right this moment, I think I'm having contractions." There was a sharp intake of breath as she put her hand on her belly, and then her Stout Fella quickly stood up beside her, offering his muscular arm to help her up gingerly.

"I'm calling the hospital to let 'em know we're on the way!" he told everyone as he pulled out his cell phone. "I've been rehearsing this in my sleep!"

"Come on, Douglas, we'll follow them," Connie said next, moving to Becca's side in a flash.

"I thought the baby wasn't due for another four or five weeks," Douglas added, following close behind. "I've had it all marked on my calendar, since I'll be the proud godfather."

"Looks like it's coming early, though," Becca managed, obviously in pain. "These things happen."

The meeting was put on hold until the Brachles and Mc-Shays had exited the front door to cries of "Text us!" "Call us!" and "Let us know what happens!" For her part, Maura Beth was genuinely conflicted since she was the godmother-to-be and felt more like going to the hospital herself. Once again, she faced the prospect of disbanding a book club event early, but she knew her mother and Cudd'n M'Dear had yet to speak.

Fortunately, Cara Lynn Mayhew seemed to be reading her mind. "Sweetheart, I'm wondering if we ought to call it a night with all this excitement. What I had to say, I can say to you in private. It was just a little essay I wrote about being thankful for having you in my life."

Maura Beth was thrilled by her mother's words. "If the rest of you wouldn't mind, I'd love to hear what my mother has to say. I think it might be the perfect way to bring things to a close."

Not surprisingly, Cudd'n M'Dear had other ideas, objecting immediately. "But what about my pitch for various charitable causes? Telethons raise a lot of money, you know. They can be very inspirational, and isn't that what we're here for?"

Maura Beth was able to think on her feet, however. "What I think you should do, cousin dear, is to leave all the contact information for your favorite charities, and I'll see that everyone here tonight gets a copy. That way, if they want to contribute, they'll be able to right away. I'm sure that's the important thing here."

"Well, I suppose that'll have to do," Cudd'n M'Dear said, though not looking particularly happy about it.

Maura Beth pressed on, realizing that indecision was definitely the wrong move with someone as unpredictable as Cudd'n M'Dear. "Then that's all settled." She gestured invitingly to her mother, and the stylish Cara Lynn Mayhew was soon behind the podium with her reading glasses on and looking down at a sheet of paper.

A mother wakes up one morning to find she has a child who is totally dependent upon her. It is a startling discovery since she thinks she is prepared for it. She has been waiting for nine months to greet this new little person in her life. But when her child finally arrives, the responsibility fully registers for the first time. The adventure is just beginning.

When I greeted my Maura Beth, I was astonished that she could be so different from me and the expectations I had for her. First there was the cute red fuzz atop her head, also the blue eyes. Where had they come from? William and I had neither. Our parents didn't have them, either. Later on, the freckles appeared. It seemed like there

*were a million of them. And then that free spirit of hers kicked in
pretty early on. It was as if a magnificent bird had flown into our lives
and was spreading its wings right there in front of us every day. I have
to say that it took us a while to realize what was going on, and we
were speechless—but in a good way.*

*I don't pretend to understand this business of genes—who inher-
its what and how. More cynical types say it's just a crapshoot. I only
know that William and I were blessed by the combination that came
together through us to create our Maura Beth. She has grown into
her own woman and made her own valid choices, and I can't wait to
see what the future holds for her now. And also the man she has chosen to spend the rest of her life with—Jeremy McShay, our son-in-
law. William and I welcome him into our family with open arms.*

*So I can tell you this much about our daughter: Cherico, Missis-
sippi, is lucky to have her, although some of you already realize
you've caught lightning in a bottle with this librarian on a mission.
May she continue to walk gracefully toward her destiny. We will always love her and what she has brought into our lives.*

As they had just before her wedding had taken place on
the deck of Connie and Douglas's lodge, mother and daughter embraced warmly, now fully connected on every level.
Then Maura Beth pulled back slightly and managed a halting,
emotional response. "What you've said . . . means the world
to me. Thank you so much . . . for coming all this way to
say it."

The rest of the gathering responded with applause and a
sprinkling of "Awws!" as William Mayhew moved forward to
put his arms around the two important women in his life.

"Photo album op, please!" he declared, handing over his
smartphone to Jeremy after shaking his hand. "This is our
payoff!"

Maura Beth allowed herself to bask in this special family
moment. How things had turned around for her since the

wedding! But it did not take long for thoughts of Becca and her baby to return. This latest meeting of The Cherry Cola Book Club needed to be officially disbanded so she and Jeremy could lend whatever support they could to the Brachles at the hospital.

21

Botulism and Populism

Was there anything more draining than the impersonal hospital waiting room game? Why, the number of worst-case scenarios the brain could conjure up was absolutely astounding!

Maura Beth and Jeremy had been sitting in the midst of her parents, Cudd'n M'Dear, Connie, and Douglas at the Cherico Memorial ER for a good half hour. Though there was no news yet on Becca from her Stout Fella, the comings and goings of Councilman Sparks's lackeys—Chunky Badham and Gopher Joe Martin—aroused more than a little curiosity among the group. First one and then the other councilman would enter through the sliding glass doors, briefly inquire at the desk, disappear inside the ER for a time, and then exit hurriedly, looking totally distracted and wild-eyed. There were moments when it all came off like a rehearsal for a classic stage farce with some unseen director demanding frantic energy levels.

"What do you suppose they're up to running around like headless chickens that way?" Connie said, unable to restrain herself any longer. "Surely, it can't have anything to do with Becca, can it?"

Maura Beth spoke up with absolute certainty. "I highly

doubt it. When it comes to the activities and priorities of those two, it's never about anyone but our beloved Councilman Sparks."

"What would that so-called man of the people be doing in the emergency room? Doesn't everyone come to him?" Cudd'n M'Dear added, tossing aside the medical magazine on recipes for diabetics she had been skimming to make the time go by. "Besides, you've led me to believe he doesn't even have a drop of blood in his veins, Maura Beth."

"I wouldn't go quite that far, but something is definitely going on." Then Maura Beth had another thought that immediately softened her attitude. "Maybe it's his wife, Evie, and he's back there with her. I just hope it's nothing serious."

"Could be a nervous breakdown after living with him all that time," Cudd'n M'Dear continued, clearly amused with herself.

Maura Beth decided not to humor Cudd'n M'Dear any further. It was so easy for the woman to get out of hand and completely hijack any conversation. "Whatever. I'm just about ready to go over to the desk and find out what's going on."

"I'm afraid that won't do you any good. There are patient confidentiality laws," Connie said. "You'd have to catch one of the councilmen on his next flyby and ask him about it."

"Well, they certainly seem to be having no trouble getting all the information they need."

Just then, Justin emerged, sauntering toward them with a shrug of his wide shoulders. "Hey, it's just false labor, folks." He sounded almost matter-of-fact about it all, even managing a big smile. "The doctor says it was brought on by a bladder infection, so he's giving her a course of antibiotics. That's way better than a premature delivery, though. We get to keep the bun in the oven a little longer."

"So everything's okay?" Maura Beth said.

"Just fine. They'll be releasing Becca soon."

Maura Beth's sigh of relief was dramatic—very much belonging to an expectant godmother. "That's all I wanted to hear."

"Yeah, she was a little rattled there for a while, but they've got her calmed down pretty good right now."

"Well, it seems we all rushed over here for nothing," Cudd'n M'Dear added in that judgmental way of hers. "I could've made my telethon speech after all, and I had it rehearsed to perfection. I think everyone would've been inspired to go out and raise money immediately."

"But you simply can't take chances with babies," Cara Lynn Mayhew said. "Believe me, cousin, when a pregnant woman tells you she thinks that baby's on the way, nothing else matters."

"Just think of false labor as a dress rehearsal," Connie pointed out. "I saw enough of them during my career. They can be a bit unnerving, but usually a case of no harm done. That bladder infection should be no big deal."

The impromptu drama continued as Justin headed back into the ER to join his wife. But no sooner had he disappeared than a distraught-looking Evie Sparks emerged, heading for the sliding glass doors.

"I'm going to see if I can find out what's going on," Maura Beth said, jumping up from her spot on the sofa. But Evie sped up as soon as she saw Maura Beth approaching, staying well ahead until she had escaped into the parking lot. At that point it seemed unwise to continue the pursuit.

"Now I really am curious," Maura Beth told the others as she returned to them. "At least we know it's not Evie back there, but she deliberately avoided me. Of course, I've always gotten a bit of a cold shoulder from her anyway."

"I guess we'll find out about it all soon enough, Maurie," Jeremy said, as everyone stood up preparing to head to their cars.

"Maybe not. I can assure you that Councilman Sparks is pretty good at keeping things from people. That's how he operates."

"Truly a man of the people in the grand tradition of our Huey P. Long," Cudd'n M'Dear added almost gleefully.

But Maura Beth wasn't in the mood for trading clever quips. "That may be, but I think our favorite populist could be in trouble back there."

Cudd'n M'Dear smirked. "Perhaps he's just getting what he deserves."

"I think the meeting tonight was an astounding success. Those stories really stuck with me, and I intend to follow through with that Lucianne woman," Jeremy was saying as he and Maura Beth snuggled in bed after one of their nightly lovemaking sessions. It always took a while for either of them to speak because of the satisfying exertion and the time it took for their pulses to wind down. The honeymoon wasn't over yet by a long shot.

Maura Beth carefully untangled herself from the warmth and firmness of his muscles and propped herself up on her pillows, biting her lip as she considered briefly. "I think you should. A collaboration could end up helping a lot of people. Meanwhile, I have an idea of my own."

"And what's that?"

"I'm going to call the hospital and ask for Councilman Sparks's room. That way I'll know if he's been admitted or not."

Jeremy frowned as he sat up as well. "I'd like to know why you're so concerned about him. We both know he certainly hasn't been all that concerned about you all these years."

"Just humor me," she told him. "Being out of the loop has cost me dearly in the past. I don't want that to happen again."

Moments later, Maura Beth found herself waiting for someone to answer in Councilman Sparks's room. "He's definitely there," she told Jeremy with sudden excitement, holding her cell phone to her ear.

Finally, a female voice said, "Hello?"

Maura Beth boldly pressed on. "Yes, this is Maura Beth McShay. I don't want to disturb him, but I just wanted to find out how Councilman Sparks is doing. I was concerned when I saw everyone coming and going at the hospital tonight and just wanted to check in."

There was no response at the other end. A good fifteen seconds passed. It was amazing how long fifteen seconds could be.

"Hello?" Maura Beth repeated. She even wondered if she had lost the connection, but her cell phone told her otherwise.

"Just a minute, please," the female voice said. There was another long pause. Then, "Miz McShay, Durden has asked me to tell you that everything is just fine, and he appreciates you calling about him. Unfortunately, he just had a little food poisoning tonight—but it's nothing serious to worry about now. They're just keeping him overnight for observation."

"Oh, I'm so glad to hear that. This is Evie, right?"

"Yes, it is." But Evie's tone of voice was definitely on the frosty side. "Now, if you'll excuse me, Miz McShay, I'm sure you can appreciate that my husband needs to get his rest, and I'm a little tired myself. Thank you for calling." Then she hung up abruptly.

Maura Beth gave Jeremy the gist of her conversation with Evie, and he said, "Food poisoning, huh? Must've been a helluva case to put him in the hospital. Not to be indelicate, but the few times I've had it over the years, I've just thrown up, and that was the end of it. Nasty business, though."

"I suppose they could be telling the truth," she told him. "My mother got a hold of some bad boiled shrimp once and ended up in the ER down in New Orleans, but I think Evie was lying. I know I surprised her, and something about the time it took her to tell me what was going on just didn't ring true. I can picture the two of them huddling at the last second to get their stories straight. At any rate, something out of the ordinary put him in the hospital."

Jeremy shrugged. "At least we know now that botulism will be the official party line." Then he gave her his most devilish smile and pointed at her. "By the way, nice detective work there. Maybe you should offer your services permanently to Sheriff Dreyfus."

Maura Beth flashed back to the way she had solved the mystery of Emma Frost and the missing tips and couldn't help but be impressed that yet another ploy of hers had worked. "Thanks, I appreciate that. Let me know if you ever need my input for something puzzling out at the high school."

Jeremy looked thoroughly amused, leaning over and gently chucking her on the arm. "Well, I would, but the most mysterious thing that ever happens out there is trying to figure out who eats all the jelly doughnuts in the teachers' lounge every morning. I mean, none of the ladies ever admits to eating even one. So I guess we must have an overweight ghost."

Later, as Maura Beth tried to fall asleep, she couldn't help wondering what had really happened to send Councilman Sparks to the hospital. Her intuition regarding the man had been serving her well as of late, even if it had been hard-won. He was so full of secrets with such a deep, dark side to him, one she had witnessed in their private encounters all too often. Nonetheless, she admitted the distinct possibility that she would never discover the truth in the matter. Some things were best left alone.

22

Enter Waddell Mack

"Don't Sell Me Short When I'm Longin' for You" was not exactly Maura Beth's cup of tea. But she had promised Periwinkle that she would at least give Waddell Mack's music a listen before the big dinner at The Twinkle. So Renette had brought her CD player to the library, and the two of them were holed up in Maura Beth's office listening to his latest hit while Marydell Crumpton worked the checkout counter with her customary efficiency.

"It's definitely twangy," Maura Beth said after they'd listened to it for the second time. "I'm not so sure about catchy, though. It just kind of wears me down emotionally the more I listen. My impression is that country music is all about wearing your emotions on your sleeve."

"I have to admit I don't listen to much of it," Renette added. "But what I have when I'm running up and down the dial on the car radio—well, it all seems to be about busted-up romances, and people who are mostly miserable because of it. I did some Googling the other day on my computer. They call it honky-tonk music sometimes. I think that's some kinda bar, but I've never been in one. I was brought up believing nothing good happens in bars."

"Well, I'm not much on bars, either. But drowning your sorrows by throwing back a couple definitely seems to be the ticket in this kind of music." Then Maura Beth began writing down some of the lyrics on a sheet of paper to amuse herself.

You don't know I'm thinking of you most every day,
But I'm just half-crazy and I guess that's my way,
I wake up each morning with my heart broke in two,
But don't sell me short when I'm longing for you.

"Periwinkle swears by this stuff," Maura Beth said, scanning what she had just written and chuckling in spite of herself. "She says her ex got her into it. I guess it's an acquired taste."

"When is this band supposed to arrive?"

"Around five-ish, I think. They have to get down to Tupelo after they finish eating to check in to their hotel, though."

Renette was staring down at the CD case as if she had just been presented with an engagement ring by some ardent suitor. "The picture of this Waddell Mack fella on the front— well, he is kinda handsome with all that curly hair and those tight jeans and those cowboy boots. You'd think he owned the world the way he's posing. Hey, with the money I bet he's making, he prob'ly does."

Maura Beth leaned across the desk and fanned Renette's face playfully. "Down, girl, down!"

"I can't help it. He looks like he's undressing me with his eyes, not to mention those dark, bushy brows. And then he's scowling just a tad bit, and I betcha he doesn't shave on purpose. I see lotsa men on TV with that scruffy look these days. Don't know if they actually are, but it makes 'em look kinda dangerous. Do you think I'm silly to think like that?"

"Well, no. But I prefer the clean-cut type, myself," Maura

Beth said. "Jeremy pretty much has to shave since he's a schoolteacher and is supposed to set an example for his students, but I've never been big on beards and mustaches, anyway. That—and tattoos. Just call me old-fashioned, I guess."

"Well, check out the titles of some of these other songs," Renette continued, handing over the CD case.

Maura Beth began reading slowly and with a bit more emphasis than was necessary. " 'The Muddy Waters of My Heart' . . . 'Gonna Crash and Burn for You, Baby' . . . 'Just a Hot Rod NASCAR Romance' . . . 'Where'd You Git That Giddyup?' . . . I think that about covers all the bases, wouldn't you say? The thing is, Periwinkle says he's all the rage right now, so who are we to turn up our noses? As a librarian, I've always been a very inclusive person."

"Yeah, I guess I am, too . . ." Renette tailed off, but Maura Beth was reading her mind anyway.

"You had a little something else to add, right?"

"Umm, well, Miz Maura Beth, I was wondering if maybe . . . I mean, I hope it's not too pushy of me, but . . ."

"You were wondering if I could sneak you into The Twinkle tonight? You're easy to read after all this time, you know."

Renette blushed and briefly averted her eyes, but she found the words anyway. "Could you? I mean, I wouldn't eat anything, if that's an issue. I wouldn't have much of an appetite anyway—I mean, with him in the room and all. It's just that this . . . thing has come over me."

Maura Beth was both amused and touched. She wasn't all that far removed from those teen years full of fleeting crushes herself. But, oh, how much better to be finally settled in life and looking forward to the future with that special someone! "Oh, I'm sure I can get Periwinkle to rustle you up a plate, young lady."

"Then I can come?"

"Absolutely. Jeremy and I will pick you up, and I'm sure we'll all have a wonderful time."

"Oh, Miz McShay, you're the best boss ever!"

Maura Beth winked smartly. "I try."

Waddell Mack was lounging on his red leather sofa with both legs sticking out in the carpeted aisle of his star bus, practically daring anyone to trip over the expensive snakeskin cowboy boots he was wearing. There was no mistaking which band was traveling through the back roads of Middle Tennessee on the way to the extreme northeast corner of Mississippi: along either side of the Prevost sleeper was his name in bright red cursive script. For many miles now, he had been daydreaming about the visit to Cherico and The Twinkle. Being the small-town boy that he was, real home cooking on the road was a rare treat, as well as a welcome respite from the franchised fare or worse that was usually available to him and his band with their hectic schedule. Indigestion seemed to come with the territory.

"You've just gotta stop by this little place called The Twinkle when you're anywhere near," his sister-in-law, the pageant-haired Bettye—who considered herself Dolly Parton's #1 fan—had told him a year or so ago after a vacation she'd taken. "It's not all that much to look at, except I thought the stars danglin' from the ceiling were kinda cute. But the food—it's pretty tasty. Oh, and if you get down to Natchez, try Fat Mama's and get you some of the tamales and wash 'em down with a Knock-You-Naked Margarita. I know you and the boys'll toss back a few. Oh, and they got the cutest old bathtub out in the side yard with lotsa flowers growin' out of it. The whole place is just a hoot'n a half!"

Waddell knew Bettye Mack was a genuine foodie. She and his brother, Milton, almost never ate at home up in Nashville. Eating out was their thing. So if they recommended a restaurant or a particular dish or drink, he knew it had to be the real thing. If he accomplished nothing else on this tour—in addition to the fact that it was a sellout—it would be to chow down in style and comfort at The Twinkle in Cherico and Fat Mama's in Natchez.

"I'm gettin' kinda hungry," Lonnie "Fingers" Gholson said as he sidled up and plopped down next to Waddell. The leather cushions made a soft, squishy sound as Lonnie shifted his weight to get more comfortable. "Hey, how much longer we gotta go, dude?"

It hardly surprised Waddell that Fingers was hungry. A tall beanpole of a man who had one of those efficient metabolisms that allowed him to eat whatever and as much as he wanted, Fingers played rhythm guitar for the band. He was also one of those prodigies who had never had a music lesson in his life. Couldn't read a note. "God give me what I got," he was always telling everyone. "And I just run with it."

Waddell checked his watch, and said, "Hold your horses. About a half hour more and we'll be there."

"I been lookin' over the menu you went online and printed out for us," Fingers continued. "Makes my stomach growl. Same for Davis, Torrey, and Lightman. We've been huddlin' in the back."

The "back," as they all called it, consisted of another bright red leather sofa strategically placed in front of a fifty-five-inch HDTV where everyone could view music videos, movies, and TV episodes as the miles rolled by. "Everyone" consisted of Johnny Davis, the bass player, Sam Torrey, the attention deficit drummer, and Trent Lightman, the fiddle player with the customary chaw in his mouth. Not to mention the quartet of twenty-something male roadies who helped with the equipment; and finally, Rankin Lowe, the band's officious manager, who had been with Waddell since the early days when the struggling singer couldn't buy a cup of coffee making the rounds on Music Row. All things considered, it was quite an entourage—one that was getting hungrier and hungrier by the minute.

"I don't wanna sound like I'm one a' those brats in the backseat on vacation, but are we there yet?" Johnny Davis said, approaching the sofa with some urgency. Unlike Fingers, Johnny was a big-boned specimen who always ate much more than was good for him—and the proof was concentrated in his overhanging belly; thus the sometimes nickname "Hulk."

"I just finished telling Fingers, we're under a half hour!" Waddell said, almost barking at him. "What are you guys watching back there? Never heard so much carrying-on in my life."

"Oh, just an oldie-but-goodie that Rankin stuck in the slot," Johnny answered. "*It's a Mad, Mad, Mad, Mad World.* They've had a few beers back there, too."

"Pure slapstick, Hulk," Waddell continued, cocking his head while remembering several typical scenes. "Banana peels, car chases, buried loot, and all that Keystone Kops stuff as I recall. But it dudd'n seem like Rankin's style."

Johnny shrugged, screwing up his mouth. "We told him we weren't in the mood for one a' those talky documentaries he likes about the history of country music, okay? So that's what he came up with instead. By the way, these folks in Cherico don't expect us to perform while we're there, do they?"

Waddell looked annoyed. "No way. They just expect us to eat plenty—and maybe autograph a picture or two for their wall. Just small-town, par-for-the-course stuff, that's all. We've been there and done that, and I wouldn't want to disappoint this nice lady—Periwinkle, she calls herself."

Johnny looked down and snorted. "Periwhat?"

"Winkle!"

"You serious?" He patted his protruding stomach. "Never mind. I'm ready to let 'er rip!"

"You referrin' to the buttons on your shirt?" Waddell said with a wicked little smirk while Johnny rolled his eyes. "I just hope this Twinkle place is ready for an all-you-can-eat outing from you guys."

Councilman Sparks was about to lose his temper with his Evie, and he had practically never done that during the course of their long marriage. But she'd been at him for the past fifteen minutes and just wouldn't let up. It was very uncharacteristic of her to nag or challenge him in any way, of course. Like Bonjour Cheri, she had always known her place. Until now.

"So the bottom line is you're not going to move a muscle all day?" Evie repeated as they eyed each other skeptically across the kitchen table. She had been trying to get him to eat something—a small bowl of cereal with sliced bananas for starters—but to no avail. Coffee was all she'd been able to manage so far—and even that he'd let cool off to lukewarm after taking a tentative sip. "You're just going to stay here in the house and feel sorry for yourself? You're not acting very much like the Master of Cherico. I never thought you'd throw that away."

Finally, he broke his silence, narrowing his eyes further. "I'm entitled to at least one day off after having my stomach pumped, okay?"

"I understand that part, but I thought you said this invitation to The Twinkle was extremely important tonight."

He dismissed her words with an abrupt, throat-slashing gesture that was startling, to say the least. "It's all pretty pointless now. Periwinkle killed my buzz permanently when she said I couldn't take the film crew into The Twinkle, so all this scrambling around at the last minute to put together a video for Spurs 'R' Us just seems like a big waste of time. And you'll have to forgive me if I don't have much of an appetite today, all things considered."

But Evie remained tenacious. For once she knew she had the upper hand. "You could at least put in an appearance and welcome this band to Cherico. Didn't you promise them the key to the city or something like that? You can do that sort of thing in your sleep. You could use last night's lie as your excuse for not staying and eating anything. I'm sure everyone will understand."

"The key to Cherico doesn't mean much anymore," he told her with a sigh of resignation. "A long time ago I promised my father and Layton Duddney that I'd look after this town, but it's dying on the vine under my watch. No way do I feel good about that."

Evie drew back and thought for a while. When she finally spoke, she did not sound happy. "You know, we've never had a talk about what that Cudd'n M'Dear person intimated at Maura Beth's wedding. That you might be having an affair. Are you having one . . . or did you?"

Councilman Sparks leaned back in his chair, allowing himself the barest hint of a smirk. His near-death experience was squeezing the truth out of him, and he was helpless to resist. "Well, I thought about it. Okay? I admit it. But I got nowhere with Maura Beth. You have the right to know that. I struck out with a woman for the first time in my life."

"I sensed something was going on with you about Maura Beth. Did that have anything at all to do with your lame suicide attempt? Was this really about your ego and not Cherico?"

All he could do was shrug. "Maybe. But who can explain such a drastic decision rationally?"

She leaned in with a deadpan expression. There was absolutely no way he was going to wiggle out of this. "You left yourself room to be saved in time, you know. You knew Bonjour Cheri and I were coming back from our walk. You could've downed a coupla more shots and a few more pills so that no amount of stomach-pumping would've saved you. I love you, Durden, but that was a half-assed suicide attempt if I ever saw one. And, by the way, I trust you'll never pull a stupid stunt like that again."

"I'm not sure you would ever understand."

Evie straightened up and set her jaw. "Maybe not. But I insist you go to The Twinkle tonight. It's exactly what you need to boost your spirits. Sitting around here and moping won't cut it. That's not the man I married." She paused to point down to Bonjour Cheri, nestled at his feet. "It's the least you can do since the two of us went to all the trouble of saving your life. Isn't that right, girl?"

Bonjour Cheri—lying as still as a fluffy white throw rug after her frenetic activity of the evening before—reacted as if she had understood every single word, making a sweet, whimpering noise.

"You two are quite an act," Councilman Sparks said, trying very hard to remain in a cantankerous mood but completely unable to do so. It was difficult to be ungrateful for being pulled back from the edge.

"Then you'll show up?"

He didn't answer right away, shifting his eyes from side to side and screwing up his mouth. "On one condition," he told her finally.

"And what's that?"

"That you come with me. You can welcome them as the First Lady of Cherico right alongside me."

"So you really need me, do you? Every wife likes to know she's appreciated now and then."

He reached across the table and grasped her hand. "Maybe

I haven't said it enough, Evie. But I guess I've always needed you. I didn't realize how much until I woke up to your pretty face in the hospital. And I was hell-bent on never waking up at all, you know."

"Well, I'm certainly glad you didn't get your way for once," she said, her face a study in relief. "Maybe something good will come of this after all." Then her features quickly hardened. "You scared the living daylights out of us. Don't you ever do anything like that again. I'll kill you if you even try!"

He managed a wry smile, reaching down to pet Bonjour Cheri's artfully clipped head. "You know, I even thought of just plain ole resigning instead of trying to off myself. I have to plead temporary insanity to that, I guess."

"You sure do. I can just picture Chunky and Gopher Joe—either one—trying to run this town without you. It'd be a farce from day one. You've done nothing but enable those two to be clueless all these years." She paused and wagged a finger vigorously. "Listen, you find a way to turn this town around instead of running away from everything—and that includes me and Bonjour Cheri. Honestly, what on earth has gotten into you?"

"That's the thing, Evie. I'm fresh outta ideas. I never thought I'd just run dry like this."

There was exasperation in her tone, but she managed a wifely smile. "The important thing is not to give up. You're always talking about your legacy. Now's the time to make sure you leave one behind."

Maura Beth was totally unprepared for Waddell Mack's relaxed charm. Her preconceived notions about what a famous country singer would be like were so far off base as to be profoundly head shaking with maybe a facepalm thrown in for good measure. Of course, Periwinkle had set the perfect mood with the singer's latest CD playing quietly in the background. Seated to his right at their table at The Twinkle—and with an obviously doting Renette to his left—Maura Beth found herself speechless as he rattled off one amusing anecdote after another. She'd never encountered such seamless banter, flavored with just the right amount of boyish Southern twang.

"Truth is, I live and breathe small towns like this. Cherico reminds me of my little hometown, at least what I could see of it as we rode in on the bus," he said between sips of his second beer. Then he drew himself up, took an exaggerated, deep breath, and exhaled against his tight pale blue shirt with the mother-of-pearl buttons. "It's what country music is all about, really. We just speak for the everyday folk the way they try to do for themselves in the shower, except we're not off-key." He loudly rapped his knuckles three times on the table, looking smug. "At least most a' the time we're not."

Renette giggled, daring to pursue his train of thought. "Now, how in the world did you know that?"

Waddell leaned over and caught her gaze playfully. No matter the size of the audience, he knew how to handle the situation, finding just the right thing to say. "What? That you sing in the shower?"

She went all crimson and quickly hung her head. "It's true. And I can't even carry a tune, no matter what. I tried out for chorus my junior year in high school, and they turned me down. I mean, I was downright awful."

"Nah, you prob'ly weren't as bad as you think. But the singin' in the shower thing—it's not hard to figure out. Here's my theory: it's the shampooing that brings it out in all of us," he continued. "We sorta get into a rhythm, if you think about it. You know, the lather, rinse, and repeat thing. They make you do it twice. Which is why I first thought I wanted to be a drummer in this crazy, mixed-up business that's as competitive as all git-out. But then my first git-tar came callin' on me as a Christmas present from my parents, and we've been uh old married couple ever since. Yep, my git-tar is my one and only old lady. I call her Miss Chordette, and I just love to tickle her."

Maura Beth couldn't help herself. The image of Waddell Mack's long fingers manipulating those strings sent a spurt of adrenaline through her veins. But she wisely refrained from commenting and hoped the excitement she was feeling wasn't showing up on her face. After all, she was a respectable, married woman.

Across the table, husband Jeremy was finishing up his last piece of cornmeal-battered catfish as everyone laughed at Waddell's musical revelations. "Glad you ordered this up, Waddell," he said. "I never much cared for catfish before, but this totally changes my mind. I'm not sure how much I've eaten already."

"Tell Miz Periwinkle down there at the other end of the table," he said, pointing in her general direction with a wink.

Periwinkle perked up as she heard her name mentioned. "Anyone need anything down there? We got plenty in the kitchen. Just say the word, and it'll appear as if by magic."

"Can't think of a thing," Waddell called out. Then he quickly surveyed the long table that had been pieced together from smaller ones by the staff of The Twinkle. "How about the rest a' you guys?"

Some of the band members and the roadies happily offered up phrases like, "No complaints!" and "We're fine!" and "Full as a tick!"

But Fingers stopped chewing long enough to raise his hand. "I'm on my second helping, Waddell. We'll see if I have room for a third." Then he turned toward the head of the table. "Guess you won't tell us what's in your batter that makes it taste so darn good, huh, Miz Periwinkle? Are you the type a' chef who gives out her recipes? If ya do, maybe I could take one home to the wife."

"Oh, I don't mind tellin' you at all," she said without a moment's hesitation. "It's no big secret. I put a little cayenne pepper and a few red pepper flakes in the batter to give it just that little kick. That's what you're tastin'. But save a little space for one of my pastry chef's sinful desserts."

She gestured toward Mr. Place a few chairs away as he smiled, nodded his head, and said, "Believe me, you'll be in Sweet Tooth Heaven."

Periwinkle quickly glanced at her watch. "And it shouldn't be long before our Councilman Sparks arrives to welcome you officially to our little town. He promised to stop by for dessert and give you the key to the city. Seems he had a little food poisoning incident last night and is trying to take it easy on himself until his stomach settles down. But no way could he ever resist a bite of one of my Parker's famous confections. You'll see for yourselves pretty soon."

In truth, Maura Beth had wondered why Councilman Sparks hadn't shown up yet, but then again, she had not had a chance to address the subject with Periwinkle, being as busy as she was all evening—the proverbial blur between the kitchen and the dining table. It sounded about right, however—Cherico's head honcho trying to make a lasting impression as Waddell and his band found themselves smack dab in the middle of a sugar high. How could they not find whatever he had to say fascinating with that kind of buzz circulating throughout their veins?

"Haul out the sweet stuff, then!" Waddell exclaimed, right on cue. "Been a long time since I've had a meal this good. Maybe I'll even be inspired to write a song about it on my next CD."

For an instant, Periwinkle looked as if she might just fall

out of her chair. "Oh, would you? That'd be too much to ask!"

Caught off-guard, Waddell resorted briefly to a frown but quickly recovered. "Maybe I just will, Miz Periwinkle. I could call it something like—oh, I don't know—'Down at Periwinkle's.' "

"Or 'Down at The Twinkle,' " Fingers put in. "I can see it movin' up the charts right now in my mind's eye." He paused dramatically and pointed to one of the mobiles dangling from the ceiling. "Wait—there it goes—straight to the top. Number one with a bullet!"

Waddell started improvising music and lyrics spontaneously, but it all sounded like he had been working on it for weeks to include in his repertoire:

Oh, down at The Twinkle,
People come tuh eat . . .
Down at The Twinkle,
The food can't be beat . . .
You can find your friends there,
Every single one . . .
Oh, go to The Twinkle when the day is done. . . .

"How do you do that?!" Periwinkle exclaimed, clasping her hands together. "Do all your songs come out of you so easy? It must be wonderful to have the sorta talent you have!"

"Oh, shucks, it ain't nothin', ma'am. I was just playin' around is all," Waddell told her while waving her off at the same time. "There's lots more to it than that, believe me."

"You bet there is," Fingers added after finishing up his coleslaw. "That sounded like a commercial. A right good one, mind you, but still a commercial that drives you crazy on TV."

Waddell pretended to be mad with a playful scowl. The two of them were good at this kind of give-and-take and enjoyed the one-upmanship. "Ah, why don't you shuddup and have some more catfish!"

"Works for me."

"Well, I'd settle for a few autographed pictures of y'all to hang on the walls," Periwinkle added.

Waddell emphatically pointed his index finger in her direction. "Now, you know good and well that's a done deal, Miz Periwinkle. And I'm gonna send a few tweets out about this place to boot. You can count on it. I hope a lot more people come here and eat under your danglin' stars!"

"Move just a little more to your right," Periwinkle told the roadies, gesturing to them while holding her smartphone in her hand. "You fellas have gotta bunch up a bit more to get in the picture." She paused briefly to frame the shot but came away shaking her head once again. "No, I still can't get you all in. There are just too many of you even for a wide shot. I can't back up far enough."

Councilman Sparks spoke up, annoyed by Periwinkle's ineffective directions. "Look, I have an idea here. Why don't you do a shot with me presenting the key to the city to Waddell first? Then Waddell and the band. Then Waddell and the roadies. That way everybody gets in at least one shot, and we finally get this thing done before midnight." The impatience in the councilman's voice was very evident, causing Evie to chastise him ever so subtly with a nudge of her elbow.

Watching from her seat at the table, Maura Beth continued to speculate on Councilman Sparks's irascible mood. He had made his entrance a few minutes earlier with Evie on his arm, looking the part well enough at that point. But his trademark reelection smile was patently missing, and when he introduced himself to Waddell and the rest of his band, he had projected an air of merely going through the motions as they all jumped up out of their seats to greet him. Perhaps, Maura

Beth reasoned, it was just a hangover from his hospital emergency of the evening before, whatever that had actually involved.

"He clearly doesn't want to be here. I know him like the back of my hand," Maura Beth had leaned across and whispered to Jeremy while all the handshaking was going on nearby but out of earshot.

When Periwinkle began to follow through with the snapshot suggestions, however, there was a slight improvement in the councilman's tone. "Waddell," he said, "I hope you'll take advantage of this key to our city anytime you're in this neck of the woods, and be sure and let us know you're coming so we can plan ahead. Lord knows, we could use some excitement in our little town."

Waddell brandished the big, plastic gold key and smiled big. "We sure will keep in touch, Councilman Sparks. I do b'lieve we can find us a way to route ourselves through Cherico on all our Deep South tours if we possibly can."

"We'll look forward to that."

"I gotta tell ya, this little restaurant here is as good as advertised. No two ways about it!"

Then Councilman Sparks nodded toward Periwinkle. "You got all the shots you need now? Seems to me like you've got plenty for your wall."

Periwinkle was beaming, holding her phone above her head like a sports trophy. "If they all turn out, I do. But even if they don't, Waddell has already signed six glossies for me."

"My tried and true head shots," Waddell added, pushing out his chest. Then he suddenly lowered his voice and cocked his head. "Except I really should update 'em, ya know. I've been sendin' these out since I was twenty-two. In case you were wonderin', I'm pushin' thirty now."

"In my opinion, you haven't changed a bit," Periwinkle told him, unable to resist the opportunity to flirt. Then she snapped her fingers, remembering her hostess duties. "Well, now that that's outta the way, are we all ready for some dessert? Our Mr. Place here has some wonderful choices for you. We have his famous crème de menthe cake, chocolate-chip crème brûlée, and chocolate éclairs with amaretto filling. Who's interested?"

When a forest of hands went up, everyone moved back to their places at the long table, and Lalie Bevins, her son, Barry, and the rest of the restaurant staff shifted into high gear taking orders.

23

Crème Brûlée Saves the Day

Councilman Sparks and his Evie had pulled up a couple of extra chairs on either side of Waddell Mack to continue their conversation with him while the dessert course was being served. Periwinkle had particularly recommended Mr. Place's chocolate-chip crème brûlée when she had been pressed further.

"Which dessert do you like best?" Fingers had asked her. "Come on, now. Cross your heart and hope to die."

And Periwinkle's answer had resulted in a flurry of crème brûlée orders, with Councilman Sparks and Evie in that number. Now, everyone had started to dig in, and the compliments were flying across the table.

"You sure didn't lie, Miz Periwinkle!" Fingers exclaimed. Then he turned in Mr. Place's direction and nodded. "My compliments to the chef!"

"I thank you," Mr. Place said. "It's fast becoming our best-selling dessert here at The Twinkle."

Meanwhile, Waddell had pulled his chair back from the table just enough so that he was face-to-face with Councilman Sparks while the two of them continued to hit it off. "My uncle, Billy Monroe Mack, was in local politics over in East Tennessee," Waddell said, carefully balancing his crème brûlée dish on his knees. "He didn't run his hometown the way you do, but he always had a vote in whatever was goin' on. I think the two a' you would've gotten along famously."

"Well, the Sparks family has been running Cherico for over seventy-five years now," Councilman Sparks continued. "I take it all very seriously. I only want what's best for our little town."

Across the table, Maura Beth exchanged furtive glances with Jeremy but said nothing. At least Councilman Sparks seemed to be rounding somewhat into form. His energy level had picked up, and there were even hints of his reelection smile now and then. She couldn't help but think—with no little amusement—that perhaps it was in his genes, and there was nothing he could do about it.

"What's the population of Cherico?" Waddell wanted to know in between bites of his dessert.

Councilman Sparks put down his spoon and shook his head. "I wish I could say five thousand and counting, but I'm afraid it's going the other way these days. We're not exactly setting the woods on fire. Unfortunately, some downtown bid'nesses are leaving and their owners are going with 'em. We're in a kinda slump, I'm afraid."

"Aw, I'm just as sorry as I can be to hear that. Seems like a real nice place to live to me."

Maura Beth could not resist speaking up. "Oh, it is, I can assure you. And things aren't completely gloomy. We've got a brand-new library going up on the shores of Lake Cherico. We're all right proud of that."

"That's just great," Waddell said just as he lifted his spoon to his lips for another mouthful of crème brûlée. "I always did like goin' to the library during the summer when I was growin' up."

And that was when it happened.

Somehow, a generous blob of Mr. Place's sensational chocolate-chip crème brûlée fell off Waddell's spoon and landed smack dab on the very respectable toe of his left cowboy boot.

"Oops!" Waddell cried out. "Looks like I made a mess. You can't take me anywhere these days!"

"And on your beautiful cowboy boot, too," Evie added, sounding as solicitous as possible as she craned her neck.

Waddell picked up his napkin and leaned down, carefully enveloping the custardy mass and tossing the wadded cloth on the table. "Oh, no harm done," he said. "It's not like it was blood or red wine or somethin' even worse. Snakeskin don't take too kindly to nasty spills like that, ya know."

"Cowboy boots are big business these days," Councilman Sparks remarked. Then without even thinking twice, he decided to elaborate. "We almost had one of the big names locate here in Cherico—Spurs 'R' Us. I thought we had it in the bag, but the CEO backed out at the last minute. We were all set for a new plant with hundreds of new jobs and a real Christmas high this year. It really would've pulled us out of the doldrums."

Waddell put his unfinished dish of crème brûlée on the table with a look of astonishment. "You're kiddin' me?"

"What? About Spurs 'R' Us? I wish I were."

Now Waddell was looking up at one of Periwinkle's mobiles, shaking his head. "When did this happen?"

"A month or so ago." But there was genuine puzzlement on Councilman Sparks's face.

"I can't believe it. Dillard did somethin' like that?!"

Councilman Sparks drew back dramatically, almost as if Waddell had sneezed on him. "You know Dillard Mills?"

"Know him? Heck, I'm one of his major investors. When I was lookin' for a smart place to put some a' my money a while back, I put a huge chunk of it in Spurs 'R' Us. Hey, I own near 'bout forty percent of the whole company, and I never leave the house without Spurs 'R' Us boots on my feet. Got a pair on right now, crème brûlée traces and all!" He pointed to the floor and then narrowed his eyes. "You mean Dillard snatched that new plant away from you folks down here and didn't tell me about it? Did you know about this, Rankin?"

At the other end of the table, Waddell's manager had a defensive look on his face. "I never have any contact with him at all, Waddell. I just concentrate on your bookings—you know that."

Waddell's easygoing charm dried up instantly as the anger continued to rise in his voice. "Maybe this is all my fault. I haven't checked in with Dillard in well over a year. I mean, the company's doin' real well—I've gotten a great return on my investment so far—so I haven't been keepin' up with it. I even missed the last stockholders' meeting. Guess it's time for me to put my hand back in."

Councilman Sparks was tentative but hopeful as he spoke up. "Does . . . could this possibly mean . . . Cherico has a chance of getting that plant to locate here after all, Waddell?"

"If I have anything to do with it, yes. I'm gonna get on this right after we wind up the tour in Tupelo and Natchez, I promise you that. Rankin, you be sure and make a note of it and remind me."

"Will do."

Councilman Sparks looked and sounded like a man reborn, finally returning to fighting form. "That'd be terrific, Waddell. I mean, if you could actually pull that off for us!"

Waddell leaned over and stuck out his hand, and the two men shook on it firmly. "Hey, if you folks down here need a big economic boost like that, I'll see to it that you get it. You can bank on it. Dillard wouldn't dare go against my wishes. No way, no how."

The excitement that quickly spread throughout the room was palpable, and Maura Beth was the first to express what everyone was thinking. "That would be some Christmas present for Cherico, Waddell. What a wonderful and generous gesture on your part."

"It's more than a gesture," he continued. "It'll be good for business, having you folks behind the plant the way you are. Spurs 'R' Us sells to the small-town guy or gal who wants that country and western, cowboy look. I can see myself doin' a print ad or two down here, too. I'll do what I can to put Cherico on the map."

"Strange the way things work out, idd'n it?" Periwinkle said. "And I'm proud The Twinkle could be a part of all this." Then she quickly surveyed the table. "Do I have any seconds on the crème brûlée, by the way? One for the road or for those sweet dreams tonight, maybe?"

Waddell laughed and hoisted his dish. "I'll take you up on that, Miz Periwinkle. Especially since I got a little sloppy with that first helping."

24

A Cherry Cola Christmas

The last thing Maura Beth had expected from Councilman Sparks was an invitation to his "Inaugural Cherico City Hall Christmas Eve Celebration." Boy, was that a mouthful! But that was precisely what had arrived in the mail addressed to Mr. and Mrs. Jeremy McShay at their little cottage on Painter Street. Now, she and Jeremy were less than an hour away from the big event and were putting the finishing touches on their Christmas outfits of choice. The PS on the invitation had read: **FUN CHRISTMAS COSTUMES OPTIONAL BUT SUGGESTED!** Was this a new and different Councilman Sparks or what?

So in that spirit, Maura Beth had decided to wear the absolutely awful green and red large, checkerboard pattern sweater Cudd'n M'Dear had sent along from New Orleans as a present.

"It's . . . well, it's just plain ole loud, and I'll bet she painstakingly knitted it herself," Maura Beth had told Jeremy the moment after it had been unwrapped and the light of day had revealed the scope of its lack of style. In addition, Cudd'n M'Dear had made sure that her idea of Christmas fashion would not be postponed until Christmas morning. *Open well before the 25th, dear Maura Beth,* the card Scotch-taped to the wrapping had read. "But since I'm not exactly sure what Councilman Sparks is up to with this first-ever holiday bash of his," Maura Beth had continued at the unveiling, "I'll happily wear it and pretend it's the most glorious garment I've ever lifted over my red head. I mean, what do I have to lose? If the party turns out to be lousy, I'll be dressed for the occasion."

For his part, Jeremy had gone more conventional—even a bit on the corny side—opting for a clip-on Santa beard and pointy green elf's cap that tilted ever so slightly to the left.

"You're a mixed metaphor if there ever was one," Maura Beth said while he was checking himself out in their full-length bedroom mirror, obviously unable to find an angle that suited him.

But he had a snappy retort at the ready. "And you are the Queen of Ugly Christmas Sweaterdom!"

"Touché!" Maura Beth chuckled and then glanced at the clock on the nightstand. "We'd better get a move on, though, if we don't want to be late."

"What's your hurry, Maurie? As you said, who knows what Councilman Sparks is up to with this party?"

To be sure, all sorts of thoughts were swirling through Maura Beth's head as she sat down to apply the finishing touches to her makeup. For the first time ever, she was considering the possibility that Councilman Sparks was actually doing something nice for everyone without expecting anything in return. Wouldn't that be a kick in the head? After all, he and the entire town of Cherico had been euphoric for a week now over the decision that Dillard Mills had made to locate the new Spurs 'R' Us plant in their little community after all—thanks to the decisive and timely intervention of Waddell Mack. The economic ripple effect had been almost immediate, causing Audra Neely to reverse her decision to close down her antique boutique and tough it out a little longer with the promise of new jobs and new citizens arriving as her incentive; Justin Brachle had further reported that Spurs 'R' Us was interested in acquiring property out at the lake to build a new apartment complex in order to provide affordable housing for prospective employees. That, in turn, would benefit the local construction industry, and things would trickle on down from there.

"Well, you have to admit that fortunes have changed for the better here in Cherico, Jeremy," Maura Beth replied. "And I have this gut feeling that our Councilman Sparks isn't conducting business as usual these days. I guess we'll never really know what went on at the hospital that night, but if he's learned a little humility as well as what true cooperation is all about as a result, then I'll go to his party, kick up my heels, and drink a toast to the future."

Jeremy's expression remained on the skeptical side, but he clearly wasn't in the mood for an argument with his wife. "I'd have to agree it would be a trip if you and Councilman Sparks were able to declare a truce once and for all. There's been way too much energy spent on unnecessary scheming—on his part, of course. You've just tried to parry the blows."

"Yep, you're absolutely right," she told him while standing up and lightly spritzing her neck with perfume. "It would definitely be a wonderful present to find under the tree." Then she gave a little gasp. "Oh, and don't forgot to act surprised when Periwinkle and Mr. Place announce their engagement tonight. She phoned me this afternoon and said this was going to be their time to finally go public with everything. It'll certainly be a relief to have it out in the open at last and not have to keep it a secret anymore."

He nodded and quickly crossed his heart. "I promise. And I certainly hope everyone is gracious to them when they get the news."

"Don't be silly. This is the twenty-first century. Periwinkle and Mr. Place are the best of Cherico."

His tone was hopeful. "And Christmas is always the perfect time for people to act on their better nature."

Maura Beth had never seen City Hall's Multi-Purpose
Event Room this spruced up before. Full of drab, faux-wood
paneling and ordinarily reserved for "rubber chicken" awards
dinners of a civic nature, it was now in full Christmas drag;
there were great holly wreaths at the windows, white votive
candles on all the tables, an enormous, fully decorated tree
with blinking white lights in one corner of the room, and the
scent of pine in the air for that essential holiday touch. Not to
mention an instrumental version of "Sleigh Ride" playing in
the background as Mr. and Mrs. Jeremy McShay presented
their invitation at the door to Councilman Sparks's secretary,
Mrs. Lottie Howard—wearing bifocals, a white wig, and a red
and white dress with *Mrs. Santa* embroidered across her am-
ple chest.

"Ho, ho, ho, and Merry Christmas. So glad you two could
make it," Lottie told them with an easy smile. "Come right on
in . . . have some eggnog or fruitcake or sugar cookies . . . or
maybe some bourbon balls and mingle to the jingle." Obviously taken with her rhyming prose, Lottie burst into giggles
like a schoolgirl. "Couldn't help myself. I've already had a little eggnog, you know . . . well, more than a little, if you
wanna know the truth. And, yes . . . I can definitely vouch for
the fact . . . it's spiked. Oh, and the bourbon balls . . . well,
they've got a kick, too."

Maura Beth returned the smile but backed up a bit as the
whiskey on Lottie's breath hit her nostrils. "I never would
have guessed."

Then Lottie cleared her throat and assumed a more serious demeanor, even though she was obviously still under the

influence. "Councilman Sparks . . . asked me to tell you to be sure and track him down when you got here. He . . . uh . . . especially wanted to speak to you tonight. Of course, I have no idea what it's about. Not even a little bit. Because . . . he's been acting so peculiar lately . . . and by that I mean he's been downright pleasant to be around at the office. Yes . . . it's true. It's been quite a while since he's barked at me about anything the way he usually does. Why, it's almost seemed like a Christmas present to me . . . from him, of course." She suppressed a small belch. "Do you . . . think maybe I should write him a little thank-you note?" She giggled again and wagged her brows in exaggerated fashion.

"Well, that's up to you, Lottie. But I wouldn't even think of missing the opportunity to find out what's on the good councilman's mind," Maura Beth answered. "This whole thing tonight—this party—it's most unexpected."

Lottie looked around briefly, then leaned in and lowered her voice just above a whisper. "Isn't it, though? Why . . . I nearly fell out of my chair when he gave me a list of things to go out and buy for . . . umm . . . the decorations. You know . . . I even asked him why he was doing this, since it's never happened before. It really hasn't. And . . . guess what? He wouldn't tell me a thing. Uh . . . nothing. But . . . I think he's gonna make some kinda speech tonight."

"No doubt. I can't remember a time when he hasn't on these auspicious public occasions." Then Maura Beth caught sight of Justin and Becca Brachle over by the eggnog table and waved at them, giving her the excuse to escape Lottie's incessant meanderings. "Well, I do believe it's high time for us to go and do a little of that mingling you mentioned, Lottie." And then she and Jeremy headed over to greet the Brachles.

"Merry Christmas, you two. And I like those antlers on your heads, Becca," Maura Beth said as they reached the table.

Becca smirked and pointed to her husband, who was taking a generous swig of his eggnog. "Merry Christmas right back to you. And, by the way, this was my Stout Fella's idea of a costume. I went along with it because I really couldn't find anything that looked halfway Christmas-y in maternity clothes. Everything I tried on made me look like a gigantic maraschino cherry."

Everyone laughed as the two men shook hands; then Jeremy ladled two cups of eggnog, handing Maura Beth hers. "Well, what's the latest on your blessed event, my real-estate friend?" Jeremy wanted to know. "You two still on schedule for mid-January?"

Justin shrugged. "It might be before then, though, the doctor says. Because of that false alarm and Becca's bladder infection, he says he won't rule out the possibility of doing a C-section to make sure nothing happens. Not that he thinks anything will. It's just that we all want him to get here safely, you know."

Jeremy exchanged glances with Maura Beth. "Him?"

Becca spoke up quickly. "Well, we both finally broke down and went for it. We told the doctor we just couldn't stand not knowing any longer. So, yes, we're having a little boy—Mark Grantham Brachle."

"If he weighs as much as I did when I arrived in my birthday suit, he'll be one *big* boy," Justin proclaimed, standing tall and looking every inch the proud father. "Hey, my Becca dudd'n call me Stout Fella for nothin', you know!"

Congratulations, hugs, and handshakes quickly followed between the two couples, and Maura Beth said, "You should have included such exciting news in your Christmas cards, especially to his godmother."

"Oh, I would have, but I'd already mailed them before we found out, sweetie," Becca explained, keeping the smile in her voice. "But we're going to spread the news right here at this party, and you're practically the first to know. We're so excited to have you as Mark's godmother, of course. We couldn't possibly have picked anyone better for the job."

Maura Beth winked. "You might as well know that I'm absolutely going to spoil him. Plus, I promise to attend every school play and athletic event he's in."

"Why do you think Justin and I chose you?"

"Fair enough."

Just then, Miss Voncille and Locke Linwood walked up, formally dressed but without a hint of a Christmas theme to their apparel.

"What, no costumes tonight?" Maura Beth asked, after everyone had exchanged greetings.

Miss Voncille managed an impish grin. "We opted for the optional option on the invitation. I'm afraid we're just not the type of couple that goes in for cutesy, right, Locke?"

"My beautiful and sensible wife speaks the truth. When you come right down to it, we're just two old fuddy-duddies," he answered, nudging her affectionately. "My tuxedo and her gold cocktail dress will just have to do."

"You most certainly are not fuddy-duddies!" Maura Beth protested. "I think the two of you are an inspiration to those of us who believe in second-chance romance, and I won't hear anything to the contrary."

Then Becca shared her news about the baby with Locke and Miss Voncille, and there were more congratulations all around. "It certainly seems to be a night for big news," Miss Voncille added when the excitement had died down. "Periwinkle Lattimore and Mr. Place are going around announcing their engagement as we speak. They just told us over there by the Christmas tree. I'm very happy for them. They've made quite a success of The Twinkle together."

As promised, Jeremy sounded surprised and delighted. "Well, that *is* big news. I think we've all hoped they would finally make it official, and now they have. Good for them!"

Maura Beth quickly backed him up. "I'm such a sucker for a good, old-fashioned romance. Of course, they've both been through so much lately. It'll be nice to see them settled and helping each other out even more."

Then Maura Beth and Jeremy continued to make the rounds, encountering in order: Renette dressed as one of Santa's diminutive elves; Marydell Crumpton in a long, flowing white gown and insisting she was The Ghost of Christmas Past; Mamie Crumpton, who caused Maura Beth to nearly do a spit take with her eggnog when she obliviously announced, "I'm a large nutcracker!"; Nora Duddney and her beau, Wally Denver, as Salvation Army bell ringers, thankfully with deadened clappers; Chunky Badham and Gopher Joe Martin, daring to describe themselves as two of the Three Wise Men—to Maura Beth's great amusement; and Connie and Douglas Mc-Shay, duplicating the outfits of several others in attendance as Mr. and Mrs. Santa Claus.

It was more than heartwarming to Maura Beth, however, to encounter Emma Frost with her Leonard on her arm—the two of them sporting a pair of red-and-white checkered Christmas sweaters that looked exactly like serviceable table-cloths at an Italian restaurant.

"Oh, my," Maura Beth said, embracing Emma warmly and then leaning in to give Leonard a peck on the cheek. "I didn't think it would be possible for anyone to outdo what I've got on. But I do believe you and Leonard win the Christmas Sweater Contest hands down."

Emma looked around the room, obviously taking Maura Beth's comment seriously. "Did we really win?"

Maura Beth laughed spiritedly. "I was just joking, sweetie. But I think your costumes suit you both perfectly."

"We . . . won somethin'?" Leonard suddenly added, looking hopefully at his wife.

"Not exactly," Emma began. "It was just . . ." Then she

exchanged smirks with Maura Beth. "Yes, Lenny, we did. Maura Beth says we won us the best costume at the party. How 'bout that?"

"Heh. Good for us."

Maura Beth reached across and patted his hand. "Absolutely, Mr. Leonard. Good for you both."

"I'm glad Christmas is almost here," Leonard said with a big smile. "I seem to remember things better this time of year."

All the socializing came to an end, however, when Councilman Sparks stepped up to the microphone with his Evie at his side. Somehow and somewhere, he had managed to find a red tuxedo with a green cummerbund and bow tie for the occasion, and she had matched his seasonal extravagance with a green silk evening gown dotted with bright red poinsettias.

"Ladies and gentlemen," he began, after clearing his throat several times. "If I may have your attention, please." It took a bit longer for the various conversations to die down before Councilman Sparks launched into his prepared speech. "Evie and I are so delighted all of you could be here tonight for what we trust will become an annual event here in Cherico. We trust you will enjoy the food and drink and catch up with each other as the year comes to an end. For 2016 will be a time of great optimism in our little town by the lake. Construction has already begun on our new library out there, which is scheduled to open on the Fourth of July. And then, construction will begin in January on our new Spurs 'R' Us cowboy boot plant, which will give our economy the boost it's needed for a long time now. This time next year, Spurs 'R' Us hopes to be rolling those boots off the assembly line, and that'll give all of us a new lease on life. Greater Cherico will rise like a phoenix!"

He was interrupted by generous applause. "I know, I know. Some of you here tonight could end up working for this great company in various capacities. And along those lines, I want to welcome our surprise special guest for this evening—one of the owners of Spurs 'R' Us and a country music star in his own right." Councilman Sparks raised his voice noticeably as he turned on his heels and gestured dramatically toward a door on the back wall. "Mr. Waddell Mack!"

The country singer emerged on cue but was hardly recognizable. A wave of laughter accompanied the applause as Waddell Mack headed toward the councilman dressed in a slimmed-down Santa Claus outfit with a big red cowboy hat and matching red Spurs 'R' Us cowboy boots. He was also carrying an acoustic guitar but had nixed the great white beard.

"Howdy, folks!" he called out. "Or should I say, 'Howdy Christmas to y'all!'?" He waited for the laughter to subside. "What I thought I'd do tonight is take some Christmas carol requests and then play and sing 'em for you. I know just about every one of 'em, since I've always been someone who loves the Christmas season. So, who wants to make the first request?"

A forest of hands went up. Waddell quickly scanned the room, finally picking Maura Beth's familiar face out of the crowd. Her request was "Away in a Manger."

"That's one of my favorites, too," he announced.

Then the audience grew very quiet as he began strumming and singing. There was a simplicity to his acoustic stylings that evoked an immediate response in Maura Beth, which she whispered to Jeremy standing beside her.

"I can almost smell the hay in the barn. He's singing like he was there witnessing it all."

It was clear that Waddell had the entire room hanging on his every well-crafted, if slightly twangy note, and several requests followed: "Silent Night," "God Rest Ye Merry Gentlemen," and "O Little Town of Bethlehem." Waddell brought them all to life masterfully, rivaling the efforts of any church choir.

Then, to everyone's surprise, Leonard Frost raised his hand and his voice at the same time. "I'd like to hear . . . . 'I'll Be Home for Christmas,' if you don't mind."

"Why, Lenny!" Emma said, leaning in to him with all the affection she could muster. "You remembered it was always our favorite."

He winked at her. "Christmas . . . it makes me remember all the good things. They seem to . . . come back to me for a while."

And then Waddell came through with an interpretation for the ages. His inflections were sunny and welcoming, yet also conveying a depth of emotion. Practically everyone in the room knew about Leonard Frost's Alzheimer's, and smiling through tears became the fashion of the moment. Except for Leonard himself, whose eyes remained dry and sparkling, his chin lifted proudly. Why, he looked like he'd won the lottery as he listened intently!

When the impromptu concert was finally over to the appreciative applause of the gathering, Maura Beth took a deep breath and gently nudged her Jeremy. "Well, that was quite a workout, wasn't it?"

"Check out my tear ducts," he told her, pointing to his face with a generous smile. "That man up there can really sing from the heart."

Councilman Sparks took control of the floor once again, taking a big, gold plastic key out of his pocket and brandishing it high above his head. "And now, will Miz Maura Beth McShay come forward, please?"

Completely taken by surprise, Maura Beth shot Jeremy a puzzled glance but dutifully approached the microphone. "Miz McShay, I'm going to do something tonight that is long overdue. You and I, we haven't always seen eye to eye on library issues these past few years. But I want it known publicly that Councilman Durden Sparks fully appreciates the efforts Maura Beth McShay has made to ensure that Cherico will be offering a first-class, state-of-the-art library to its citizens. For that reason I present to her this evening the key to the city of Cherico. Perhaps some of you will think this is only symbolic. But I want Miz McShay to know that my door will always be open to her and that she can expect the full cooperation of City Hall for the foreseeable future on any project she deems worthy." Then with a little bow, he handed over the key to a blushing, speechless Maura Beth.

It took her a while to compose herself, but she finally came through as she stood behind the mike. "I will try my best not to start off with something trite like, 'I don't know what to say.' "

There was brief, muted laughter and then she continued. "Because I do know what to say. I accept this key in the spirit in which it was given. For a job well done. Since I came to Cherico nearly seven years ago, fresh out of college but without an ounce of real-world experience, it has been my goal to be the most professional librarian I could possibly be. And I do feel I've taken that to another level by working hard to bring a twenty-first-century library to Cherico. Mission accomplished. And I can't wait for all of you here tonight to start using this great new facility next summer when we'll open it with a flourish—fireworks and all." She turned to face Councilman Sparks and nodded graciously. "Thank you for truly being on board with this project and for finally being aboveboard with me, Councilman. You have no idea what it means to me. I truly consider Cherico my home now."

Once again the room exploded with appreciative applause as Maura Beth and Councilman Sparks firmly shook hands and then briefly embraced. It appeared that a new era in Cherico had begun at long last.

Surprisingly, Chunky Badham stepped up to the mike, looking slightly comical in his elaborate Wise Man outfit. There was way too much shiny blue fabric covering him, resembling a floor-length evening gown that had not been fitted properly, and the turban atop his head looked like it might fall off any second. But he quickly got down to business with his comments.

"I just wanted to say," he began, "that Durden Sparks, he's always been my role model for gettin' things done in our little town of Greater Cherico, as we like to call it. I think it's best to know your limitations in life, and I learned early on when I got into politics that I was a follower, not a leader. That's been Durden's gift to me. Delegatin' what he knew I could do best. My wife and kids've had security because a' that, and I just wanted to take this opportunity to thank him publicly for it." Polite applause immediately followed.

Apparently inspired by Chunky's testimonial, Gopher Joe Martin—whose silvery Wise Man costume fit him way too snugly—motioned for the mike next. "As long as we're handin' out kudos here at Christmastime, I wanted to tell all a' y'all about somethin' Durden did for me and my family one time. My wife, Lydia, well, she got real sick a few years back. Woman's troubles that I'm sure I don't have to go into, ya know. Well, I got so in the red with it all that I couldn't even afford the insurance deductibles. But Durden—well, he took care of 'em out of his own pocket. Lydia and I've never forgotten his kindness." He gestured toward his wife out in the audience. "Raise your hand, honey. Let 'em know you're still healthy and happy—and we're solvent because a' Durden. Come on now, don't be shy. We're among good friends here."

Lydia Martin, a plump, middle-aged woman with helmet

hair sprouting reindeer antlers, put her hand up, tentatively at first, but then waved it vigorously to the applause and buzzing of the room.

Councilman Sparks took the mike from Gopher Joe and seemed at a loss for words for what may have been a first during his lengthy political career. "Well . . . umm . . . fellas . . . you really surprised me with all that . . ."

"Don't be embarrassed, Durden!" a voice from the crowd cried out. "I have something I'd like to say myself!"

Mamie Crumpton stepped up in her "large nutcracker" outfit and seized the mike. "The Crumpton family has long been indebted to Charles Durden Sparks. Our families go way back, and our houses are practically next to each other on Perry Street. But that's not the point. There are things that our good councilman has done for Cherico that he never mentions because he just thinks it's part of his job. Taking care of our little town, that is. He's gotten streets and roads paved that were falling apart, he's taken trips at his own expense to visit company CEOs in an effort to get them to move their plants here, and on a personal note . . ."

She paused for an awkward length of time but finally cleared her throat, heaved her chest, and resumed. "Well, the truth is—and my sister, Marydell, doesn't even know about this—I had made some investments with a broker up in Memphis a few years ago who was—well, he was a con artist is what he was—a snake-oil salesman if there ever was one. And he was about to abscond with a huge chunk of the money our parents had left us. When I told Durden about it, he took it upon himself to go up there in person and put the fear of God in this man. To make a long story short, we got our money back. So what I'm trying to say is that come hell or high water, Durden Sparks does care about Cherico, whether they have a little money or lots of money. He's told me more than once that he only wants to be a good steward for us, and I be-

lieve that's what he's tried to be to the best of his ability."
Mamie quickly handed over the mike. "And that's all I wanted
to say."

Councilman Sparks momentarily looked stumped, managing a weak smile as the room continued to buzz. "Well . . .
that was a mouthful, Mamie. I'm not sure I completely measure up. I'm no George Bailey, you know. Maybe some of you
have even thought of me as Mr. Potter now and then. There
have even been times lately where I've had a bad day or two
and doubted my effectiveness."

Mamie shook her head vigorously, wagging her finger for
emphasis. "Nonsense, Durden Sparks. You're the first person
everyone looks to when there's a crisis. They expect you to
have all the answers, even if you don't. Every town should
have someone like you looking after it."

Finally, Councilman Sparks came to his senses as his old
mojo kicked in. "Well, I'm all about the legacy my father and
Layton Duddney left me a long time ago, and that's the truth.
From the beginning, I've always been determined to make
something out of Cherico one way or another. Maybe I've
made my share of mistakes, but I've also learned from 'em."

Waddell Mack chimed in, enthusiastically patting the
councilman on the shoulder. "I like the way you romanced
your little town to try and get Spurs 'R' Us to locate here, and
by gosh darn, you did it. So I'll be right proud to call it my
second home from here on out, or these boots I'm wearin'
tonight aren't bright red! Oh, and I'll plan on doin' at least
two concerts a year down here in Cherico. And I'll donate all
the proceeds to whatever project this little town needs doin'
the most. You just let me know what it is, and I'll help you
get it done. Now, how's that for a Christmas present to all a'
you folks!?"

Out in the audience, Maura Beth was one of many who
felt the spirit of the season bubbling up and spilling over.

Wherever she looked, right and left, everyone returned her smile effortlessly. Why, she wondered with a certain sense of awe, couldn't it always be like this?

Maura Beth was propped up against her pillows, catching her breath after a very satisfying session of Christmas Eve lovemaking with her Jeremy. He was content to wind down in silence as well, staring over at her affectionately. Then she grabbed a sheet of paper from her nightstand and held it in front of her face, looking virtually mesmerized.

"Now what have you got there?" Jeremy asked, inching a bit closer to her to get a glimpse.

"It's the Christmas newsletter we received from Locke and Miss Voncille. It made quite an impression on me when it came a few days ago. I wanted to read it again before falling asleep tonight."

Jeremy briefly reviewed its contents in his head and nodded enthusiastically. "Yep, I have to admit it sure wasn't your ordinary newsletter full of snippets about vacations and raises at work and how much the children have grown and what good grades they got in school this year. It was pretty powerful and moving stuff there at the end, I seem to recall."

"Would you like for me to read it out loud before we turn out the lights so Santa can come down the chimney and visit us?" The smile on her face was utterly irresistible, like that of a small child eagerly anticipating Christmas morning.

He returned her smile in kind. "Sure."

She sat up even straighter and cleared her throat. "Okay, then. I'll skip down to the part that really grabbed both of us:

>   Voncille and I wanted to share with all of you—
> our good friends—another essay my Pamela
> wrote in her journal the week before she died a

few years ago. Her clarity of vision at such a time has always seemed remarkable to me. We think it especially makes sense here at Christmastime when we send out our best wishes to so many people who are reflecting upon the passage of another year and their lives in general. She wrote the following:

> Like empty space that is unsullied by its contents, or water that is unaffected by the fish that swim through it, the mind of God is beyond all form. Like space, it is equally present in the objects therein. That which is omnipotent, omniscient, and omnipresent is not vulnerable to threat or emotional upset. Thus, God is not prone to revenge, jealousy, hatred, violence, vanity, egotism, or the need for adulation or compliments. The beneficiary of worshipping is the worshipper. God is totally and absolutely complete and has no needs or desires. God is not unhappy or upset if you have never heard of him or don't believe in him.
> —Pamela Alden Linwood, August 2011"

Maura Beth exhaled dramatically after she had finished. "Well, I'm not sure Pamela Linwood had all the answers—I mean, who does?—but she had obviously given life a great deal of thought to write that. I remember being so impressed with what Locke shared of hers a few weeks ago. She certainly faced her own mortality in an inspiring way. I've always thought of myself as an outside-the-box girl, too. I think that's the best Christmas card I've ever read. It's empowering in some way I can't quite put my finger on."

"I have to agree with you," Jeremy said, snuggling up against her and lightly kissing her forehead.

Maura Beth glanced at the clock on her nightstand and made a soft purring sound. "Well, it's midnight, sweetheart. Christmas Day is officially here. So what do you think? Shall we settle down for a long winter's nap? Last time I looked, I don't believe a creature was stirring."

He chuckled, picking up on her theme. "Not even a mouse?"

"Let's hope not."

"You just talked me into it," he told her, and this time they enjoyed a sweet, lingering kiss.

"Merry Christmas, sweetheart," she said as she drew back ever so slightly. "I can't wait to begin another year with you."

"Merry Christmas and Happy New Year to you, too, Maurie. It just keeps getting better and better for us."

And then, with her loving, grown-up companion by her side, she turned out the light, hoping to revisit the Christmas dreams of her girlhood one more time.

Recipes from Fat Mama's Tamales and The Twinkle, Twinkle Café

This time around, we offer a famous recipe from an actual restaurant, Fat Mama's Tamales, in Natchez, Mississippi (www.FatMamasTamales.com), as well as another from my fictional restaurant creation, The Twinkle, Twinkle Café in Cherico, Mississippi. Both are perfect for entertaining large and small groups and well worth the try. In fact, we suggest a menu consisting of both recipes for your next party, along with wine.

Fat Mama's
Homemade Tamale Recipe

Ingredients you will need . . .

2 pounds beef
2 pounds pork
2 tablespoons garlic, minced
1 cup yellow onions, chopped
Salt
Black pepper
Red pepper
10 cups masa harina (corn flour)
3 cups lard or shortening
Corn husks

Making tamales is a labor of love and is time-consuming. Please keep in mind that it will require 5 to 6 hours from start to finish. So take off your instant gratification hat. The meat and masa (dough) are prepared separately, then combined to make the tamales. We suggest you invite friends and family over when making tamales so it is as much a social event as it is a good day's work in the kitchen!

MEAT MIXTURE

Ingredients (from the above) you will need . . .

2 pounds beef
2 pounds pork
2 tablespoons garlic, minced
1 cup yellow onions, chopped
Salt, black pepper, red pepper to taste

Combine beef, pork, 2 tablespoons of minced garlic, 1 cup of chopped onions, and salt, black pepper, and red pepper to taste in a large pot and cover with water. Bring pot to a boil, then reduce heat and simmer for 3½ hours. After 3½ hours, remove pot from heat and allow to cool. Once moderately cool, remove and strain meat from liquid and shred. Be sure to keep the strained liquid for use in your masa later. Once you have shredded the meat mixture, place in refrigerator to cool.

DOUGH (MASA HARINA)

Ingredients (from the above) you will need . . .

10 cups masa harina (corn flour)
3 cups lard or shortening
1 tablespoon salt
1 tablespoon black pepper
Red pepper to taste
Seasoned water that meat was cooked in

Mix your 10 cups of masa harina, 3 cups of lard or shortening, 1 tablespoon of salt, 1 tablespoon of black pepper, and red pepper to taste in a large container. Slowly add the hot strained liquid from the meat mixture and mix thoroughly. We suggest that the masa have the same consistency as thick cornbread. Allow to cool once masa has reached desired consistency.

CORN SCHUCKS /HUSKS·

Wash the corn shucks under running water, removing the corn silks, and then soak in a big pot of hot, but not boiling, water for at least 3 hours in order to soften the shuck so it is easy to handle. This step can be done while the meat is cooking. Once the shucks are pliable, you can lay them out to be filled with the dough and meat mixture. Spread the dough (masa harina) on with a knife; then spread the meat mixture over the masa. The meat mixture will be heavier and thicker than the masa mixture. Once the masa and meat are applied to the shuck, the narrow end of the shuck is folded up and the shuck is then rolled up from side to side. Tie the tamales in bundles of six with a string prior to the final step.

FINAL STEP

Once the tamales are all bundled, place them in a steam basket and cook them over water. It is important that the water is not completely steamed away at any time. Keep the steamer full of water so the tamales do not dry out. They are best served hot right out of the pot. Suggestion for libation: ice-cold beer.

—Courtesy David Gammill, Natchez, Mississippi

The Twinkle, Twinkle Café's
Baby Kale, Spinach, and Blueberry Salad

Ingredients you will need . . .

15-ounce bag or package of baby kale (do not use mature
  kale)
15-ounce bag or package of baby spinach
Dried dill weed
1 11-ounce package of fresh blueberries
2 ounces Feta cheese crumbles
Balsamic vinaigrette dressing (any bottled brand)

Wash baby kale and spinach leaves; place in very large salad bowl. Sprinkle dried dill weed throughout. Wash blueberries and distribute throughout salad. Sprinkle Feta cheese throughout; drizzle dressing to taste. Toss everything together lightly, but do not bruise or crush blueberries. This recipe serves up to six. Halve ingredients, except dill weed and cheese crumbles, to serve two or three. An excellent light dinner party selection and a cool accompaniment to any hot tamales being served.

—Courtesy Marion Good, Oxford, Mississippi

A CHERRY COLA CHRISTMAS

Ashton Lee

ABOUT THIS GUIDE

The suggested questions are included to
enhance your group's reading of Ashton Lee's
A Cherry Cola Christmas!

DISCUSSION QUESTIONS

1. Did you have wedding turmoil similar to that experienced by Maura Beth in this novel?

2. Discuss the concept of "relatives coming out of the woodwork" for weddings and funerals.

3. Have you had an unusual spiritual experience similar to the ones discussed in this novel?

4. Do you think weddings have gotten out of hand to some extent and that Maura Beth is right about wanting to take a simpler approach?

5. Pamela Linwood has made "appearances" in each of the first four novels in the series even though she is deceased. Discuss her importance to the series in your estimation.

6. Do you see Maura Beth and Jeremy as "making it" as a married couple?

7. What would you most like to have happen in future novels?

8. If this series were made into a movie, what actors do you see portraying Maura Beth, Councilman Sparks and Periwinkle Lattimore? Feel free to suggest actors for other roles as well.

9. In your opinion, what is the most important quality to have to make a marriage truly work?

10. Have you learned more about the inner workings and problems of libraries because of this series?

11. Has the series made you want to support your local library more?

12. Has your opinion of any character changed for the better or worse because of this fourth novel?